A Dishonorable Discharge

A Novel of Love and War

Larry R. Sherman

HISTORICAL FICTION 13
BENNINGTON, VERMONT
2015

First Edition published in 2015 by the Merriam Press

First Edition

ISBN 9781576382837
LCCN
Merriam Press #HF13-P

This work was designed, produced, and published in
the United States of America by the

Merriam Press
133 Elm Street Suite 3R
Bennington VT 05201

E-mail: ray@merriam-press.com
Web site: merriam-press.com

The Merriam Press publishes new manuscripts on historical subjects, especially military history and with an emphasis on World War II, as well as reprinting previously published works, including reports, documents, manuals, articles and other materials on historical topics.

Dedication

I would like to dedicate this book to my wife, Irene, without whose help it would never have been finished.

Acknowledgments

I want to thank Mrs. Barbara Spurr for her continued encouragement. Without her inspiration, the book would not be readable.

Furthermore, without Ray Merriam's assistance, the pictures concerning the War would not be as clear and as useful as they are.

Chapter 1

Germany

April 1945

CAPTAIN Walter Steinberg wrote to his wife Ashley, *"I'm back in the hospital again. We were transferred to the Seventh Army and crossed the Rhine on March 30. There was almost no opposition to the crossing, but it got worse each day. Vladimir was hit by a sniper and could not operate the 37 mm cannon until the wound healed. Since I am the best backup for the rifle, I took the gunner's position and Vladimir agreed to operate the radio until he healed.*

"On the third day, the armored car was hit by a 50 mm antitank shell. Jacob Cooper was instantaneous killed. Bill Johnson suffered a scalpel wound from shrapnel, and I was also wounded. We got to an aid station fast and neither Bill nor I have any long-lasting wounds. The doctors did a good job of stopping the bleeding and we both should be back with the patrol in about two weeks.

"Ed Smith told me that in the firefight they fired a thousand rounds of .50 caliber ammunition. One of the jeeps was hit, and that they found four dead Germans when an infantry company reached the engagement.

"I'm having problems seeing. The doctors think it is shell shock since I was not hit in the head. They have given me reading glasses to help see for a few days.

"Love, Walt."

Ashley wrote to Chaplain Henry Weidman, whom they had met in Paris, and told him that Walt was wounded again. Weidman answered the letter immediately,

"I had not heard that Walt had been wounded a second time. He is in Germany and I am still in Paris. However, I think I can arrange to visit him and shall try to do so in the next week. I just

need to find someone to handle my duties while I am gone. I will write again as soon as I see him.

"Faithfully, Henry Weidman."

Five days after Weidman received Ashley's letter, he entered Walt's ward. He announced, "Ashley told me that you were wounded again. I made arrangements to come as soon as possible. I had to find another chaplain to take my rounds for me. Tell me about the wound!"

"Thank you for coming; I never expected you to travel all the way from Paris just to see me."

"That's a Chaplain's job. To visit the wounded especially if they know them. Ashley did not give me any details."

"I don't think I gave her any. I wrote to her, as soon as, possible that I was in the hospital and that the wound will heal in about two weeks. I am not seriously hurt. I was hurt much worse last August when the jeep rolled on top of me and broke my leg."

"Tell me about the current wound."

"My first sergeant was hit by a sniper and could not operate the 37 mm cannon. His wound was not serious and he stayed with the patrol. I took the gunner's position in the armored car and he operated the radio. We were hit by an anti-tank shell. It killed Corporal Jacob Cooper, the driver, and wounded Bill Johnson and me "Our jeeps opened fire with their fifties before the Germans could fire a second shell; however, one of the jeeps was eventually destroyed. My patrol fired more than a thousand rounds of .50 caliber ammo and killed at least four Nazis. An infantry company joined in the firefight and the Germans either ran or were killed. Ed Smith gave me most of the details about the conflict when he visited the field hospital. Bill and I were taken to a field hospital and doctors patched us up. I hope to get back with the unit by the time they get new vehicles. The medics moved me here to Offenburg the day after I was wounded because the facility is better than in a field hospital. The doctors do not know how badly I was hurt and I have not told Ashley about the damage. The doctors want to wait to see if the nerves still operate. I've needed reading glasses to see printed material. The medical people think it is nerves. For the last two days have not used them. I will no longer need them once I am dismissed from the hospital."

Before he rejoined the patrol, Walt answered Ashley's letters. When he got to the patrol, he wrote,

A Dishonorable Discharge

I think the War is coming to an end. I have been sitting here near the Czech border for two days waiting to move the 763 patrol. No one has any orders. The men come to see me every day and are still lamenting Jacob's death. He was well liked; we feel it was unfair that he was killed so close to the end of the War.

The doctors have not told me anything about any long term problems with my wound. I will write to you when I have more information. I think a lot about my whole life especially before the War and my love for you.

With all my love, Walt.

While waiting to make a patrol, he contemplated about his life. He was born in June 1920 in Marietta, Ohio and attended St. Peter's Evangelical Lutheran Church as his family had done for four generations. He served as an acolyte in grade school and high school. Many of his activities were centered at the church and the church school. He enrolled in scout troop #83 sponsored by the church. He received his Eagle Award as a senior in high school. When he was a fresh tenderfoot scout (age 12), he was selected to go on a big camporee. He was the youngest scout in the patrol. It was an arduous weekend for it started to rain before they left home and continued until they returned. When they checked into camp, an elderly scout leader came to inspect the boy's packs. The older man, Edward Benedict, walked in front of each boy and carefully looked at him. Walt remembered that he had four red and brass service stars on his left lapel. Each star indicated that the man was in the Boy Scouts for five years or a total of twenty years. He was nice to everyone and assigned the patrol to the White Pines resident camp where they were permitted to use the lentos to protect them from the rain. They had trouble keeping a fire going but the patrol survived the weekend, despite the weather. The next year Walt was a first class scout and the camporee was held in ideal weather. When the patrol entered camp, Mr. Benedict came to inspect it. He now had four red stars and one green one. Each year Mr. Benedict inspected the incoming patrol and each year he added one more green star to his uniform. When Walt was sixteen and became a staff member, he got to know Mr. Benedict, who was totally devoted to the scout program. When Walt graduated from college before going to army boot camp, he accompanied his troop to camp as an assistant scoutmaster. Mr. Benedict still inspected the patrols and had six red stars. At Chapel the next morning, the camp director came onto the stage end announced, "I have bad news. Mr. Benedict died in his sleep last evening. He began to feel bad during dinner and retied early. You might have notice there are flowers on the chapel altar. Mr. Benedict went into the woods and picked them yesterday afternoon. He has been coming to camp every Saturday for the past twenty five years to pick flowers for the altar. Sometimes there were no units in the camp and it was empty. Mr. Benedict never asked; he just put flowers or greens on the altar as his devotion to God and his contribution to those in camp. Let us stand for a minute of silent and pray for this great scouter." Walt remembered seeing flowers or green on the altar whenever he was in camp but never associated it with the devout man.

His troop went camping two or three times every month. Walt learned all the skills and was asked to teach the younger boys. When he was sixteen, he went to work at scout camp. The first year he worked in the kitchen for the entire summer season, but his second year he became the scout assistant to the scout-craft director. In college, he became the provisional scout master and director of the scout craft area. He attended summer camp eight years as a boy and as a leader before graduating from college. His time in camp allowed him to earn some of the merit badges he needed for his eagle, like swimming and lifesaving, which were difficult to earn unless one had access to a good aquatics program. He earned a Bronze and Gold Palm in the two years after he received his Eagle. Scouting was his primary activity and he loved the adventures.

He attended public schools throughout his entire twelve years. Even though his grades were always in the top 25%, he was not popular with the other students. In high school, he tried to get dates but never had any luck. When he was fourteen, he had a scout court of honor and went directly to the school dance in his uniform. Upon entering the gym, he met Janet Moore, who was in his Latin class. He asked her for a dance and she consented. When the music stopped, she proclaimed, "You look very handsome in your uniform." Late in October that year, when he was an usher in church, he saw Janet sitting with her parents. After the service, he stopped to talk to the three of them and asked Janet, "Are you a member of the parish?"

"Yes, I am in the girl's Sunday school class!"

"I'm in the boy's class. Since I am either an acolyte or directors of the ushers, I need to leave the class before everyone gathers for the Sunday school closing. I come every Sunday; do you come regularly?"

"About twice a month, when my parents come to church."

"Will you go for a walk with me to Fort Harmar this afternoon?"

"Yes. What time will you be at my house?"

"Is two PM convenient?"

Janet turned to her parents, "May I go for a walk with Walt at two?"

"Yes. Just be home before 5:30. I will serve dinner at that time," answered her mother.

Walt appeared at her door at 2 PM. He wore Levis, a gray sport shirt, light wind breaker, and same shoes that he had worn in church. Janet wore blue slacks, a pink sweater with a high collar, saddle shoes, and light pink lipstick. Walt could not determine if the lip covering was the same that she wore for church and had just freshen it or if she had put on fresh lipstick for the afternoon walk. They walked slowly to the Muskingum River; then crossed the bridge to the reconstructed eighteenth century Fort. The path to the Fort was lined with flower beds, but they had not been maintained since Labor Day and looked rather shabby. There were two obsolete 75 mm artillery pieces from World War I sitting on either side of the path. Walt thought the guns were inappropriate since the Fort had originally been built in 1785.

Janet defended the guns existence with the statement, "The park commission does not have much money; the artillery pieces were probably donated to the park because they were of no use. You see that they have not mowed the grass and the shrubby has not been trimmed in more than a month."

Walt was silent. When they reached the door to the Fort, there was a "Closed" sign on the door. In small print at the bottom of the sign, it stated "This monument is opened from Memorial Day to Labor Day and at other select times." It was now late October.

The couple strolled back to the city and conversed about the church and school. Walt informed Janet that his ancestors had belonged to the Lutheran parish since the Civil War. She disclosed that her family had come to the city ten years previous but had only joined the parish two years previous. He now knew why he had not noticed her. He told her that he usually had to meet his parents, who sang in the choir, immediately after the service and did not find time to see who might be in the congregation. She informed him that she would try to find him at church functions. Nothing came of the "pledges."

The couple amiable parted at Janet's door and promised to take a hike together in the woods near the city. Walt never found the time to date her again. However, during the next autumn while walking home and shuffling his feet thorough the freshly fallen leaves in the street, she saw him and reprimanded him, "You ought to lift your feet and not drag them through the leaves." He was startled but shrugged his shoulders and continued walking. However, he carefully lifted his feet so that they no longer kicked the leaves. He was slightly embarrassed by her verbal criticism.

Two year later, he asked her to attend the senior prom with him. She declined his invitation because she had already accepted another date. She was 5'4," had brown eyes, a flawless complexion, wore her light brown hair in a reverse flip, and wore no makeup except a bright red lipstick, which never seemed to smear even when she was eating. She was voted the best dressed girl when she graduated from high school. She was also an excellent student and earned almost all A in her courses. Upon graduating she attended Normal School and taught first grade for two years before leaving to work as a floor supervisor in the parachute plant in the northern part of the city.

After Janet turned him down for the prom, Walt asked Alice Baker, who was in his Physics lab, to accompany him to the prom. She was not as pretty as Janet but she accepted the invitation. Walt bought a new blue suit and wore a black bow tie. At a distance the blue suit looked like a tuxedo but had the wrong cut. When he picked up Alice on the night of the prom, she looked as nice as any of the girls in their class. She was wearing a white formal evening gown; it could have been mistaken for a wedding dress except that it had a red trim on the collar, sleeves, and hem. She had gone to a beauty parlor and had her hair styled in a very fashionable style. She wore two inch white heels and painted her lips and nails red. Walt was very pleased that he had invited her be his date. He got sexually excited when she took his arm. When the evening came to a close, she passionately kissed him at her front door. As usual Walt spent the summer in scout camp, but on the two occasions that he was at home, he called her for a date. She was not able to accept either of his invitation but encouraged him to try again. During his first weekend home as a freshman in college, he accepted his invitation for a date. On the date she was good looking, but Walt did not think she was as pretty as on the prom night. He took her to a movie. She passionately kissed him at the door. He phoned her when home at Christmas break but her mother told him that she had become engaged to a young man who was in training to be a river boat pilot.

When Walt was sixteen, his father came home from work and announced, "I had a visit from the Treasury boys!"

"Oh! What's up?"

"They had a tip that a barge with bootleg whisky was docking and needed my assistance. I checked the records and the same barge had been coming to town about every other month. The cargo was listed as syrup. The agents accompanied me when I checked the barge; they insisted in opening a few cases. They were filled with moonshine. There were five hundred cases of the stuff on the barge. That would be 6000 bottles and worth more than $12,000[1] on the illegal liquor market. The treasury confiscated the liquor and hauled it to a federal warehouse. Since the papers were always in order, I never checked the crates."

"Won't it be easier to haul the booze by truck?"

"I don't know. I suspect that they have been using the barge even before prohibition was repealed three years ago. I would have to go down to the city archives to find out what occurred more than a year ago. The barge came from Morgantown, West Virginia. The whisky was probably produced in stills in the mountains of West Virginia and loaded on the barge in Morgantown. The captain gave us a bottle of Scotch last Christmas. I have a feeling that the treasury was tipped off by someone, maybe a disgruntled employee or a customer. As I said, the barge brought the 'syrup' every other month and it could have been going on for ten or twelve years. Nothing was ever out of order and I had no reason to suspect that it was illegal whisky."

Walt commented, "Never a dull moment."

Upon graduating from high school, Walt entered Buckeye University as a business major; at the end of the first year, he switched his major to Industrial Engineering. He was not good at drafting and had to redraw each of his engineering drawings three times before they were accepted by the instructor. He earned an A in Math and History but rarely earned an A in the other subjects. His engineering classes took too much time that he never studied as much as he thought he should in other studies. He never made the dean's list but came within a few tenths of a point during his last semesters. Many of his fellow students joined social fraternities, but he never had the time or money. He joined the Alpha Phi Omega fraternity,[2] and held several minor offices. He never tried to hold a major elevated position because his engineering classes required too much time.

---

[1] 1935 value
[2] Associated with the Boy Scouts.

He was not a good swimmer but participated in track and cross country in both high school and college. He rarely placed and during his four years in college only contributed four or five points to the school's score. He was mainly a team member who worked hard and inspired other students. He rarely procured dates in college and when he did ask the coeds, most of them rejected his advances. He concentrated on his studies in defense of his poor social skills. However, since he was on the track and cross country teams, he was invited to many parties at frat houses during his senior year. Unfortunately, he did not have close relationships with any co-eds and often skipped the parties because he did not have a date.

Walt was a senior in college and home on the weekend that the Japanese attacked Pearl Harbor (December 7, 1941). He had come home to talk to people at the new parachute plant about an engineering position. The plant was being built in the northern portion of the city but was not finished. The personnel office agreed to contact him at the end of February when they would start to hire permanent employees. Walt and his father were waiting for a late Sunday afternoon dinner when the announcer interrupted the New York Philharmonic concert to announce that Pearl Harbor had been attacked. They switched radio stations in an effort to get more information but to no avail. His father had agreed to drive him back to school; they kept the radio tuned to national broadcasting stations during the whole trip back to the university campus. There was nothing new about the attack. They listened to Eleanor Roosevelt's short NBC talk that she delivered each week. She had little to say except that the Japanese had attacked Pearl Harbor. She declared, "For months the White House knew something would happen and that the American people would meet the need.[3]" Walt commented as they separated, "They'll need to finish the parachute plant now that there is a War. If you hear anything about my application, please call me immediately."

At a cabinet meeting on November 10, the Secretary of State, Cordell Hull, noted that negotiations with Japan had reached an impasse. The possibility of war was discussed in the following weeks but everyone expected the Philippines to be the Japanese target. In actuality, besides Pearl Harbor, the Japanese attacked the Philippines, Guam,

---

[3] D.K. Goodwin. *No Ordinary Time*. Touchstone, NY, 2008, p. 291.

A DISHONORABLE DISCHARGE

Wake Island, and Midway Island on that Sunday or on December 8.[4] Guam would fall in a few days. Wake Island fell before the end of December and the Philippines in May. The Battle for Midway Island in June would be the turning point in the Pacific War.

The President had met with Churchill in August, 1941, and they agreed that if/when the USA entered the War; the defeat of Germany would be the primary objective. Roosevelt began to worry that the plan to first fight Germany would not transpire; however, on December 11 both Germany and Italy declared War on the USA. Roosevelt moved forward with the plan that had been formulated prior to the Pearl Harbor attack.

On Christmas Eve Walt went to a candlelight service at the Methodist Church with a high school friend and on Christmas morning went with his parents to Communion in St. Peter's Church. The pastor preached a sermon based on the Pearl Harbor attack and quoted part of Roosevelt's "Day of Infamy" speech. Even though Walt had heard the speech, the sermon really put American patriotism strongly in his mind. At dinner, he told his parents that he wanted to do something for the War effort and felt that a position in the parachute plant was his best option.

One evening during the vacation, he visited the home of a student whose father was a lawyer. Good-humoredly everyone drank liquor that the friend served from his father's liquor cabinet. A younger girl, Jennifer, drank too much and fell while leaving the house. She was not hurt; however, Walt, and another friend had to take her home. The evening taught him that he needed to be very careful when and where he drank.

During the first week in February, 1942, Walt received a draft notice. He appealed it because he would graduate in June with a degree in engineering. The president of the draft board notified him that he was being deferred until the end of June. The board members suggested that he go to boot camp at Fort Benning, Georgia at the end of June and enter the officer's training school in August after his initial training.

Walt turned twenty two during graduation week. Everyone in his family came to his college graduation, including his sixteen year old

---

[4] Most of the targets were on the western side of the International Date Line but were only a few hours later than Pearl Harbor.

sister, Abigail. Since he had three weeks until he left for basic training, he worked for his father or attended scout camp. The port traffic had significantly increased with the outbreak of the War. Furthermore, his father had lost two employees, one was drafted and the other left to work in the War industry. He received $0.85/hour and often worked sixty hours a week on the docks. His job was thankless since he had to decide who would be the first to dock and be loaded or unloaded. No matter how he arrived at his decisions, someone was always unhappy. He was actually ecstatic to leave for boot camp and escape the bickering on the water front.

During the first day at Fort Benning, the master sergeant asked the raw recruits, "Who among you was a Boy Scout?"

Walt and six other men raised their hands. The sergeant separated four men from the group, and then asked, "Who has the highest scout rank?"

Walt answered, "I am an Eagle Scout."

"Good you are now in charge to teach the other men how to raise a flag. You are responsible for the flag ceremony tomorrow morning."

Walt and the other men practiced raising and lowering the flag. After the evening ceremony the next day, the sergeant stated, "That was the best flag ceremony that I have seen by new recruits in many months. I am assigning you men the job of teaching everyone else how to run a flag ceremony by the time we leave basic training."

Someone asked, "Why do we all need to know a flag ceremony?"

The sergeant was annoyed and shouted, "Because some general may ask to have a flag raised or lowered and will pick the four men nearest to his vehicle. Anyone could be in the group! If any of you mess up the ceremony, I'll personally kick your butt." No one made any further remarks. Every afternoon prior to retreat, Walt and the other three men rehearsed flag raising and lowering with the other men in the company. At graduation, the sergeant congratulated Walt's group for a *job well done*.

To Walt, the basic training was a bore but realized it was necessary. Most of the instruction involved material that he had used in the Boy Scouts or in college. He went directly to officer training school without a leave at the end of his basic training. He was good in orienteering and map reading due to his Boy Scout training. He could also find every major star on an astronomical map. He was also an excellent pistol shot. Since he had studied most of the non-military tasks in scouts or in college, he maintained a 90% average at OTS even though there was no real grading. The captain sought him out one day to congratulated him on his fine scores while stopping for coffee and let him know about the unofficial grade. He was recognized for his excellent work when he received his Second Lieutenant's Bar. His family did not attend the graduation and he arrived home at 2:30 AM the day after the graduation.

When at home while stopping for coffee, he met Janet Moore at a local restaurant. He asked her for a date and took her to an alumni dance. He wore his uniform and reminded her that she had once told him that he looked handsome in a uniform. She laughed and told him, "You look even better in an army officer uniform than in a scout uniform." At the end of the date, he asked her for a kiss and she consented. He gave her a passionate kiss. He had another date with her before the leave came to an end and took her to a melodrama performed by a local amateur acting group. After the play, the two had coffee and a hamburger in a small café and laughed at the flubs that the actors had made during the silly scenes in the play. He asked her for a third date, but she declined because she worked nights in the parachute plant and could not arrange a time to meet with him. He offered to write to her when he reached his assignment in Colorado. She indicated that she would look for the letter. Upon arrival at camp, he wrote her a letter but she never answered it, and he never tried to make contact with her in the future.

Upon graduating from OTS, Walt expected to be assigned to a parachute training group at Fort Bennington, but to his surprised, he was ordered to report at the end of his leave to Fort Carson, Colorado. When he arrived at Fort Carson early in November, 1942, he was assign by the duty of officer to be the CO for Reconnaissance Patrol #763. He was sent to building 222A. There were two entrances to the barracks. There were two rooms. One room had ten cots and the second room with a single cot and a small desk for the CO. The second entrance to the barrack led to rooms that were duplicates and numbered 222B.

Six member of his patrol were waiting for him in the barracks. They introduced themselves. Corporal Edward Smith from Cleveland, Ohio. Pfc. Edwin Yavorski from Detroit, Michigan. Pfc. Edwin Scalise from Athens, Georgia, Pfc. Michael Goldsmith from Columbus, Missouri, Pfc. Nicholas Van Warden from NYC, and Pfc. Peter Audernreid from Townsend, Maryland. Shortly after 1400 hours, the sergeant from the reception center took the men to the vehicle depot to request the jeeps and armored car[5] that would make up their patrol unit. Walt sat in the passenger seat of the jeep and the other men crowded in the back. They were dropped off at the administration building and told that the sergeant inside would escort them to their vehicles.

Walt introduced himself to the sergeant who led the men to the back of the building where there were hundreds of numbered jeeps, armored cars, tanks, and trucks. He led them through the rows of jeeps to #4727 and announced, "This will be your command vehicles. Lt. Steinberg, you will need a driver and a gunner. The jeep needs to be adapted with a .50 caliber machine gun and a radio. Who will be your driver?"

"I assume it will be Corporal Smith since he is the highest ranking of the enlisted men."

"Good. Corporal Smith Take the jeep to the front of the building. If the other three men in your unit arrive, assembly them out front."

They found Jeep #5566 and Jeep #4931 and Privates Edwin Yavorski and Peter Audernreid became their driver. They went to the lines of armored cars and found car #942. Jacob Cooper, from Allentown, Pennsylvania was assigned as the driver, but since he had not arrived, the sergeant put the other men inside and drove the vehicle to the front of the depot. He informed them that it was known as an M8, had six wheels, a turret with limited rotation, but needed a .50 caliber MG and a 37 mm cannon.

Walt entered the depot with the sergeant, who pull out a map of the base and marked where the unit was to go for weapons. The other three men had arrived by the time Walt emerged from the building. He assigned Nicholas Van Warden, Mike Goldsmith, and Edwin Scalise as the gunners. Jacob Cooper took over as the driver of the armored car. Since he had never driven anything but a family automobile, he required instruction in driving the larger vehicle. William Johnson from Carpus, California became the machine gunner and Vladimir Livingston from Pittsburgh became the armored car gunner. The convoy slowly moved from the depot to the equipment storage warehouse. A sergeant walked along the row of parked vehicles talking to the officers and marking the unit's numbers on a clipboard. He had a map of the base and instructed each group where they were to park

---

[5] M8

their vehicles, how to cover the jeeps, and what they needed to do each morning to inspect the vehicles. Walt and his group waited idly for more than an hour. The sergeant returned and told them to move their vehicles to the assigned parking place and to return at 0730 the next morning for their equipment.

The next morning they returned to the warehouse and within an hour had four .50 caliber MG and the 37 mm cannon for the armored car. They slowly drove to the equipment field to install the weapons. For thirty minutes, a corporal instructed them concerning installing the weapons and how to maintain them. They started their training by firing the weapons at a target at the end of the field. After thirty minutes with few target hits, they were instructed to yield the field to another reconnaissance group and told to cruise around the base to learn the egocentrics of their vehicles. By lunch time they had burned the better part of a tank of gasoline. They parked at a fuel depot and hiked to the mess hall for lunch. They spent three days learning to drive the vehicles and tried to determine the best speed for scouting. They were also issued three Thompson submachine guns, five rifles, and two .45 caliber pistols. They spent part of each day on the range learning to shoot as fast and as accurate as possible.

They were still learning to use their weapons and vehicles when they received an announcement that U.S. forces had landed in Algeria at Oran. An officer's meeting was called and a major detailed much information that had not yet been appeared in the press.

In the subsequent weeks, the 763 unit learned to drive their jeeps and armored car at reckless speeds and to fire their weapons without stopping. They started to function as a team. At the end of their three months training, they were congratulated for their evolution and informed that they were remaining at the Fort Carson to train other units. After training the second group of rookies, Walt and his men were given promotions. Walt was promoted to First Lieutenant, Ed was promoted to sergeant, and both Livingston and Scalise were promoted to corporal. The other men with given permanent PFC distinction which meant that they would be promoted the next time a rank change was approved. After training two more recon groups, they were finally given a four day pass and were told that they could visit Denver. Throughout their training the group had learned to work together.

In March 1944, Walt was promoted to Captain and everyone else received another strip. They were given a thirty day leave and told to report to Fort AP Hill in Virginia. Walt went home to Marietta but did little except visit with his family. He could not find any of the girls with whom he attended high school and only visited a local pub twice to drink beer with old friends.

When the patrol group gathered in AP Hill, they were ordered to take their vehicles to Norfolk to be loaded on a liberty ship for transport to England. They were put on a French ship that had been built in 1915 and was in a West African port when France surrendered; it sailed for Brazil and plied between Brazilian ports and the Caribbean until the USA entered the War. At that time, it sailed to Florida and began carrying troop to England and Africa. The ship was designed for one thousand passengers, but the army jammed eight thousand men onto the ship. The enlisted men slept four to a tier. The officers lived a little better, but four men were assigned to a room that was designed for a couple. The men were allowed on deck for four thirty minute breaks during the day for a smoke. Meals were served twenty four hours a day. The food was fairly good but had often set for hours on the counter before being served. After seven days at sea the men disembarked in Liverpool. Everyone needed exercise to get back in shape. They drilled and did exercises for three days until their equipment arrived. They were ordered to cross England and were barracked at a village *Brighten on the Lake* in Kent.

The convoys driving south were given priority on the roads. They were taking troops to disembarking ports in southern England. The 763 patrol would sit for hours in small villages while south moving traffic moved at a snail's pace. As soon as, they stopped along the roads, the villagers offered them cups of tea while they waited to move. When night came, they pitched their tents in a vacant field or even on a large lawn and dug slit trenches for latrines. When they moved east of London, the traffic finally disappeared and they moved at 30 mph.

Brighten on the Lake had a population of only 300 inhabitants. It was an odd name since there was no lake near the village; in fact there were no real streams. When Walt asked about the name, he was told, "Legend has it that the name arose in 1066 to confuse the Normans. The Saxons knew that the Normans required good water after the Battle of Hasting. Once they arrived at the village, they discovered there was no water, not even a small stream. They had nothing to care for their men or animals. They suffered terrible during that first night because there were only two wells in the village that had been dug by the Romans. Good water only became available to the village at the end of the nineteenth century when the Kent County Water Company piped running water to every building in the village. Within two days after the 763 patrol arrived, two more patrols arrive. The Nazis attempted to bomb the town but did little damage—most of the bombs fell in vacant fields. The villagers assumed that Irish fifth columnist reported the arrival of the Americans. No one ever explained how the Irish knew that fresh American patrols had arrived in Kent.

Time seemed to have stopped in the village in the middle of the nineteenth century. When free, the men in the patrols liked to walk through the gardens. Birds, flowers, hedges, and gardens best described *Brighten on the Lake*. There were flowers blooming everywhere. Some of the gardens were centuries old and were beautiful. The original owners had constructed formal gardens and they were still maintained. Every house had peas, lettuce, and early spring vegetables. They were planted on hilled rows where they absorbed more sun than if planted on the bare ground. There was an eighteenth century manor house at the west end of the village. It had been built by an aristocratic family and was occupied through many generations by the same family. During the 1920s the owner ran into financial problems and sold the house to a land management company. The latter cut the manor into apartments but never filled them until the blitz (August/September, 1940) when Londoners, who had lost their dwellings, came to the village. In late 1942 and early 1943, when air raid diminished, most of the tenants migrated back to the city. When the patrol arrived, there were only four families living in the manor house. Walt wrote to his parents twice a week and they returned his letters on a regular basis. He told them about the village in a manner that he felt that the censers would not delete the information. His biggest complaint in his letters was the weather. It rained two out of three days. It never rained hard, just enough to make everyone miserable.

Neither of the other two patrols in the village had been trained by the 763 men at Fort Carson. Since Walt had his Captain bars, he was put in command of the three patrols. He contacted the regimental headquarters each day and relayed the duties for each group. One unit (#2811) was commanded by a First Lieutenant and the other (#3101) by a Second Lieutenant. There were six large tents at the east edge of the village for the enlisted men and three smaller tents for the officers. The officers had a small table, a cot and two chairs in their tents. Walt filled out his reports and counseled the men in the tent. He let the other men in his patrol use his tent when they wanted to write home and desired a quiet place to work. The large tents had a table where the men could sit and eat their meals in bad weather, which was most of the time. A mess truck arrived about 1800 hours each evening with a meal for all thirty men. It also came at 0700 hours each morning with a hot breakfast. When the patrols had not returned from their scouting, the truck left pots of food for the patrols to eat at the end of the day. However, none of the meals were really very good. The men sometimes refused to eat. When this happened they carried the food to a field where more than a dozen hogs were kept.

The recon patrols were attached to the Eighteenth Army, a bogus unit set up in Kent and eastern English counties to confuse the German into thinking that the invasion would occur near Pas-de-Calais, directly across the English Channel. The patrols traveled over all of SE England sending fictitious reports about units that did not exist or overstated the effort for those few that actually existed. The information confused the German, who estimated, that thirty Allied divisions existed in the Eighteenth Army and were posed for the invasion. In reality, there were only a few thousand communication personnel with the recon groups at *Brighten on the Lake* as part of the deception units. Each day Walt and his officers made radio and verbal reports to the Regimental Headquarters. The radio reports were always wrong and sent in simple code so that the Germans could decode the messages and plot the non-existed units on their intelligence maps. The regiment HQ often returned the messages at frequency monitored by the Germans giving details which only further confused the issue. Everyone knew that less than ten percent of the information had substance. It became a game and the men were overjoyed when told that the German had accepted their irrelevant reports. However, sometimes the data was so bad that even the men in the patrols realized no one would believe the report. They did know that at least fifty percent of the bogus transmissions were used to strengthen the Nazi divisions across the channel.

Three times a week, the enlisted men were allowed to visit a local pub named St. Arnold's. The men tried to eat in the pub as often as possible. With the strict rationing, they were only allowed one meal a week and had to bring food to prevent consuming too much civilian food. The officers ate their one meal a week in the White Deer Tavern which had a complete dinner menus; however, there was actually only one dish each day even though the menus listed ten to fifteen dishes. The civilians were required to present ration coupons when they enjoyed a dinner and the American always brought some kind of food. One evening there was duck on the tavern menu. It tasted like duck and Walt asked where they obtained the fowl. The cook explained she fashioned the duck from cans of Spam and favored it sufficiently with spices and other condiments so that everyone thought they were eating duck. Lamb or mutton was served several days each week. Chicken, beef, or pork appeared occasional. There were always potatoes, peas either fresh or canned, and strawberries in May, June, and July. There was lots of bread but no butter. Most days there was white margarine which came from either the USA or Canada. Beer was unlimited but hard liquor was rationed to one drink per customer each day but only if a full dinner was ordered.

Walt tried to determine where the names originated for the eating establishments but no one had a good tale. He was told that the names existed before anyone in the village was born and had been just accepted by everyone.

St. Arnold's pub always served something that looked and tasted like a potato chip, hard boiled eggs in a red beet pickle juice, and pickled pig's feet. The potato chip was salty but did not taste like anything the Americans had ever eaten and was not liked by them. The owner only told the American that he procured the items without ration coupons but was limited in the amount that he could get each week. The English patrons liked the little munchies but the favor was not conducive to American taste and the enlisted men only ate the food when their meal at the bivouac area was too bad. The eggs were the most desirable, but the owner only allowed each patron to buy one each week. He kept good records and if anyone, including the Americans, tried to break the rule, he refused to serve them beer for the rest of the evening. When there were no eggs, the enlisted men ate pig's feet but only in protest. Because St. Arnold's was the only pub in the village, everyone both English and Americans began to enjoy each other's presence, jokes, and laughter.

The one cook in the White Deer Tavern was in her mid-fifties and named Lorraine. She was twenty pounds overweight, never used any makeup, came to work in a washed off house dress, wore aprons with birds or flowers, and rarely talked to the American officers. The other cook was named Mrs. Lewis—no one knew her first name—was in her early sixties; she usually wore nice colored dresses and a white apron. She had a nice figure but was not bosomy. Walt thought she looked like a nicely dressed upper middle class woman. Her hair was short, curly, and an off strawberry blond in color. There never seemed to be a strand out of place. Her face was always nicely made-up, with pink lips, and smooth cheeks with a touch of pink. Since she had no eyebrows, she drew them with a brown eyebrow pencil. Sometimes she wore pink nail polish. She liked to stop at tables and talk to the patrons, especially the American officers. Her husband worked in an aircraft factory in Newcastle and her son was an officer on a motor torpedo boat (MTB) in the Adriatic Sea. Her daughter was married to a shipyard worker and lived in Edinburgh.

Mrs. Lewis was an excellent cook and baker. She would go mushroom hunting in the fields and woods around the village and used the fungus in most of her dishes. She made sweet raised yeast bread every day. It came out of the oven in her house at 1430 just before she left for the walk to the White Deer Tavern. Everyone tried to get to the tavern at that time to buy her rolls even when they could not stay to buy a meal. Walt asked her where she got the sugar for her rolls. She answered, "From British Islands in the Caribbean. Three years ago, sugar was extremely difficult to procure. There were severe shortage in 1941 & '42, but when the U-boat menace was eliminated, American and Canadian ships delivered sufficient sugar to meet our needs. The American shipped us saccharin even before they entered the war and we had to use it in our tea until early this year. Many taverns still will not serve sugar with tea and only place saccharin on the table. We are a little better and have some sugar for our tea as well as sweets like my rolls. I make sweet rolls because there are few ration restrictions concerning the other ingredients. I like to bake but can't do much with the rationing. Maybe after the War, I can go back to making cookies and cakes."

"Does Loraine bake?"

"Not normally. She lives with an elderly couple whose children are in the military. I am not sure where. She never has time to bake; at least that is her excuse. She is a good cook but will not experiment. At the end of each day, she takes home dinner for the elderly couple. I am not sure what she does about ration coupons. She does not talk about it and I never asked. A few weeks ago a policeman brought us a deer that had been killed by a motorist. The policeman knew Loraine by name so he might have been a relative. She spent most of the day cutting up the deer and cooked the venison for everyone. It was nice to eat something besides mutton. My husband gets a few extra coupons because of his job. With them and what I take home from the tavern, we eat quite well—considering that there is a War."

"What does your son tell you about the War?"

"Nothing or at least the censors do not allow anything through. He has gone to most of the Roman ruins in Southern Italy but except for a short trip to Sicily, I don't know anything."

"Do you pick the flowers that are on the tables most evening?"

"No. The owner does. He goes through the village each morning and negotiates with the home owners for permission to pick flowers. I don't know if he pays for them. I better get back to work. See you next time you can come for a meal."

Walt thought that Mrs. Lewis was charming and tried to visit the tavern as frequently as possible just to talk to her.

A cat walked into the 763 patrol encampment on the fourth day after their arrival. It was black and white. She meowed until Vladimir opened a can of K rations and fed her. The cat became attached to the patrol. She would rub against Nick's leg and softly purr. She entered Walt's tent and liked to lie on his table. She slept in the enlisted men's tent. She preferred the foot of Nick's bed; but if he was not in bed when she wanted to retire, she would go to someone else's bed. On the third day after her arrived, she went to Jeep 5566 and meowed until Edwin threw her onto Peter's lap. They named her *Band –Aid* because she had a black tail with a white ring the size of a Band-Aid bandage four inches from the end. By the time the patrol left the village, she answered to her name. Whenever she heard the jeep engines start, she crawled into the empty seat in one of the jeeps and made herself comfortable. She sat there throughout the whole patrol and only left the jeep when necessary. After her first patrol, she came to the jeeps each morning. She let everyone know that she was going on the day's excursion. Band-Aid began to ride on the front seat of the jeep where she could see the countryside. When the men went to mess in the evening, she would sit quietly until they brought her food. She normally licked the plate clean then sauntered back to a tent to sleep. While the men ate breakfast, the cat usually caught a mouse and laid it beside the jeep in which she wanted to ride that day. The men became very attached to her but did not know what to do with her when the orders came to prepare for transfer to France.

On May 31, Walt wrote his father,

> "We had another patrol today. We drove about 50 miles but it was terrible. There was a misty rain and the temperature was in the low 50s. We had to leave the jeeps open and scan the sky for German planes. I wore my poncho, but it did not keep me dry. My helmet shed water from my face but it kept dripping down my neck. We made some uninteresting investigations but had nothing to report to regimental HQ at the end of the day. We were all happy to get back to camp and get out of our wet clothing."

Another time, he wrote, *"We have adopted a stray cat. We have named it Band-Aid because it has a white ring about its black tail about the size of the bandage. We feed her K rations or from the mess that is delivered each day. She likes to go on patrols with us. She likes Nick and sleeps on his cot. Everyone likes to play with her and she certainly makes the days less boring. We don't know what we will do with her when we have to move out of our camp but maybe we can find a villager who will take her."* Walt went to the White Deer Tavern and asked Mrs. Lewis to take the cat home. She agreed to take it off their hands the day that the order came to move.

One day after being established at *Brighten on the Lake*, the patrol visited an American Artillery unit of 155 mm Long Toms in St. Margaret's, a small village a few miles south of Dover. Before the War, St. Margaret's was a retirement community for civil servants. None of the houses were old with most being built at the end of the 19th century or early 20th century. There was no real beach at the village, just a narrow strip of sand between high tide and the bluffs behind the hamlet. When the Germans occupied the cliffs on the French side of the channel, they started to shell the villages near the channel; but since there was nothing in St. Margaret's, they rarely wasted ammunition on the hamlet. Most of the villagers moved a few miles back from the bluffs to avoid the possibility of being a casualty. A few houses had been turned into hospitals and aid stations before and during the Battle of Britain but most were now vacate. A few airman, ether Allied or Germans were still being pulled from the channel but unless the wounds were trivial, they were usually transferred immediately to big hospitals in the tunnels carved below the Dover cliffs. Minor injuries/wounds were treated by the two nurses in St. Margaret and then sent to centers in Kent that were out of range of the German artillery. There were a few bomb shelters that the villagers had dug in 1940 but very few would give protection to anyone looking for real shelter if the Germans actually tried to hit the town.

There were four 155 mm Long Toms[6] in the artillery unit. Walt talked to Captain George Gumbart, who was the CO of the unit. Walt stated, "We're Recon Group 763 and have been driving all over Kent radioing reports on the units that we visit. Today we were sent here to report on your ability to support an invasion across the channel."

---

[6] 155 mm Long Toms were artillery with a range of more than 20 miles and fired a 56 pound warhead.

A Dishonorable Discharge

"Ha!" Laughed Captain Gumbart, "We can't support anything. We have four artillery pieces and enough ammunition to fire four or five volleys each day. When the Germans return fire, we hide in the dugouts and don't even try to return the fire. If we did, we would be out of ammunition in less than twenty five minutes. We are here to be a nuisance and not much more. Now if you really want to see supporting artillery, you should visit the big guns that the British have up on the White Cliffs." The Captain pointed to the Dover Cliffs about two miles north of St. Margaret. "We usually wait until late morning most days before we start to fire. The hazy usually disappears and we can see the French coast. Do you have a set of binoculars?"

"Yes, they're in my jeep."

"Get them and you can see what we can do."

Walt retrieved his binoculars and George ordered his men to load the 155 mms. He looked across the channel, and then stated, "Can you see the concrete and stone building on the cliff directly across from us?"

"Yes."

"That's the German observation post; we try to shell it several times a week. As soon as we start to fire, the Germans run to a deep shelter a short distance behind the observation post. Sometimes they don't see the flash of our guns and we have killed or wounded a few of them. However, most to the time the shells fall harmlessly on the cliff. Oh! We destroy or damage the tower once a week but the Krauts usually rebuild it during the night after the shelling. Like I said, we're a nuisance; but it keeps them guessing. I bet they know that you are here but have chosen to save the ammunition."

The artillery men were ready and George shouted, "Fire three rounds."

Walt watched and saw some Germans vacate the observation post. The first shell crashed into the facility before everyone escaped. The artillery men quickly reloaded their weapons and executed a second firing. Immediately they reloaded a third set of shells and fired. Walt saw some of them smash into the observation post and saw dust rise from the shell bursts. George's attention was only on the cliffs and Walt could not see what he was trying to determine. After two minutes, George announced, "It looks as if they are not going to return the shell fire. The gun flashes give us enough time to hide. As I said earlier, most of the time they do not want to waste the ammunition. Two weeks ago, they hit one of our guns and it had to be replaced. None of my men were causalities. We were hiding in the trenches. I usually watch to see if they are going to return our fire. At other times, I station a man at the siren to let us know when they are firing on us. It takes several minutes for the shells to transverse the Channel. If we see gun flashes, we have sufficient time to take cover. I would not be surprised if the Germans are just as bored are we are with this cat and mouse game."

The Captain saw Band-Aid and explained, "Hey, there's a cat in the jeep!"

"It's a stray that we adopted. It likes to take patrols with us. We all try to pet it several times a day. It even sleeps on our beds at night. Is there anything, we should see while we are here?"

"No. I think you should report that we need more ammo. German E-boats cruise the channel at night. We fire on them but run out of ammo just as we get the right range. They move rapidly and are gone before we can stop them. It's frustrating. But if they gave us more ammo, we might be able to hit one. Don't radio the request. If the Krauts intercept it, they will know that we can't fight an artillery duel."

"We're on these patrols to report failures. I'll try to get the ammo for you. But I am not sure I can do anything."

"It's a bore being here but I guess we serve a purpose. Will you be back in a few days?"

"I don't know but there are three patrols stationed in our village. Unless we get orders to move out, one of our patrols will be back to make a false report in the next few weeks."

When returning to their base, Walt sent the following message to the intelligence officer; "The ten Long Toms fired thirty six shells and destroyed a German bunker. The artillery is in an excellent position to support the invasion." He knew it was not true but sent it anyway. He hoped the Germans would be confused with the propaganda message even if they knew it was false.

Walt requested more ammunition for the artillery pieces. He received a strong, "Hmmm!" when the intelligence officer heard the request. Two weeks later one of the other recon patrols made a visit to St. Margaret's and Captain Gumbart sent a thank you to Walt since they now had sufficient ammo to do their job.

The patrols traveled throughout all the Eastern counties. On one patrol, they approached a unit which appeared to have hundreds of tanks, armored vehicles, and artillery. When the men entered the park, they discovered the equipment were decoys. Wooden frames were covered with camouflage tarps to look like military vehicles. In the air, no one could determine that the equipment was decoys. Even as the patrol approached the camp, they did not realize that it was bogus until less than 250 yards away. Walt reported that there was a division and that it was waiting for orders to move to a loading area for the invasion.

One morning, they were told to search through Kent with no particular unit to visit. They found an RAF base at Cranbrook. When they showed their orders, passes, etc., they were allowed to enter the base but needed to lock down the machine guns and leave the armored car and Thompsons at the gate. They crowded into the three jeeps with the cat and drove about the base. There were three squadrons of Spitfires and two squadrons of A-20s. The 763 men walked about the hangers and planes. The British flyers and armorers were quite willing to talk about their exploits. For more than a month, they were flying missions against airfield in Northern France. They usually approached at tree top level early in the morning or late in the afternoon. They estimated that they destroyed more than fifty enemy planes on the ground and another twenty in the air. Their tally was small; however, there were more than fifty allied airfields within one hundred miles and if everyone had the same record as this group the allies would have destroyed more than 3500 enemy planes. They knew that it was not true but it made good propaganda.

Ed asked an armorer, "Has your base been attacked recently?"

"Yes, last February, five FW 190s strafed us. They destroyed three planes and wounded six men. I think one of the wounded died; but since none of the wounded has returned to the base, it is only a rumor."

"Have you lost planes on missions?"

"Oh, yes! We lose a plane almost every other day. Most are lost in the low level attacks. The Germans are good at throwing up small AA fire. Some days 100% of the planes have holes or parts missing. We work long hours and can keep most of the planes in the air."

Walt addressed his men, "You can walk around the base and talk to the RAF men. Just stay out of their way. I want to talk to the base commander to see what I can put into my report."

Walt moved to the base commander's post. The guard at the gate needed approval before the recon group could enter the base and he checked with the CO. The Colonel welcomed Walt into his office. Walt explained that he ran a Recon Patrol to make fictitious reports to confuse the Germans. The CO knew about the patrol.

Both officers worked on the details for the report. They added extra data to exaggerate the observation but needed to make it believable. The CO and Walt agreed that Walt would increase the number of planes at the base from 50 to 75, and that they made 200 sorties a day, and that they lost three planes in the last week but had over 1000 bombs and truck loads of ammo stashed away behind buildings and in tunnels. They knew the information was false; however, it would confuse the Nazis about when and where the RAF would attack in their preparation for the invasion. Walt gave the CO the frequency that he used to transmit his reports and the patrol exited the base at 1530 hours.

Chapter 2

England, 1944

The Recon Patrol at Dover

JUNE 6 was a nasty day and Walt cancelled all patrols. The men set up a pinochle card game tournament in the largest tent in the bivouac area. Pinochle was selected because all but two of the enlisted men knew how to play the game. The two novices were paired up with experienced players. The men played a normal one hundred twenty point game. They threw nickels into the pot at the start of each hand. They divided the pot in half for each game with one half going into the tournament jackpot and the other half being distributed between the game winners. There were fifteen teams (30 men) in the tournament. At the end of each game, half of the poorest teams were eliminated. After two hours, Ed and Nick were still in the tournament representing the 763 recon group. Their opponents were from the 1152 group, who won the final game. The winners divided $26.60 between themselves. Not much money, but the games kept each recon group rooting all day for its members. The games were fun but the men were happy when it came to an end at 1530. The enlisted men celebrated the competition by going to St. Arnold's pub for a beer. Walt told them that they could drink several beers that evening; providing the pub manager had no objections. Walt went to the White Deer Tavern. He met Mrs. Lewis at the door. She had not only painted her face but also painted her nails a dark pink. She asked, "Are you here to celebrate the invasion?"

"No, What invasion?"

"The British and Americans have landed on the Normandy Beaches. My husband came home an hour ago and was jubilant about the invasion. You did not know?"

"No. The weather was too bad for a patrol, so we spent the day playing cards. We never turned on the radios."

"We'll need to correct that. I'll get the radio from the kitchen."

Loraine accompanied Mrs. Lewis when she returned. They dialed the BBC news station in London. It gave some details. Most of the news came from German broadcasts and told very little about the invasion. There were five invasion beaches but neither the movement off the beaches nor the casualties were broadcasted. The first battle report had arrived by carrier pigeon late in the morning. The listeners would need to wait until the next day to acquire real news about the invasion. There were few conversations between the news personnel located on the ships and their London office but no one gave any real details.

Everyone was jubilant at the tavern. The cooks had made a pot roast with fresh beef, potatoes, carrots, celery, and onions. There was lots of gravy. They served it with a salad made from local greens that had a vinegar and oil dressing. No one knew what the oil composition was; they assumed it had come from either Canadian or American soldiers who contributed it to the tavern's food supply to help by-pass the rationing. For desert, Mrs. Lewis made a *Rich Almond Cake* that had butter, flour, sugar, eggs, almonds, and almond extract. To help celebrated the historical event, the tavern owner served coffee which he had obtained from generous soldiers. Mrs. Lewis told the patrons that everything was rationed but they had saved the food for a special engagement. They felt that the invasion was such a day for the use of the hoarded food.

Walt ate his dinner and joyously celebrated with everyone in the tavern. As the help cleaned off the tables, he ambled over to St. Arnold's pub to join his patrol.

Earlier in the day, when the enlisted men entered St. Arnold's, an Englishman in a tweed suit shouted, "Why aren't you in the invasion?"

"Invasion?"

"Yes. The British and American hit the beaches in Normandy. Didn't you hear about it?"

"No. The weather was terrible and we did not go on a patrol today. We only have radios in the armored car and in the command jeep. We never turned them on because we did not make a patrol."

"The BBC has been broadcasting nothing but the invasion since 9:00 o'clock this morning. We have a radio behind the bar set to the BBC London news station. Come with me!" He led the way to the bar. There were many interviews with correspondents and service men who served on many fronts but little about the invasion itself.

Walt joined the men of the 763 unit two hours after they entered the pub. Everyone was joyfully celebrating the invasion. Lots of beer was flowing; however, this day there were no pickled eggs.

A man about fifty years of age stood on a table shouting, "I was on the Iron Duke, Admiral Jellicoe's flagship, at the Battle of Jutland in 1916. I was a gunner's mate and fired the 6 inch secondary armament. We saw very little in the fight. The battle was mostly between the big guns, the 12 and 15 inchers. We watched the big shells strike the German Battleships. We damaged or sunk every one of those dreadnoughts in that battle. Everyone on our ship got a medal for our work."

Someone shouted, "Didn't the Royal Navy lose the Queen Mary and the Indefatigable?"

"I don't know. I just know that we beat those bastards."

Another ex-soldier stood up, I was in the 5th Army when the Huns attacked in March 1918. I was stationed near Ypres. Although the Germans broke through at a number of places, my battalion held. We machine gunned or blew the bastards to pieces as they tried to cross the no-man's-land. They shelled us and a number of men were killed. We never left the trenches but held day after day. The Huns finally quit after two weeks of fighting. We had to go into the no-man's-land to bury the dead. The stench was terrible. But they never tried to break our line again. I was fortunate, I wasn't wounded. After the attack we just sat in our trenches until the Armistice."

A man with one leg took the floor and announced, "I was in the Dieppe Raid in August '42. The slaughter was terrible. There was no pre-invasion bombardment and the Nazis were waiting for us. The Canadians dropped like flies. I was on a destroyer and we were hit three times. I lost my leg when a shell came through the radio room where I was stationed. The other two men in the room were killed. We had good medics on the ship and they saved my life. Now, I go to man an anti-aircraft gun four nights a week."

Others told War stories that continued until the owner closed the pub early on June 7.

By 1500 hours, the Saturday following the invasion, all the patrols returned early to *Brighten on the Lake*. Walt contracted regimental HQ. They had no orders and told him to give the patrols off on the Sunday. He decided to attend the morning service at the local parish church of the Church of England. He asked how many men would like to join him. About half the men raised their hands and he felt like he needed to warn the vicar. He arrived at St. Agnes Church at 1715 hours and the vicar was leading Evening Prayer. The church was a typical 18th century stone church; however, it was clean whereas all the other stone buildings in the village were black from smoke and dirt. Walt assumed the church had been cleaned just before the War began but was never given the details.

There were two parishioners in the congregation and a teenage boy assisted at the altar. Walt stood at the door until the service ended. The vicar removed his stole and surplice, and then walked down the main aisle. He spoke to one of the women then greeted Walt, "I'm William Mainer, the vicar of St. Agnes. What can I do for you?"

"I'm Captain Walter Steinberg, the CO for the patrols stationed in the village. We have no patrols scheduled for tomorrow and would like to attend your church. I have checked with my men and 15-20 want to accompany me. I thought I had better warn you that there will be that many Americans."

"That was nice of you. Because of the invasion on Tuesday, I anticipate more people than normal. With you and your men, we could have a full house. Is there any special requests that you have?"

"Yes, we would like special prayers for those involved in the invasion."

"I have already included them. Since we are holding Morning Prayer, the prayers will be prayed after the sermon and before the offertory. Are any of the men Episcopalians?"

"I don't know. I'm Lutheran and I know one man is a Methodist but I don't have any idea what the other men profess."

"Understandable, thanks. I shall have Mr. Caldwell, our lay-reader; give instructions on finding the pages in the Prayer Book and Hymnal. If I arrange a tea after the service, will your men attend?"

"I'm sure they will."

"I'll ask Mrs. Lewis if she will make some sweet bread to serve with the tea."

"I've eaten her bread at the White Deer Tavern. It is excellent. Will she have enough sugar?"

"We'll know tomorrow. She is a good parishioner and does almost everything I ask."

Walt returned to camp and announced that the patrols would gather at 0930 hours and march to church. Everyone was ordered to wear their parade uniforms or the best uniform that they had. He also told them that if the weather permitted, tea and sweet bread would be served on the church lawn.

The men gathered at 0930 hours. There were twenty one of them. They formed into three squads of seven men and marched to the church. Walt and the other officers followed in the rear. He was very proud of them. They entered the church and sat together as instructed by the usher. Walt and the two lieutenants sat together in the last row of the military troupe. They arrived ten minutes before the service began and sat quietly until the choir began the procession. During the ten minutes, Walt studied the church. There was a raised pulpit on the right and a wooden lectern on the left. There was a large framed print of St. Agnes behind the lectern. There were four plain glass windows on the sides of the church but no stained glass elsewhere, even in the window behind the altar. The altar was simple and covered with a white frontal. There were two candles on the altar and two teenage boys entered to light the candles just after the soldiers were seated.

At exactly 1000 hours, a choir of six people entered the sanctuary singing *Onward Christian Soldiers*. Mr. Caldwell announced where all the prayers, hymns, etc. were located in the Prayer Book and Hymnal. The Vicar preached a sermon on the duty to God, the need for military personal to keep their Christian faith, and to love everyone even on the battlefield. The sermon was quite patriotic but gave the message that the enemy might also have to rationalize their beliefs just as the Allied soldiers did. Just before the offertory, he delivered a long prayer asking God's protection for the men on the battlefield especially in Normandy and to help those behind the lines to aid the fighting with their prayers and physical support. The service closed with Luther's hymn, *God is our Fortress in Ages Past*.

Even though the soldiers marched into the church with excellent military disciple, there was no order in leaving the church. There were 35 parishioners and they all wanted to speak with the servicemen. People ambled to the front door and the vicar shook everyone's hand. He asked them to stay for tea and sweet bread on the lawn in front of the church. When the officers reached the vicar, he thanked them for bringing their men and asked them to come again. He offered to visit their camp for a short morning or evening prayer service. The officers were embarrassed by the congeniality but agreed to consider his enthusiastic offer. On the lawn were three tables; tea and sweet bread was displayed on one, cups and plates on the other for everyone to select, and the third table was used for the dirty dishes. Walt found Mrs. Lewis and asked, "Did the sweet bread preparation take all your sugar ration?"

"A good deal of it but I'll get more this week."

"Maybe I can replace it. I'll try to get a bag of sugar from the commissary and have one of the men deliver it to you on Tuesday or Wednesday. The supply people give us little things if we don't ask for too much or we assure them that it will not be sold on the black market. I'll tell them it is for the Church and don't expect to have any difficulty."

"Thank you."

The recon patrols returned to their bivouacs area in little groups. Unlike the march to the church, there was no military semblance in the return. As the three officers returned, Walt commented, "The vicar offered to visit us and lead either a morning or evening prayer services. We have not seen a chaplain since we arrived in *Brighten on the Lake*. I think it would be nice to accept his offer. What do you think?"

A Second Lieutenant answered, "I'm an Episcopalian and have not heard an Anglican Service since March, 1943, when I entered the army. I'm in favor but I may be prejudice."

The other officer thought it was a good idea but did not know how to arrange a service because most days the patrols were scheduled in the early morning; no one knew when they would return. In bad weather the patrols were sometimes cancelled and that might be a good time to consider a service but again it was rare to know before 0800 hours on any day.

Walt continued, "I think I can make arrangements. I'll need your assistance to get the men to attend the service—like today."

The next day he contacted the commissary and asked for a bag of sugar to replace the material used in the sweet bread. The next day, they sent him a ten pound bag of sugar and he asked Ed to take the sack over to Mrs. Lewis's home. She was overjoyed since she had not seen that much sugar at one time since the Battle of Britain began in 1940.

Ten days later Walt arranged early on a Wednesday morning for the patrols to return to their base by 1500 hours. He told the two lieutenants that he would schedule a service and then contacted the vicar. The latter with Mr. Caldwell, two altar boys, and three women came to the bivouac area at 1600 hours. They pulled a table out of a tent and the vicar set up an altar. The boys lit the candles but the wind blew them out within two minutes. The parishioners brought twenty Prayer Books and Mr. Caldwell announced every section. The service lasted just over thirty minutes and the officers requested that the parishioners stay and have dinner with the GIs. Walt warned the mess crew as soon as they returned from the patrol that they would have visitors for dinner. The meal was better than usual. There was a repeat of the Evening Prayer service on July 4 and the vicar prayed a special prayer for the American Independence Day. Most of the men personally thanked the vicar for the special service to commemorate the American Holiday

Day. Walt was beaming with pride as the local Anglicans left the bivouac area.

There were days between D-day and July 4 that the 763 recon patrol had no duties. On the whole, the weather was terrible. When it was nice and there were no patrols, the men took walking tours of *Brighten on the Lake* or the nearby villages and visited many gardens, some of which had been in existence for hundreds of years.

Mike met a young girl on one of the walks in *Brighten on the Lake*. He asked her to show the men the village. She consented. Walt asked her age. She was sixteen and Walt told the men that they were not allowed to do anything except to use her as a guide. At the end of an hour, she suggested that they enter St. Arnold's pub. Everyone was thirsty and she addressed the bartender by name and had him serve a glass of local ale to everyone including herself. Walt paid for the ale. The young girl recapped that there was no age limit for drinking beer in English taverns. The men had a delightful time talking to the young lady. When they asked her a question, she sought one of the men in the tavern that she personal knew could give an answer. She knew them all by their Christian names which indicated that she was well known by everyone in the village.

On July 5, Walt received orders to have all the patrols vehicles serviced. The Kent County service park was full of jeeps, trucks, armored vehicles, etc. He was told that it would take two days before their vehicles would be ready to move and was told to return the next evening to determine the progress in getting his vehicles ready to move to France. The men set up their pup tents in a nearby field and walked to the service area. There was nothing to see near the service area that was not like *Brighten on the Lake*. However, the village was not as pretty as their former bivouac area.

At 1300 hours on July 6, the Glenn Miller Band arrived at the service area to provide the GIs with a show. The 763 patrol elbowed their way thought the attendees until they were only a few feet from the stage. At the beginning of the performance, an army signal corps broadcaster come onto the stage and announced, "We are recording this show to be sent to the Army Forces Radio Network. There will be no cheers, whistles, etc. except when given the signal by the announcer. He will raise his hand, one finger means clap, two means you may add a little noise — *a little-noise* — and three fingers means you can do whatever you wish. Do not stand or leave your seats during the performance." To Walt's surprise everyone followed the announcer's signals. There were no cheers, whistles, etc. except as instructed by the signal corps broadcaster. The band opened the show with *In the Mood*, the Miller theme song. Ray McKinley sang *And Her Tears Flowed Like Wine* and Johnny Desmond sang *Long Ago and Far Away*. The band played *Moonlight Serenade, Guns in the Sky, With My Head in the Clouds, Sweet Afton, Juke Box Saturday Night*, and many more popular tunes.

When the performance was over Glenn Miller announced that he would meet with the enlisted men in the big tent in the service area. He added that SSgts McKinley and Desmond would meet with the officers in the mess tent. Walt's patrol broke up and went to their locations as required by ranks.

Walt walked into the mess tent with the other officers. There were less than eighty men in the crowd and Johnny Desmond took the stage center to talk about the band. He was the descendent of an Italian Jew, was born in Detroit, and his real name was Giovanni Alfredo de Simone. He started to sing in his own band on January 3, 1942. He told the officers that he had arrived in Scotland on June 21, having been shipped over on the HMS Queen Elizabeth. He had gone to London, stayed in the Sloane Court Hotel, the same one that Walter Cronkite occupied during part of the winter. The first night, he watched the buss bombs.[7] Fortunately he left the hotel to join the band the next day and two days after he left the hotel, it was destroyed by a V-1 bomb. Ray McKinley did not get a chance to say anything because the mess tent personal moved everyone out so they could set up for the evening meal.

When the vehicles were finished, the patrol drove to Southampton for transportation to France. The tents were pulled down as soon as the patrols left. Walt knew that the orders to move would put them into the fighting but he did not know when or where. During the drive to Southampton, Walt asked Ed if he knew anything about Desmond. Ed told him, "When Desmond first came to join Miller's band, the later told him to get a haircut. He made Desmond go back for three haircuts before Miller was satisfied. Miller's band looked great and his men do their part to be an example of military discipline. Miller always insisted that each member of the band display the highest standards."

---

[7] V-1 flying bombs. Sometimes called "doddle bugs."

A DISHONORABLE DISCHARGE

Walt stated, "I've never hear Desmond sing before yesterday. I was very impressed with his voice. I'd like to hear the band again but we'll need to wait until they come to France."

"Miller told us that he was traveling to France as soon as the army could provide him with transportation. Maybe we can attend the performance."

The patrols vehicles were loaded on a LST and arrived at Cherbourg, Normandy on July 16. Each patrol drove to a different staging area. The 763 drove to Carteret on the West Coast of the peninsula to join in the front line training. Most of the enlisted men needed physical training because of the easy conditions in Kent and went to a physical training class for part of each day. Walt went to the officer's briefings. Much of the talk was about how to avoid casualties for armor units and still reach their objectives. Since the instruction was irrelevant, Walt went to the colonel in charge and told him that he was the CO of a reconnaissance patrol. He asked if there was better training for him. The colonel told him that there was a recon training session for all ranks on the other side of the camp at 0830 hours each morning. The next morning all the members in the 763 unit went to the recon training session even though the enlisted men were not required to be at the meeting.

The colonel in charge of the recon training session repeated what Walt and his men had learned at Fort Carson. A recon patrol sought out German defenses but had poor firepower power with which to fight. However, they had speed but little or no firepower. Once they had completed their observations, their job was to get out of the area before they sustained any causalities. Their main purposes were to locate German units, then transmit the information to the regimental headquarters. "You are expected to run. In Sicily the recon patrols had one of the lowest casualty lists of any of the specialized group. We want you to meet their record, in France."

"Don't the Krauts have recon patrols?" asked one of the officers.

"Yes, but they have fuel and other problem. Thus the number of patrols is smaller than ours. Furthermore, their vehicles are slower. I doubt if they can move more than 45 mph on French roads. They also tend to bunch, so they are susceptible to concentrated artillery fire. In Sicily, we probably destroyed two of their units for every one that we lost."

He showed some newsreels taken in Sicily illustrating the difference between the two opponents. In most patrols, a jeep led the patrol and was followed by an armored car, then the other jeeps. One officer rose and asked, "All the films that you showed, indicate open country. Normandy is full of hedgerows. How do we operate?"

"In hedgerow country, you must be very careful. Since the armored car can withstand light machine gun fire, most scout units, here in Normandy, are led by their armored car. It is easier to make films of moving units in farm land; thus I showed the Sicilian films. Furthermore, we are now concentrating for a major attack. If it successes, we'll be in open farm land like those in the film."

"When and where will the attack occur?" asked the same officer at the back of the gathering.

"I don't know and if I did, I would not tell you."

The chief officer continued, "You don't have room to maneuver along the roads along the west coast of the Normandy peninsula. You need to try running your patrols on the other French roads. French roads especially in Normandy are much poorer than in either the UK or the USA. Your drivers need to know what is expected of them. We'll post unit numbers each morning at 0630 hours. If your number is on the list, you need to try to manipulate that day along the French roads. If your number is not on the list, you are to report to this tent at 0830 hours for further instructions. The better trained that you are, the more likely it is that you will be in coming back from a patrol. Now find your men and start telling them about the job they need to do."

For the next eight days, the 763 group primarily assignment was searching for hidden "enemy" imitations on the back French roads. They were quite successful and twice they were complimented by the colonel in charge of training. They now realized that all their training in the USA and Kent had paid off. They returned to the reconnaissance patrol headquarters each evening and ate in the mess tent. The meals were terrible, much worse than in Kent. The worse was breakfast with powdered eggs, rubbery sausage, and bad coffee served with caked sugar and powdered milk. However, most of the time, it was served with saccharin and tinned milk. The latter made it a little better—not good—just better. Most of the eggs for breakfast were reconstituted with powdered milk. They were terrible. There was usually Spam with mustard served for all meals and rarely hot dogs with catsup in the evening. There were lots of canned fruit juices and normally fresh baked biscuits. The nourishment was adequate but the taste was terrible. There was no seasoning in the food and it was boring at best. Because there was no seasoning in the food, and there were only limited quantities of salt or pepper on the tables, there was nothing to make the food more palatable. In taste, the K rations and C rations eaten on patrol were not much better. The men complained continuously but no one listened. The worse part of being in France was that they were not allowed to go to any of the French restaurants for a reprieve from the bad army food. While traveling through the French villages, the patrol occasionally had the opportunity to either buy or trade army food for hard boiled eggs, bread, and wine from the villagers. There was never sufficient food for the men in the patrol but after bartering for good food they always felt better than waiting for Army dinners. The 763 men could never determine if the food was as bad as they claimed or if, in Kent, they could always go to the tavern or pub and acquire good food. This was especially true when they felt that the meals were inedible. In Normandy, meals were always available at all hours of the day and night. They usually consisted of canned beef, boiled rice, and canned beans or carrots even in the morning.

On July 22, the Glenn Miller Band came to the Carteret area to put on a concert. Walt learned about the scheduled concert several days ahead of its general announcement. The 763 patrol was at the stage before anyone else arrived. In fact, they probably had beat most units in learning about the concert. Miller opened the concert with his theme song, *In the Mood*, then played *Star Dust*, and the *White Cliffs of Dover*. Baritone soloist Ray McKinney sang *Beat Me Daddy*, *Eight to the Bar*, *Get along Little Doggie*, and *Peggy the Pinup Girl*. Johnny Desmond sang *Symphony* and *All the Things You Are*. After thirty minutes, everyone, including Walt, was surprised to see Marlene Dietrich come on to the stage. She was as pretty as ever. Jimmy Steward once said she wore too much makeup, but no one in the audience cared. The crowd went wild with calls, shouts, whistles, and clapping. As she calmed the audience, she announced, "I want to sing the ballad, *Lilli Marlene*. I know it is very popular song among American troops because it makes you think about the women you left behind. However, I think you should know that the ballad was initially commissioned by Joseph Goebbels in 1940. Hitler was very pleased. It was frequently played on radio Berlin and was recorded by British and American artists. I started to sing it late last year. Hitler hates me and after I began to sing it, he forbids it to be played on German radio stations. He even put a price of $250,000 on my head in the hope that someone would stop me from singing the ballad. Let me sing it!"

The audience went wild. It took five minutes to calm them down. Marlene sang the song and followed it with four more. After the fourth tune, Walt saw perspiration on her forehead. She exited the stage and only returned at the end of the program to sing *Auf Wieder-sehen* and wave good-bye to the GIs. Miller closed the program with *Goodbye Little Darlin' Goodbye*. The 763 patrol was extremely overex-cited and spend hours talking about the show when they should have been asleep.

The next few days transpired as the previous seven. The Norman-dy Break Out attack was scheduled for July 25 and the 763 patrol was told to be ready to move at a moment's notice. It was two days after the breakout before they reached St. Lo. The roads were jammed with vehicles and the only vehicles that received priority from the MPs, were ambulances and repair trucks. The rest waited, including the 763 patrol! It was late in the morning of the 27th before they reached the 10th Armored headquarters in St. Lo. To their joy, the road was clear to the east. After receiving orders and radio frequencies from the regi-mental headquarters, they moved out a 30 mph. In 30 minutes, they reached a front line armored battalion that was waiting for fuel. The Lt. Colonel told Walt that the Germans were about two miles ahead but he knew nothing else. He gave Walt his radio frequency then told him to see what he could find and try to return to him before night fall. The 763 recon carefully moved forward with Walt's jeep, 4727, in front followed by the armored car the other two jeeps, 4931 and 5566 at 75 yards intervals in the rear. They moved at 15 mph with one man standing by the machine gun at all times in each vehicle.

The road was mostly broken macadam. The lead jeep could see about a mile and a half ahead. Every 20 minutes, they stopped even though they could not see anything suspicious. Walt reported to the regimental intelligence their position and lack of enemy. They traveled four miles before they saw a group of retreating Germans on the road ahead of them. They assumed it was the enemy that they were sent to find. They made their report. The regimental intelligence officer switched them to the armored column that they had left earlier in the day. Walt announced, "We see the Krauts about a mile ahead of us. We will try to find out the number and be back with you immediately." Walt switched the armored car to the lead vehicle which crept ahead at 10 mph. They drove up a very small hill and could see fifteen or twen-ty Nazi vehicles, a self-propelled gun, and a mortar squad. The Ger-mans had not seen the recon unit. Walt radioed, "We still see them about a mile ahead of us but they can't see us. We are on a small hill and will need to retreat as soon as they turn that artillery piece around. We can fire a few 37 mm rounds which should put them into a defensive position. They'll likely stay in their current position until it is dark enough to slip away."

The Lieutenant Colonel replied, "We are still not ready to follow you. It will be 30 to 60 minutes before I can get my men on the road. Why don't you keep watching them? If they turn around—RUN! If they do nothing, just keep them in sight. We still have four hours of daylight."

"Roger. We'll report in twenty minutes unless something really happens."

The Germans moved half a mile, then turned the gun around. Walt saw it move and waved his men back across the hill. Walt and Ed slowly crept to the crest of the hill where they could see the German unit. There was a small stream eight feet wide in front of the German line. The enemy started to dig in a defensive position on the far side of the stream. Ed kept watching and Walt returned to the radio to let the battalion know that the Germans had started to dig into a defensive position.

The Colonel asked, "Can you fire a few rounds with your little cannon? I have started to move some of my men down the road. It will be an hour until we reach you, unless there are snipers or mines along the road."

"We can fire but if they move on us, we will need to retreat. We are currently hid behind the crest of the small hill but it is only twelve feet high so we have no protection even from rifle or machine gun fire."

"We're moving out. Give us an update in twenty minutes unless something significant happens."

Walt carefully directed the armored car so that the Germans, now digging in, were within its sights. They fired two quick rounds then move back 50 feet so that they were out of the German vision. One round hit a truck but did not appear to do any damage. The other flew over the top of the whole company and Walt could not determine where it hit. The Germans opened fire with a machine gun. A few rounds hit the dirt in front of Walt but there was nothing to hit but dirt since he was as tight against the ground as possible. Ed crawled up to him and whispered, "If they open with that 75 mm, we need to get out of here."

"Are you sure it's a 75 mm?"

"I think it's called a Panzerjäger 38 Marder III. I've seen pictures of them in the UK. The Krauts have a lot of them in Russia. They can stop anything, but they don't carry much ammo, maybe 30 rounds.

Thus in a concerted attack they either flee or are knocked out. I think there is a machine gun on the top. I don't think our 37 mm will penetrate the armor."

Walt ordered, "Have Yavorski move about 50 yards to our right and carefully watch their movement. Remind him that he has to stay below the crest of the hill or he's a goner."

Walt carefully appraised the enemy. He now knew that Ed was correct. The artillery piece was a 75 mm. It was not particular aimed at anything so their commander must also be waiting to see what the patrol was going to do. As he studied the German movements, he saw dust about five miles behind the German unit.

Yavorski saw it at the same time and motioned to Walt. The machine gunner from his jeep crawled over to Walt and asked, "Is that a relief column moving up to support those two companies?"

"I don't know but it looks like it. Let's watch them for another five minutes before I make a report. You need to return to your jeep. I know that Yavorski is watching but if it's a big group, we need to get out of here in a hurry."

"Yes, sir."

Walt scanned the road behind himself. He thought he saw dust but it was still far away. He couldn't be sure if it was the battalion on the move. He stood up, walked to the jeep, and called the Colonel. "I think the Krauts have reinforcements coming up. We see dust but cannot distinguish anything. How far behind us are you?"

"My whole unit is on the move. We should be with you in less than an hour. What have the Krauts done?"

"We fired two rounds and they answered with some machine gun and rifle fire. They did not hit anything. They are not taking-up a very good position. They are either waiting for the reinforcements or dark in order to escape. We can fire a few more rounds so that they know that we are still here."

"Go ahead. Check with me in ten minutes."

Walt ordered, "Move the armored car to the crest of the hill, rapidly fire two rounds, and retreat as fast as possible." The men prepared the armored car, then leaped to the crest, fired two quick rounds, and retreated. Neither shell hit anything. The armored car moved 50 yards west on the road. Walt watched the Germans fire two 75 mm rounds. They went over their heads and crashed almost a mile behind their hiding place. A mortar round fell 100 yards behind the 763 vehicles. Walt quickly radioed the battalion, "They have started to mortar our position. We cannot stay much longer. We can see dust about a mile and a half behind us. Is that you?"

"Yes, you better get out before they get the range."

"Roger!"

"Retreat." Walt shouted!

All vehicles moved as fast as possible back to the road that they used to reach the crest of the hill; two more mortar rounds landed where they had just been making their observations. The 763 patrol didn't stop running until they met the battalion's lead Sherman tank. The tank commander asked for information. Walt explained that the Germans were over the crest of the hill that was barely visible about a mile to the east. As he talked, a mortar round landed 300 yards in front of the tank. The commander got on his radio and six infantry men climbed on the back of the tank as it headed for the crest of the hill where Walt had made his observations. Five more tanks with infantry on top followed and they raised a great deal of dust as they moved through the fields on either side of the road. The 763 patrol sat and watched the battalion move forward. The first tank moved across the crest of the hill and opened fire as the Colonel pulled alongside of Walt's jeep. He shouted, "Good work Captain. I think we can take care of the firefight at this point. You need to check with regimental headquarters."

Walt radioed the intelligence people. They ordered him to move to a road two miles north of their current position and locate a place to spend the night. The next day was basically a repeat of their first day on the front. They moved three miles east and ran into two German squads guarding the road at the western entry to a small village. The Germans saw the 763 patrol approach and fired on Walt's jeep. One bullet smashed the head lamp on the left side. Ed ran the jeep into the field as fast as possible and Nicholas opened fire with their .50 caliber. Jacob trained the 37 mm on the row of houses where the small caliber fire originated and fired three quick rounds. They waited for five minutes. No further fire came from the German line and the 763 unit inched through the field. As they reached the village, a number of villagers emerged from the buildings and started to shout. Yavorski was fluent in French and started to talk with them. He discovered that when the 763 patrol opened fire with their 37 mm, the Germans fled the village. They had nothing to challenge the small cannon.

The French offered the men wine. They started to have a good time enjoying the French hospitality. Everyone was pouring wine into the canteen cups and some of the women climbed into the jeeps and kissed the men. A pretty woman about 20 came up to Ed and kissed him. Walt tried to shut down the noise created by his men's exuberance and the cheering French. However, after 40 seconds, he gave up and ordered Nick to drive him about the village. Nick asked, "Why don't you let me stay with the other men. They're having a good time!"

"Someone needs to check to see if the Krauts have laid a trap for us. I'd have a hard time getting Ed back in the jeep. As soon as we finish the tour, you can join the fun."

Walt sat with the Thompson submachine gun on his lap. Nick laid on the horn in an effort to keep the villagers from crowding the jeep. At one point, there were so many jubilant French that Walt fired a few rounds into the air to get the natives to retreat to the doorways. It took Walt and Nick 30 minutes to completely survey every road and dead end alley in the town. There was nothing but jubilant French. The Germans had fled. One French woman, who spoke in broken English, explained that the occupation soldiers only had rifles. She felt that they fled in the two staff cars because they could not put up a defense against an armored car and heavy machine guns.

Walt returned to where the men were drinking wine and eating the sweets offered them by the populace. He pulled to the side of the road and fired five .45 slugs into the air. Everything fell silent. He stood up and demanded order. He granted the men another twenty minutes of revelry but articulated that they needed to move east. They did not pay much attention to him.

A man about fifty years of age emerged from a house and held up a picture of a wrecked train. He told everyone that he was the one that wrecked the train. He had secretly removed the bolts from the rails at night. When the train ran over the section without the bolts, the engine rolled over and caught on fire. The rest of train was demolished and some of the cars caught on fire. The Nazis never determined how or who had caused the wreck. The man was praised by everyone, who slapped him on the shoulders. His wine glass overflowed with the pale red beverage.

After two hours, the French citizens returned to their homes and the 763 patrol moved east. As Walt passed through the center of the village, a Frenchman in uniform rushed to his jeep. The man was carrying an obsolete rifle and asked to join the recon group. He explained that when France surrendered in 1940, he hid his uniform and rifle and now wanted to hunt Nazis. Walt told him that he could not accept a volunteer but agreed to call the regimental CO. The later told the

Frenchman to wait until the next day. He would be inducted into the French army as soon as a recruiter could sign him into the rapidly forming French army. The man was disappointed but there wasn't much that anyone could do.

The 763 patrol moved two miles east of the village. They came to a small stream. The bridge across the stream had been blown. The jeeps roared down the three and as half foot bank, sped through the six inches of water, and up the far side. The armored car slowly drove down the bank and moved slowly through the water but it could not ascend the bank on the east side of the stream. Walt ordered the three jeeps to attach tow lines to the armored car. It moved but could not ascend the bank. The six men pushed the car. It climbed the bank but all the men were dirty and wet. As they washed in the stream, three tanks came down the road and forded the stream; as the second tank climbed the bank, the sergeant whose head was out of the tank shouted, "Get a horse. They never get stuck." The tank crews roared with laughter. The 763 unit maneuvered drown the road at 25 mph. A mile further, they found the three tanks parked at the side of the road. They needed fuel. As the recon patrol pasted them and stopped, one of the Walt's men shouted, "Get a horse. They don't need petro!" The whole crew laughed and pulled to a stop twenty five yards in front of the tankers.

Walt expected to have trouble between the tank crew and his men but they just joked about the difficulties that kept their vehicles from moving. The tanker made hot water and everyone enjoyed hot chocolate or coffee before a fuel truck arrived. Everyone topped off their vehicles including the jeeps.

Since the recon group saw nothing for the next few miles, they pulled into an orchard. They waited ninety minutes for the tankers but the latter did not appear. They assumed the tanks had taken a different road. Walt made his report; and received permission to set up camp until the next morning. They pitched their pup tents, made supper from K rations, set their guard; and went to bed before the sun had completely set. The grass was six inches high and made a nice bed. The men took their tommy guns and rifles to bed with them. At 0230 hours, they were awakening by a violent thunder storm that lasted twenty minutes. Edwin was standing watch and crawled into a jeep with a canvas roof. As the sky lighted in the eastern sky from the early morning sun, they hear firing of either artillery or tanks. They could not see anything and it ceased within fifteen minutes. They never did determine the source of the explosions.

There were spider webs over everything that stuck more than six inches above the ground. The rain drops on the webs in the early morning sun light glistened like little diamonds. It was beautiful and peaceful. The men ate cold C rations. They had not covered two of the jeeps and everything was wet; however, nothing was damaged. Walt pulled a box of hand grenades from one of the jeeps, pried off the top with his bayonet and gave each man two of them with the comment, "If we have a firefight as we did yesterday, you will need these." There was a ground fog, so the patrol moved very slowly because they could only see about 1000 yards ahead.

They drove east for ten miles and saw nothing except a few farmers working in their fields. They stopped and asked if the natives had seen any Germans but all the answers were negative. Late in the afternoon they entered a village about a mile square. No one was on the streets. In the center of the town was a church whose north wall was a pile of rubble. Walt halted the column and all the gunners walked into the church. It was two hundred feet long and sixty feet wide. It looked like a late 17th or early 18th century church. Except for the missing wall, it was well kept. As the men walked about the church looking at the statues and paintings of the Stations of the Cross, the priest entered from the sacristy. He asked in French, "What do you want?"

Ed Yavorski walked over to the priest and answered in French, "We're recon group 763 and looking for German defenses. We have just entered the town but have seen no one. Have the Germans retreated and where are the villagers? They usually flock to our vehicles when we enter an unoccupied town."

"The Germans left last evening. They took a number of villagers as hostages with them. The rest of the villagers are hiding. The town suffered some shelling early in the day but none has occurred for about four hours."

"Let me call Captain Steinberg. He's the commander of our unit."

Walt walked over to where the two men were talking. A conversation started between him and the priest with Ed as the translator. "We need a place to spend the night. We often sleep in our tents in a field but if we may, we'd like to use the church tonight. It is a better bivouac area."

"You may stay the night but you must keep the church clean. I have a Mass at 0730 hours."

"We'll dig latrines outside and bury everything before we leave in the morning. How did the church get damaged?"

"The railroad runs 30 meters behind the church. There was a train sitting there two or three months ago. The Allied bombed it. One bomb hit the church. Since the Germans needed the RR they repaired it, but they would not allow us to repair the church. So far, since there is no real damage except to the blasted wall, we have been able to use the church. I hope the American will let us repair the church."

"I am sure they will. In fact if an engineering company comes through the town, they will hang tarps over the hole and try to get you lumber to start the reconstruction. I'll call the regimental HQ and see if I can arrange for engineers to be here tomorrow."

Walt went to the radio and was told that his request for the engineering company would be considered. He then ordered two men to dig a small slit trench latrine and everyone dragged bedrolls into the church. They prepared coffee in the yard and heated K rations for dinner. Since the Germans were gone, they stationed only one guard. In the twilight, they studied the church a little better. It was built of granite in cruciform architecture. The marble altar set in the nave and there were twenty seats in the choir. There were no pews in the church. There was a painting of Elizabeth and Mary over the altar but it looked modern. The Stations of the Cross were small painting two feet square. Ed Scalise explained that two stations were missing. Everyone assumed that they should hang where the wall had collapsed. Overall the church was very plain and probably had little historic value except that it met the town's needs. As the sun began to set, several parishioners emerged from their cellars and came to inquire about the patrol. Ed was busy talking to them but obtained no useful information. He did not translate most of the conversations.

Early the next morning, the patrol packed their gear and was leaving the church as the priest entered to say Mass. The men waited until the Mass commenced before driving east. Ten parishioners attended the Mass.

At 0930 hours, they ran into two companies of infantry that were hiding in the brush and low three foot banks alongside the road. They were pinned down by German artillery pieces located on the west side of a village. The 763 unit joined the hiding infantry. The senior company commander, Lt. Edward Spade, told Walt that he could not advance since there was open ground between his company and the German defenses. "I have no artillery and am low on supplies. Furthermore, my men only have two 60 mm mortars besides their rifles and light machine guns. I called for air support and armor more than an hour ago but none had arrived. Do you have any suggestions?"

"Hum! We have a 37 mm cannon on the armored car and several fifties. I guess that's a little more than you have?"

"Yes, but we can't cross the fields. When I tried earlier, I lost eight men and never fired a shot."

"We need to know what the Krauts have and how fast they can fire. Maybe we can decoy a jeep out into the open?"

"Will one of your men drive it?"

"Yes, if I ask them?"

Walt and Spade crawled forward with Peter Audernreid until they could carefully see the edge of the village. They thought they could see the muzzle of a 40 mm artillery pieces. Peter was chewing on a cigar that had long gone out and suggested, "I think I can take one of the jeeps and get them to fire on us. I can maneuver in a manner that I don't think they can hit me. If you guys carefully watch, I think you can identify the gun's location. I won't be able to see much because I need to move very fast to avoid the shells. You need to time their ability to fire. I'll have Edwin fire continuously at them so that they can't get a good shot."

"Good, we'll watch."

Peter shouted, "Edwin bring a BAR some extra clips and a canteen. We have a job!" They climbed into the jeep after throwing the BAR and extra clips onto the passenger seat. Edwin checked the machine gun. Pete spun the wheels and the jeep leaped onto the road in front of the crouched infantry men. Pete raced the jeep rapidly forward for 75 yards then made a 90° turn and drove up the embankment for 35 yards. He reversed and came back to the road. The Germans took the bait and tried to hit the jeep but Peter was too quick at making twists and turns and Edwin keep pumping the .50 calibers slugs into the buildings where they thought the artillery piece was hiding. After the second 90° degree turn, he raced back to the hiding infantry. An artillery shell exploded on the road just as the two men reached a safe position. The whole adventure took less than three minutes before the jeep roared back to where the units were crouching.

Peter crawled up to Walt and Spade, who were still scanning the village edge with their field glasses. Edward Spade explained, "That was some driving. Where did you learn that?"

"Weren't nothing. I drove in demolitions derbies before the War. Could you spot the guns?"

Spade answered, "We think so! I got sixty two and seventy four seconds between rounds. Walt, what did you get?"

A DISHONORABLE DISCHARGE

"I got sixty five and sixty six seconds. It takes them about 65 seconds between rounds. Send Vladimir up here."

The armor car driver crawled to where the two officers were laying. Pete followed. Walt handed he driver the field glasses. The three men carefully scanned the village edge. Vladimir was certain that he could identify the muzzles of the guns. He explained, "I think we can move rapidly enough down the road and fire the 37 mm fast enough to knock out the artillery. We will need 15 seconds head start then follow with the other jeeps with their fifties firing. The infantry can run, hide, then run some more behind the jeeps."

Walt stated, "I think the two artillery pieces are only 40 mms and are hid in the building at the end of the first row of houses. They can fire at a rate of about 65 seconds. You can get two round off in that time. We need a decoy so that you can emerge during their first reloading." Turning to Pete, he asked, "Can you run a decoy like you just did but move away from the guns?"

"It's done." The two enlisted men crawled back to the vehicles followed by Lt. Spade. He ordered his men to be ready to move as some as the armored car started to race up the road.

The 763 men spaced out their vehicles in a line. The infantry companies had two jeeps with .30 calibers, and they followed the 763 jeeps. The mortar crews set up their guns and started to drop mortar bombs as close to the buildings as possible. The 763 armored car and Pete's jeep leaped out of hiding and raced down the road with the other jeeps firing as they moved into sight. Everyone moved left and right to prevent the Germans from getting a bead on them. Walt watched nervously. Timing was essential if the 37 mm did not hit the artillery pieces, there would be twenty five or thirty casualties before everyone could take cover.

Within three minutes, the artillery pieces ceased firing and there were holes in the buildings where Walt thought the enemy guns were setup. Vladimir continued to pump shells into the German positions. The jeeps continued to fire until they came close to the buildings; the six men jumped out of the jeeps fifty yards in front of the buildings and hid behind the jeeps, holding their Thompsons and BARs. They continued to fire into the holes which were formed by the small artillery shells. The infantry rapidly moved in front of the jeeps. The complete engagement was over in twenty minutes.

Once the artillery pieces were destroyed, the German infantry ran through the village without regard for their safety. A few German soldiers put up a defense with grenades and rifles but the American infantry overran them within a few minutes. The 763 patrol machine gunned a few Germans but the whole assault was really an infantry effort. Most of the Germans fled. As the MPs attempted to line up prisoners, a French man walked over to the line, pulled out a pistol, and shot one of the Germans in the face. Everyone was agape and the MP disarmed the man. One of the interpreters asked the man why he shot the soldier. He answered, "That soldier raped my 15 year old daughter." The MP escorted the man to the company commander and when the 763 patrol finished searched the village, the man was walking home. No one wanted to challenge him about the murder.

Walt had his unit line up to determine their losses. The armored car left front tire was flat. Either a machine gun or rifle bullet had hit it. Edwin had blood on his face but it was a small graze high on his head and he did not know he had been hit until the blood dripped off his chin. Most of the .50 caliber and .45 caliber[8] ammo was gone. One of the jeeps had six holes in its hood and another had holes below the door. The damage was minor but the patrol would need to hole-up until an ammo truck and fuel truck arrived. Walt reported to regimental headquarters. They said they would send the service vehicles and that they should be in the village before dark. If possible, the recon unit could move west towards the regimental headquarters and meet the service truck on the main highway.

The German prisoners were taken to a large store that served as an interrogation building. They told the interrogating officer that there was less than a company in the village and that they started to flee when the artillery pieces were destroyed. They only had three light machine guns besides the two 40 mm artillery pieces plus rifles and grenades. They were short of ammo and knew that there was hundreds of American pinned down in the brush. Walt walked into the interrogation building but since he could not understand German, he returned to where his men were resting.

The two senior army officers congratulated the recon group for its assistance. They indicated that they would let the regimental commander know how well the patrol had assisted them. The infantry company captain asked, "Where did you guys learn all these tricks?"

"We trained dozens of recon squads at Fort Carson, Colorado. We did it for over two years and learned everything that a patrol unit can

---

[8] Thompson ammo.

and cannot do. We learned to work together and we really developed techniques that any recon group should be able to do."

"You are modest. I have seen several groups and none worked as you and your men did. I will tell the regimental Colonel about your good work."

Walt ordered the jeeps to move to the side of the road. Vladimir felt it was best to leave the armored car where it sat in the field so that further damage would not occur. The group waited two hours until repair and supply vehicles came to the village. It took another hour to refuel, arm, and make emergency repairs to the vehicles. By 1600 hours, they were ready to move west to the regimental HQ in Domfront. They left their vehicles at the service center. Since there were no orders, they headed to the Red Cross tent for rest. Edwin went to the first aid tent to have his wound bandaged. He joined the men in less than thirty minutes. He told them that he was eligible for a Purple Heart. The men all laughed and he explained that he requested that they not give it to him. Everyone congratulated him on his "bravery."

The Red Cross tent was a large white tent with a red cross painted on its roof. It was normally respected by the Luftwaffe and was not subject to strafing. It was a safe haven for the men to rest. The tent was divided into a large enlisted men's section and a smaller officer's section separated by a simple canvas sheet. Before the group separated, Walt told the sergeants, "We will need to find a place to sleep. Inquire and see what you can find. I'll do the same."

Walt entered the officer's section and accepted a donut and a cup of coffee in a porcelain cup from a well-dressed middle aged woman in a Red Cross uniform. He then looked for a place to sit. There were twenty officers in the section. He saw two nurses sitting by themselves near the rear exit. He ambled over to their small table and asked, "May I join you?"

The older women about 30, with wavy brown hair and bright red lips, answered, "Certainly; however, you will need to find another chair, that one is broken." She pointed to the third chair at the table. Walt placed his coffee and donut on the table, found a sturdy chair, and pulled it up to the table. As he sat down, the younger of the women wiped the powdered sugar from her face and asked, "Who are you?" Walt took a slip of coffee and gasped from a burnt tongue. "I should have warned you. The coffee is very hot," stated the younger nurse.

Walt grunted then found his voice, "I'm Captain Walter Steinberg. I command the number 763 reconnaissance patrol. We just returned to

Domfront for fuel and ammo. Our vehicles were slightly damaged in combat earlier in the day and may need a day or so to be repaired."

The younger nurse, who had a pretty face, beautifully manicured long unpainted nails, but wore no lipstick, stated, "I'm Lt. Ashley Miller. We're attached to the field hospital setup in the school across the road at the back of this tent. We just arrived today. As yet, we don't have many patients, so we walked over here for coffee. Our shift is actually finished until tomorrow morning. That is, unless they bring a lot of causalities and call us back during the night."

"You'll probably receive some men from the firefight that we just finished."

Walt looked to the older nurse who stated, "Not by the time we left. They may not have gotten here. Oh! I'm Captain Elaine Shook; I'm the head nurse with this unit. Were there many wounded in your combat engagement?"

"I don't know. We saw three or four men lying by the road. Since we had no real way to transport them, we let the ambulances that were attached to the infantry battalion pick them up. None looked as if they were seriously wounded, but I did not look close enough to make a real assessment. Corpsmen were working on them and we left before the ambulances arrived."

Ashley asked while fingering a gold earring, "To who are you attached?"

"We're officially attached to the 826th Regiment of the 10th Armored Division but we go wherever they tell us to go. We never know from one day to the next where we will be assigned or whom we will need to assist. We hunt for Krauts defenses, make an evaluation of the number of enemy, the equipment they possess, and then run. This morning we ran into a couple of companies that were pinned down by two German artillery piece and a few machine guns. There were about sixty enemy troops. We felt we could destroy the artillery with our 37 mm cannon. My men are good; we did the job with about fifty rounds of cannon ammo. The German defenses fell apart as soon as we destroyed the artillery pieces. They were not mobile and after we destroyed their artillery pieces, they did not put up a fight. However, we burned most of our ammo and fuel. We came back for ammo and other supplies. Where do you women came from?"

Ashley was dressed in a good-looking form fitting white uniform which showed her 33-29-34 figure and answered first, "I'm from Memphis, Tennessee. I took my nursing training at South Central Hospital. I was studying for a BS in Nursing; when in November, 1942, I decided to join the army. I was sent to Sicily in 1943. We arrived in Palermo a few days after it was liberated. I worked in a large Italian Hospital but was never sent to a field hospital. Most of my work was routine–like I had in the USA. The real serious cases never came to our hospital; they were loaded on hospital ships and sent back to the USA. We had a lot of civilian patients; some were wounded but most suffered from neglected sicknesses. My major problem was understanding the translator.

"When the campaign came to an end, I was sent to England to await the invasion. I worked in a hospital in Bath. We had hundreds of minor casualties, who were recovering from their wounds or diseases so that they could be sent back to their units. We had Americans, British, Canadians, Poles, French, and even a few Israelis; until I got to Bath, I did not know that the Jews in Palestine had raised several battalions to fight in North Africa. I landed in France on D + 8 and started to work in a field hospital near St. Mere Eglise. We only moved to the front on July 27. Our field hospital moves every few days."

Elaine was 5'2," had blue eyes, a round face with high forehead, eyebrows with a smooth natural look, cute dimples, and her cheeks possessed a natural pink so that she did not need makeup to enhance her appearance. She had a squatty neck but a very pleasing smile. She was not pretty but was cute. However, she chewed her nails; they were bitten back to the quick and looked rather ugly. Her uniform was slightly soiled which showed that she had been handling patients even if there were not many in the field hospital. She told Walt, "I was at Fort Meade, Maryland. I've been in the army for ten years. I entered immediately after I graduated from nursing school. I wanted a career where I did not have to be an MD assistant. The army was very rewarding. I was sent to England in January to head up a nursing unit. I had twenty five nurses working for me in Southampton. I came to France on June 22 to help set up another field hospital. They needed experienced nurses when the breakout occurred and I volunteered to go to the front. Ashley and I met while waiting for transportation. We immediately became friends."

Ashley, who had a long face, ears that were very close to her head and tiny gold earrings in pierced ears, stated, "We usually show a movie every night. Why don't you bring your men? If you can't find room, ask for me and I'll find you chairs."

"We'll have to see what the regimental commander has for us but if we don't have to move out until morning, we'll be there. What time do you start and what are you showing?"

"We start at 2030 hours but sometimes it is not dark enough. I have no idea what will be shown. The Signal Corps brings the movie and we show whatever they bring."

Ed entered and Walt left with the entire 763 patrol. They found a mess tent and had a hot meal. Walt and Ed walked back to the regimental headquarters and were told that they had no order but to return at daylight. The men found a bivouac area then walked about the town and at 2015, found the school that was being used as a hospital. There were only 30 men and nurses waiting for the movie. There was no separation by ranks and the entire 763 patrol sat together. Just before the picture started, Ashley arrived, she had put on fresh red lipstick but not as bright as Elaine's and was still wearing her nursing uniform. She pulled up a chair alongside of Walt. She removed a small pair of wire glasses from a glass case in her pocket and said, "I need glasses for seeing movies and for some reading. I almost never wear them in the hospital; however, I often leave them stuck on top of my head and often ask, 'Where did I leave my glasses?' It's embarrassing when someone tells me that they are on top of my head."

The movie was *The White Cliffs of Dover*, a typical propaganda movie but the plot was good. It was about an American woman, played by Irene Dunne, who married a British army officer in World War I, and was now working in a hospital. The military brought in the casualties from the Dieppe Raid. Her son, played by Peter Lawford, was one of the fatally wounded men. When the movie culminated, Ashley suggested, "Why don't you come to the nurse's quarters with me and we can serve you a cup of coffee?"

"We only have two jeeps for the ten of us."

"Bring your sergeant. I am sure the rest can crowd into the other jeep."

Walt and Ed walked with Ashley to the little house next to the school. There were four nurses including Elaine, who was wearing sweat pants, a sweat shirt, and sandals, in the kitchen drinking coffee. They made room for the three newcomers. The conversation was centered on the August 4 issue of the *Stars and Strips* that had circulated in the hospital. The American 2nd division was approaching Brest and its U-boat pens but the greatest concern was the V-1 buzz bombs, which had plowed into seven hospitals in the London area. Some of the hospitals were military but most were civilian. The bombs killed several people. Walt and Ed had not seen the paper. The women also talked about the breakout and the low casualty list.

Walt assessed Ashley, who sat next to him in good light. Her hair was blond but longer on top and brown at the nap of her neck; he realized that it was severely sun bleached. He face was narrow with a short neck. She wore a gold bracelet and a gold wrist watch whose dial was quite large. After fifteen minutes, Ashley comment, "I need to get to bed. We serve breakfast at 0700 hours and I must be at my station by 0730 hours. If you're in the area, please come back. We try to show a movie every evening."

"I have no idea where we will be on any day, but I will hunt for you if I can. What is your unit number?"

"Number 1411."

As they walked to the door, Walt commented, "Your pretty enough for me to want to kiss you. I know it's an inappropriate remark but it is the way I feel."

"Maybe next time that you are here; I'll let you." She giggled.

Walt added as they separated, "That's a good reason to find time to return for a movie."

Chapter 3

France, August 1944

Wounded

THE 763 patrol returned to scouting the roads to the east of the regiment HQ. The patrol moved to the small village of St. Jerome where they came across four partly burned Sherman tanks. There were six men standing by the road. The patrol stopped. The tanker CO announced, "We were hit by an 88 mm that was hid in the brush." He pointed to a line of trees and brush 300 yards on the left. "The Nazis destroyed two tanks before we saw them and could return the fire. Fortunately, there was a company of infantry with a Priest[9] and other vehicles behind us. They started to fire on the Krauts but the 88 mm hit two more of our tanks before the infantry mortars and howitzer got the range. We lost sixteen men—six wounded and ten killed. The Germans lost thirty men but I don't know how many of the infantry were hit during the firefight. Ambulances came up behind the infantry and took the wounded to a field hospital before I could count the causalities."

"If you don't need us, we'll try to catch the infantry and scout for them."

"Go ahead. We're waiting for a tank retriever unit to determine if these are junk (he waved across the burned tanks) or if they can be repaired."

They caught the infantry and two tanks in a battle two miles down the road. The company had no use for the recon patrol. It retreated to a cross roads and then drove south.

They were on the road for three days. They were driving cautiously on a nice two lane highway when Walt spotted a low flying plane

---

[9] The "Priest," officially Motor Carriage, Howitzer, 105mm, was a self-propelled artillery piece. It mounted a 105 mm howitzer and a .50 caliber machine gun.

directly in front of the patrol. The vehicles scattered in all directions. As the plane came closer, Walt saw the white star on the wing; it was smoking and landed a hundred yards behind the patrol. Everyone turned around and hastily drove to the wreck. The pilot was climbing out. He fell in the dirt. As Walt's jeep pulled alongside of the wreck, he shouted, "Are you wounded?"

The pilot stood up and shouted, "Naw! I was hit by light flax and it smashed the oil line. I was flying low and could not gain altitude. I was looking for a place to land. When I saw your convoy, I decided to put the plane down. It didn't catch fire, so I guess it can be repaired. Do you have a radio?"

"Yes."

"I'm Lt. Gerald Pitman. Report that I crashed landed and need assistance. My shoulder hurts but I don't think it is broken."

Walt got on the radio. "A P-47 has crashed a few hundred yards behind my patrol. The pilot is Lt. Pitman and not seriously hurt. The plane did not catch fire. What should I do?"

"Stay with the pilot. We'll send a staff jeep to retrieve the man. We should be there in thirty minutes." Forty five minutes later, the 763 unit was back on patrol and never saw the pilot again. On a return trip, they observed that the fighter was gone.

Although the patrol identified a number of German emplacements, they rarely participated in any of the fighting and just reported what they saw. By Friday afternoon, they were low on ammo and fuel. They could have found a service depot near to their location but Walt decided to return to Domfront. Thus they could attend the movie and he could see Ashley. As they entered the town, they passed a farmer's market; Walt stopped the column and purchased a dozen carnations. The men kidded him about returning to see the nurse. He blushed but said nothing. They parked their vehicles outside of the hospital and Walt ran into the reception area to leave the flowers. He enclosed a note, *"Pretty flowers for a pretty face. We'll be at the movie tonight! Walt Steinberg."* As he climbed back into the jeep, he told Ed, "I guess roses would have been better than carnations but at this time of the year they are difficult to find." Everyone laughed.

It was 1800 hours by the time that they checked into the service center. While the men serviced the vehicles, Walt and Ed walked over to the regimental headquarters and asked for orders. The place was in disarray. The sergeant informed them, "We're planning to move in the morning. Bring back your unit at 0600 hours to help us."

"Is the hospital also moving?"

"I don't know. Probably, as soon as they can move the wounded to a more permanent facility. They have asked for twenty ambulances for tomorrow. I don't have any further information. I might have more in the morning."

Walt and his men found a hot meal at the service center. It was much better than they experience in Carteret. At 2030 hours, they entered the movie. Again Ashley joined them just after the movie began. She was wearing WAC shoes, a tan army uniform which showed no bust line, red lipstick, and combed her hair back as far as it would go: her hair was too short but the style emphasized her narrow face and pink cheeks. She looked very nice but not good enough, except for Walt, to serve as a pinup girl. He was very interested in her. She dug her glasses out of her shirt pocket and adjusted them so she could see the screen. The signal corps showed *Destroyer*, a movie starting Edward G. Robinson and Glenn Ford. Walt had seen the movie before he left the USA but did not care; he wanted to see Ashley. At the end of the movie, he asked, "Is there coffee tonight?"

"Certainly."

"We brought all three jeeps so my men will not need to crowd into one jeep."

"Bring your sergeant. I'll catch Elaine and tell her that you are coming for coffee."

Walt recapped the instructions to his men about the morning patrol then he and Ed followed Ashley. Elaine joined the three other military personnel as they entered the school house kitchen. Five nurses were in the kitchen. It was too crowded for four more people; thus Walt and Ashley poured themselves a cup of coffee and withdrew to the front steps of the school house. Ashley opened the conversation, "What did you do for the last three days? We had a large number of causalities. I wondered if you were in any of the firefights."

"We patrolled the roads east of here. We ran into a tank company that was badly shot up. You might have gotten their casualties. We moved south and found a downed P-47. We helped the pilot get back to his squadron. We located a number of Nazi units. They fired on us twice but we just radioed their location and ran. We suffered no casualties and our equipment was not really damaged. We needed fuel and ammo so we returned to Domfront. We could have gone to nearer supply depot but I did not know where to find any."

"Was I part of your decision?"

"Yes. You promised me a kiss if I came back. I came to collect it.'

"I don't think I promised; I think I offered to think about it."

"Hum! This is going to a conflict of wills. I think my memory is better than yours!" commented the Captain.

"Okay, if it will shut you up, I'll give you a light kiss but only because you brought me flowers."

Walt adjusted himself and Ashley gave him a light kiss on his left cheek. He objected, "That wasn't much."

"You got your kiss; now shut up," Ashley giggled.

Walt joking remarked, "If I bring you flowers next time, will I obtain a better kiss."

"I don't know; let's see what the flowers look like," she laughed heartily.

"What did you do with the flowers?"

"I put them in a vase and set them on a table in the room that I share with three other nurses."

"Couldn't you display them in a better place?"

"No, this is a field hospital. We don't have officer or nursing areas except for the registration portion of the tent. Back in Memphis, I had an office where I could exhibit items."

Walt changed the subject, "The regimental headquarters are moving forward tomorrow. Are you moving with them?"

"Yes, as soon as we can transport the wounded to a more permanent hospital. We have ordered ambulances for tomorrow but I doubt if we will move everyone. It will probably be Saturday or Sunday before we can start to pack our gear and find transportation. We hope to be set up at the new location by Monday evening. Do you know where the headquarters is going?"

"No. We were told to be to there at 0600 hours and to travel with them. We have four fifties on our vehicles and they could use the AA guns. However, we have only seen two kraut planes since we moved out of St. Lo more than a week ago. I think the regimental officers are being awful careful. However, orders are orders, so we will add our firepower to theirs. How tall are you?"

"Five foot four. That's irrelevant, why did you asked?"

"Just curious. I though you and Elaine were the same height. Tonight I notice a small mole on the right side of your face just below the nose. I had not noticed it until this evening."

"I have had it all my life. Most people do not see it. Several people have suggested that I have it removed, but I'm afraid that the surgery might leave a scar which would be much more evident than the mole."

"That's a good reason. I cannot see it unless I am very close to you; like when you kissed me."

"Where do you come from?"

"I grew up in Marietta, Ohio. It is a river port on the Ohio River but its heyday was during the riverboat era. The railroads put an end to most of the river traffic. My father works for the Port Authority but had little to do until the War broke out. Now he is very busy. In the last letter that I received from him, he told me that he had not gone to church for three weeks because he had to work 12-14 hours every day. The port has a good railroad connection and is busy ferrying finished War materials to the Gulf of Mexico or raw materials to the industry up north.

"I was in college when the Japanese attacked Pearl Harbor and was drafted as soon as I graduated. I became the CO of the 763 patrol in November, 1942. Not much of a story. Oh! My father often needed help but I preferred to work at Boy Scout Camp as a counselor."

"What rank were you in the Boy Scouts?"

"I earned my Eagle Award in November, 1937. It earned me a position as a platoon leader in basic training. With the administrative position, I avoided much of the abuse suffered by the other recruits when the staff sergeants were not pleased with the conscripts' progress."

"Are you going back to Marietta after the War?"

"I don't know. My degree is in Industrial Engineering. The only job I was offered before I was drafted was in the parachute plant. When the War comes to an end, it will close. I will probably need to look for a position someplace else. Are you going back to Memphis?"

"Most likely. I had a position in a small hospital before I joined the army but I think I would rather work for a private physician. My parents told me that each week there are lots of ads in the newspaper. Oh! My father operates a small cotton gin. He works hard from November through February but spend most of the rest of the year repairing equipment or selling the by-products, like cotton seeds. Does your mother work?"

"Not really. She mends clothing for a local dry cleaner but has become very busy since the War began. People want to repair their clothing rather than try to find new. Does your mother work? "

"Part time. She keeps the books for the cotton gin that my father operates. The owner comes to see her about once a week to sign checks. She only works 10-15 hour a week."

By this time Elaine and Ed emerged from the kitchen; Walt and Ashley shook hands and agreed to meet again in the next few weeks.

As they entered the nursing quarters, Elaine asked Ashley, "Are you interested in Walt?"

"Maybe! He's a nice guy."

Early the next morning, the regimental command moved out.
They had one quadruped .50 caliber MG and one dual 37 mm anti-
aircraft battery. They put Walt's jeep and the armored car in the front
of the column where they could position their guns as AA and the
other two jeeps in the rear. There were eight trucks and about 60 men.
Walt realized that they needed his patrol since the regimental command was very short of ordnance either against aircraft or pockets of
Germans who might want to attack a lightly armed convoy. They
drove nearly 60 miles than pulled into a field near Laval. The regimental commander searched out Walt and gave the order, "I want your
patrol to scout the back roads within five miles of our command post.
We'll have the radio setup in 15 minutes so that you can contact us.
Mark your map where you have reconnoitered and be back by 1600
hours. If you see anything, contact us immediately."

The 763 patrol moved east along the back roads. At 1240 hours,
they entered a farm yard; four German soldiers came out of the barn
with their hands up. The soldiers had been left behind when their battalion moved east. They had hid in the barn for two days, had nothing
to eat, and very little to drink. They surrendered because they felt that
they had no chance of linking up with their combat unit.

Walt radioed headquarters, "I have four German soldiers who surrendered to us. Their unit abandoned them. What are we to do?"

"There's a battalion four miles east on the main road. Take them
there and the MPs will relieve you of them. We'll radio the battalion
and tell them that you are coming."

The recon men locked down the machine guns in the two rear
jeeps, then herded the four Germans into the back seats. The jeep gunners assumed the co-pilot's seats with sub machine guns on their laps.
Twenty minutes later, they rolled into the battalion resting at the side
of a road and turned their POW over to a MP. The MP scratched his
head. "I'm not sure what I can do with them but will find a POW
stockade someplace." Walt radioed regimental headquarters and then
went back to scouting the back roads. They saw nothing but a few
American army trucks and arrived at HQ at 1614 hours. They delivered their report and the CO congratulated them for a "Well Done"
job. He then ordered the men to scout a road parallel to the main road
three miles north of where the HQ was located

They drove five miles and saw nothing. They pulled off the road and set up camp for the night. Prior to dawn, they rose, ate cold C rations, and move out at ten mph.

They scouted the back roads and the main highway. They passed a number of infantry battalions marching to the east and saw two armored units parked at the side of the road. They passed four M18 Hellcats.[10] The latter could move at over 30 mph and had a 76 mm gun which could stop anything but a Tiger tank. There were hundreds in France but these were the first combat vehicles of this type that the 763 men observed.

No one had any orders for them. The next day they spotted a German patrol which fired upon the Americans with their 20 mm AA gun. The German gunners were accurate and hit the middle wheel on the left side of the armored car. They also knocked the hood (bonnet) off jeep 4931; the hood hit Mike Goldsmith as it flew back and gave him a nasty gash on his shoulder and head. The 4227 jeep had five bullet holes and the 5566 had a punctured tire. The 763 recon groups returned the fire with everything they had. The German patrol turned and retreated east. As they move away, Walt saw a soldier rise up with his rifle. He took careful aim with his colt .45 and with the first shot, hit the German in the head. When examining the soldier, that Walt had shot, Vladimir saw one large hole in the soldier's head. The 763 fellows knew that he died instantaneously.

The men carefully treated Mike's wounds, replace the punctured tires, and surveyed the damage to the other vehicles. They realized that their vehicles needed repairs before moving forward again. They limped back to the service area near the regimental headquarters. Walt stopped to buy carnations. He delivered them and Mike to the field hospital before making his report. The hospital and service area were less than 100 yards from the HQ.

Mike was put to bed in the hospital and the other men went to the movies that night. Walt had time to see Ashley and Elaine during the coffee social after the movies. This time when no one was in sight, Ashley permitted him to give her a mildly passionate kiss.

Ashley asked, "What do you know about the Falaise counterattack?"

"Not much. We were south of the fighting and were not ordered into the area; probably because an armored car is worthless in a real

---

[10] M18 was a self-propelled tracked antitank Motor Gun Carriage which mounted a 76 mm antitank gun and a .50 caliber machine gun.

firefight. I do know that the British sent a number of their armored cars along the roads. The British armored cars have only four wheels but can get bogged down more easily than our M8. It does have a 37 mm gun like our cars.

"The Canadians attacked on August 7 and sought to seize Falaise; it's about 70 miles NW of here. The initial object was to cut off the German counterattack towards Vire, which is on the road to St. Lo. About 40,000 Nazis regrouped. Our American troops were already in Le Mans. There were four or five divisions in the area and no one was worried about the German movements. I saw pictures of hundreds of tanks, trucks, cars, *et cetera* that were wrecked along the roads. Everywhere there were dead men and horses. I've been told that there were more than 10,000 dead and 50,000 prisoners taken in the pocket."

"We must have had 300 to 400 casualties in our hospital. All our beds were full. Everyone worked 16-18 hours and we are still tired. Most of the causalities brought to us were American but we had some French, Poles, and Canadians. At the beginning of the fight, we had more Germans than Allies. When we ran out of facilities, we sent the wounded to other clinics. We are now moving the minor wounded out of the hospital. Where are you going this time?"

"I don't know; the regiment had no orders when I stopped earlier. All our vehicles were damaged in the fire fight where Mike was wounded. We'll be here several days while they are repaired. I assume we will be sent on the same scouting missions that we have been doing for the last several weeks. The front line is moving very rapidly. Are you going to move again?"

"I doubt it. The rumor is that we will move to the Paris area once it is liberated. However, it is only a rumor and means nothing until it is translated into real orders."

"I know what you mean. There were lots of rumors at Ft. Carson while we were training the new recon units. About 90% were wrong. "

One afternoon while visiting Mike, Walt met Elaine alone and asked, "Why don't you paint your nails a bright red? It might help you to stop chewing them."

"Most nurses do not paint their nails."

"You're in charge, who's going to tell you what to do?"

"I had not thought of it that way. I'll give it some thought."

It took three days to repair everything. By that time, Mike's wounds had healed sufficiently that he rejoined the unit as the vehicles were able to move out on a patrol.

Late in the morning of August 27, the 763 patrol was moving along a narrow stream on their right. There was a small forest ahead. There was also a ten foot embankment on their left. The visibility was very poor. They moved at 15 mph and the men manned the .50s in all the vehicles. Walt carefully studied everything he could see but realized that they could be ambushed. He stopped the column ever mile and a half, climbed the embankment, and scanned the area in front and to the north. Most of the time, he saw nothing but a few French farmers tending their fields. After 30 minutes, he stopped and saw a cloud of dust on the road north of them; it looked like a battalion moving to a new position. He learned from a radio message that a friendly battalion was heading for the junction of the Husine River and stream that the patrol was following. However, even though he had a good map, he could not identify the name of the stream and he could not estimate where he might meet up with the battalion.

The patrol continued to move forward feeling a little more secure with the knowledge that a battalion was less than two miles north of them. Suddenly a mortar shell exploded on the embankment on their left and showered everyone with dirt. Before they could react, a second shell hit the embankment less than five feet from the command jeep. Walt was thrown out of the jeep and down the embankment into the stream. The jeep rolled down the edge of the stream and landed on top of him. Nicholas was thrown out of the back of the jeep and landed on his shoulder; however, except for bruises and a few scratches, he was not seriously hurt. Ed fell out of the left side of the jeep, hit the ground hard, and hear a loud snap. His left forearm was broken.

The armored car's 37 mm cannon erupted and Jacob poured eight shells into the woods where he thought the Germans may have set up the mortar. The other men fired the two machine guns into the brush with the hope that they might also hit something. There was nothing to see and the firing became indiscriminate. As Jacob positioned the 37 mm to cover them, the two undamaged jeeps roared down the three foot embankment and across the stream into the brush. They continued to fire their MG as they moved forward. When the trees became too thick to drive through, the drivers grabbed their Thompsons and bounded through the woods on foot. As soon as the jeeps were out of sight, they slowed and carefully advanced to a level spot, 70 yards from the stream. It looked like an ideal site for a mortar setup. There was debris and two empty shell casings but no enemy soldiers. It appeared as if the enemy mortar squad had made a hasty retreat after the 37 mm cannon started to fissure the trees. There was no evidence of either dead or wounded. They assumed the enemy squad had escaped without any causality. Ten yards beyond the site was a dirt trail. It had tire tracks from either a staff car or a light truck. The two men felt sure that the Krauts had escaped, so they hiked back to their jeeps. They now needed to determine how badly Walt and Ed were injured.

Ed sat on the embankment: his left arm hanging uselessly by his side. Nicholas had propped himself against the front of the armored car. As the two jeeps reached the road, the three men in the armored car emerged and all seven uninjured men descended the small embankment into the stream. The men carefully lifted the jeep off of Walt and dumped it right side up on the road. The radio was a wreck, petrol was leaking from a small hole in the gas tank, and the .50 caliber ammo was scattered all over the area. The Thompson lay in the creek with K rations, and scattered hand grenades. Two men retrieved the stretcher from the back of the armored car. Four men carefully lifted Walt and deposited his wet body onto the stretcher. He had several broken ribs, a compound fractured leg, and a broken arm. They splinted the arms and leg as best they could, taped gauze over the slow bleeding wound to inhibit, if not stop, the blood flow, gave him a shot of morphine, and carried him to the road. They tied him to the stretcher, and then carefully placed it on the rear of jeep 5566.

Jacob tried to start Walt's jeep. The engine ran for a moment, coughed, and died. It turned over a second time and kept running. The six men pushed it until it faced west. It needed repairs but it continued to run with a few occasional coughs and some sputtering. Walt was under extreme pain. He ordered the patrol to leave him and chase the fleeing Germans: however, Jacob, who was now the highest ranking enlisted men countermanded the order, had the vehicles turn around, and headed for the field hospital in Laval. Ed took the shotgun seat in Jeep 4747 at the rear of the convoy. His pain was not intense and he refused a morphine shot. Nick drove the battered jeep in the third position. Even though they could only move at 15 mph, Nick had some difficulty remaining within sight of rest of the convoy. To everyone's surprise, they did not pass any infantry or armored units until they were within sight of the field hospital and regimental headquarters. The drive was very tedious. The ruts in the roads made the jeeps bounce and each time they hit a hole, Walt and Ed let out a moan. Twice the patrol stopped to see if they could help the injured, but the latter denied everything but a few sips of water. It took them over two hours to reach the hospital.

Ed walked into the hospital entrance and sat down as a nurse looked at his limp broken arm. He was exhausted and nearly collapsed; the examining nurse caught him before he fell and guided him to a bed. She removed his dirty clothing as a doctor approached the bed. The nurse started to wash the dirt off of him and the doctor examined his arm. The only significant injury was the broken arm; he also had a few insignificant scratches and bruises.

Nick's wounds were less than Ed's. A nurse washed them off poured antiseptic over them and bandaged them. He gave a short report to the attending nurse, "We were attacked by a Nazi mortar squad. The shells hit the embankment and our jeep rolled over on top of Captain Steinberg. Sergeant Smith and I were thrown clear of the jeep." When he finished his report, he was told to go to the Red Cross tent for coffee and donuts to calm his nerves.

Walt was in terrible pain from riding on the stretcher tied to back of the jeep. Four of the 763 men carried Walt directly into the examining room behind the reception area. Two doctors gave him narcotics to reduce the pain and looked at his broken bones. The four carriers were dismissed and along with the other three men followed Nick to the Red Cross tent.

Jacob was now the highest ranking member of the patrol. He left the table after fifteen minutes to make a report at the regimental headquarters. He returned after a few minutes. The officer in charge asked him to fill out the forms for a Purple Heart for Walt and Ed. He was then told to let the patrol members relax until the next morning. The men spent forty five minutes reviewing the day's events. They were extremely concerned that Walt's wounds were more serious than they perceived and that he might not survive the night. It was the first time that the recon group had suffered serious causalities.

Ed's and Nick's wounds were not serious. In fact, Jacob refused to fill out the Purple Heart papers for Nick. After everyone had calmed down, they took the vehicles to the service area for repairs. Jeep 4727 needed extensive repairs. The service mechanic estimated it would probably not be ready for patrols for four weeks; possibility, when Walt and Nick were well enough to return to the unit.

A Dishonorable Discharge

Chapter 4

Marietta, Ohio

August 1944

EVERYTHING was wet from a strong thunder shower that had just passed through Marietta in the morning. The sun was starting to reappear when the doorbell rang at the Steinberg's home on Maple Drive. Since Walt's mother, Helen, was a housewife, she wore a washed off house dress with fading blue flowers. She was canning peaches that she had bought earlier in the day at the farmer's market. She rushed to the door to answer it because she needed to take the jars out of the canner. She threw open the door. A Western Union messenger stood on the bottom step, "A telegram for Mr. or Mrs. Steinberg. Are you Mrs. Steinberg?"

"Yes."

"Sign here." The messenger boy pointed to a line on his clip board.

Helen scribbled her name and asked, "Is the telegram from the War Department?"

"I'm not sure but likely. Most of the telegrams that I deliver are from either the War or Navy Departments. I see by the star in your window that you have a son serving in the military. Where?"

"He's in the army someplace in France."

She knew she had to be discrete about what she told the messenger boy. If she told him too much, he might tell someone who would accuse Walt of breaking military secrecy. She knew that he was attached to the 10th Armored Division and from the newspaper articles; both she and her husband knew he had been part of the American breakout and was racing across France. Even though there was a fight known as the Falaise pocket, they knew he was not involved in the battle. Walt had told them a little about the country through which he was traveling and from the description they knew it was not near Falaise. The newspapers estimated that 40,000 Wehrmacht troops had tried to escape through the small pocket between the British and American armies. There were photographs of dead Germans and ruined German equipment in all the weekly news magazines. One of the correspondents hinted that the information about the fights was delayed for 48 hours by Allied commanders to make it impossible to know the losses on both sides. .

"I need to be going. I have two more delivers on Maple Drive." The young man ran to his motorcycle.

Helen tore open the envelope as she hasty moved back to the kitchen. She had to wait until she retrieved her glasses from the kitchen counter before she could read the message. It stated:

> *The Secretary of War expresses his deep regrets to inform you that your son, Captain Walter Glenn. Steinberg was wounded in action on August 27 in France.*

She did not reread the telegram but laid it on the corner of the kitchen table and took off her glasses. She thought "It is only three days. I did not think they responded that fast." She returned to her freshly canned peaches. She removed them from the canister and placed them on the counter to cool. She took each jar and tightened the lids so that they would seal properly. When all the jars were tightly sealed and cooling, she called her husband, Frank, and notified him that Walt had been wounded.

She proceeded to prepare another batch of peaches. She had just placed the last of the peaches in the canner when her daughter, Abigail, came into the house after teaching a swimming lesson at the local pool. She asked, "Is anything new?"

"Yes, your brother has been wounded!"

"How bad?"

"I don't know. The telegram from the War Department lies on the table. It doesn't say anything."

Abby quickly read the yellow paper. "They don't tell you anything."

"That's what I said. I guess we'll have to wait until we get a letter from Walt to find out what happened. It will be a hard two weeks waiting to hear from him."

"He might be sent home."

"That's a possibility. We will need to wait until we get more information before we can make predictions."

"In his last letter, he told us that he had met a nice nurse. Did he purposely get wounded so that she would have to take care of him?"

She giggled. He mother gave her a censured look; then returned to her canning rather than create an embarrassing conversation. Abby ran out of the kitchen still laughing.

Frank came home for his dinner at 5:30. He asked, "Did you try to find out any more about Walt's wounds? "

"No. I am not sure what can be done. Pearl Lange's son was wounded at Mt. Casino in Italy. She belongs to the church and waited three weeks for a letter from her son to find out what happened. As you know, he lost a leg and arrived in the USA about two months later. We'll have to wait and see what happened. Do you think they will deliver our letters if we write to Walt's former address?"

"Of course. He is wounded and in a hospital. They'll find him and deliver the letters. In the last War,[11] they tried to expedite delivery to the wounded. They knew that it helped morale. There are all kinds of ads asking families to write to the GIs. I would expect that it is more important now that he is wounded. I'll write a note this evening."

After dinner, Frank wrote a short letter to his son. He let him know that they had received a telegram from the War Department and would be looking for his letter. He continued by telling Walt that his sister was doing very well as a swimming instructor and that twelve river boats had docked in Marietta that day. The latter was difficult because there were insufficient piers but that they had all tied up by the time he traveled home.

The local newspaper learned about the telegram and listed Walter G. Steinberg as a casualty in France. It was an abbreviated note in a short paragraph that listed eight other military personal from the Marietta area as causalities. No details were given for any of them.

After the telegram arrived, Helen phoned the pastor of St. Peter's church and requested that Walt's name be added to the list of causalities from the parish. The next Sunday morning his name appeared in the prayer list among the many members of the parish that were either wounded or killed. Each Sunday morning after the service, the pastor queried the Steinberg's if they had any further news. The first two Sundays, Helen shook her head but on the third Sunday, she told the Pastor that she had received a form letter from a regimental chaplain telling her that he had a number of broken bones but no other news. The letter, a typical military airmail letter, was written on the 10th Armored Division stationary. It had been microfilmed in France and

---

[11] World War I.

printed in the USA. The chaplain explained that more information would be forth coming in a few days. It was informative in that it informed them that Walt had not lost any organs or limbs but needed to rest and let time heal the wounds. There was nothing specific about the injuries.

Walt's first letter arrived two weeks after the chaplain's. He did not say much except that his only wounds were broken bones. The second letter came five days later:

Dear Mom, Dad, and Abby,

I want you to know that I am healing. My ribs are still tapped but there is no pain. The doctors expect to remove the tape in 6-10 days. My arm is in a cast but I have limited use of my hand. It itches. I no longer need anyone to assist me in eating and I can move the chess pieces when I play the game. A non-com comes almost every day to play and I am getting better at playing chess. I may try to enter a tournament when I get home.

My leg is slowly healing. The doctors feel I will be walking with a cane in about six weeks. I expect to be back with my recon group early in October.

Lots of love, Walt

Two days before Walt's second letter arrived, Frank called home in the mid-afternoon. "A riverboat ran into a barrage full of railroad cars and the barge sank. I don't know when I will be home. It is one of the worse accidents that I have seen since I have been working on the river. I will need to be at the site for the next few hours. I love you."

At nine PM, he finally came home. Helen had kept dinner for him. While he ate, he told her. "I don't know how the two collided. The riverboat came from Pittsburgh with a load of specialty steel. Its bow is crushed. I put it into a dock on the outskirts of town. It will need to be repaired before the Coast Guard will allow it to ply the river again. No one was hurt on the boat but it is a mess. The barge was loaded with RR cars full of barrels filled with petroleum products but I don't know what was in them. I suspect they contain chemicals but they are not under my jurisdiction so I had no listing of the contents. We called the Corps of Army Engineers immediately upon being notified of the wreck. They dispatched a barge with a crane as soon as I told them what happened. The crane had to come from Covington, Kentucky and did not arrive until 8:30. They are planning to work all night.

They hope to pull the RR cars out of the river and move them to shore. The river is not deep but if the barrels got smashed it could contaminate everything for hundreds of miles. Since there was nothing I can do until morning, I came home. I'll have to be back at dawn."

Frank rose before dawn, ate a hasty breakfast, and was at the wharf as it turned light. All but two of the railroad cars had been moved to the shore and fortunately none of the barrels had broken open. He spent the entire day trying to collect data on the accident. He arrived home at 6:20 that evening and before he went to bed wrote Walt a letter about the accident.

Dear Walt,

A riverboat and a barge collided in the river. Apparently the barge was moving twelve railroad cars full of 55 gallon drums of chemicals to the RR siding. The barge captain turned towards the mooring and the riverboat ran into him. One of the barge crewmen was seriously hurt and one of the riverboat crew was hurt. I put the riverboat into dock #22. I will need to have it repaired before the Coast Guard will allow it to move. The Corps of Army Engineers brought a crane and moved all the railroad cars to the river bank. Most are still sitting there. They are not seriously damaged, so I suppose that they will be moved as soon as they can be loaded onto the tracks. This was the worse wreck that I have seen in my thirty years of working on the wharfs. Fortunately it will all be cleaned up by next weekend. As you once, said, 'There is never a dull moment in this business...'

Janet Moore got married but I don't know anything else. It was a small ceremony in the church. I only know about it because the flowers on the altar were left after the wedding and there was a notice in the bulletin that the flowers came from her wedding.

Love, Dad

When Walt was home in April, he told the family that he was heading for England but did not know anything else. He knew the Allies were preparing for the invasion but everything was unsubstantial rumors at Fort Carson like those that circulated about the Sicily and Italy before the Mediterranean invasions. The most important rumor about the Mediterranean activities was that the invasion would occur in Sardinia rather than Italy. One of the officers in the intelligence office had good information, so good, that the men were surprised when the actual invasion occurred at Salerno, Italy. Because of the bad rumors, Walt began to discount anything until an official announcement was made on the base. Actually, he began to believe that the French invasion would not occur until warm weather arrived in July

He came home at Easter during his freshman year in college. He had always attended some of the Easter service at St. Peter's Church but had too many commitments to go to all of them. Being in college, he was free for the entire Passion Week. He went to the Tenebrae Service and to Communion at dawn on Easter morning. He spent more hours in church during the spring of 1939 than he had at any previous Easter. His mother always went with him and his father attended when possible. To him the music was excellent during the holiday season and helped him feel that God had blessed hm.

To his surprise, Janet Moore and her parents came to his parent's home for dinner on Easter Day in 1939. Walt's mother and Mrs. Moore had become good friend knitting scarves, sweaters, and hats for the poorer inmates in the county home. She invited the Moore family to dinner partly because Walt had expressed an interest in Janet while he was still in high school. Again nothing came of the parental effort to be matchmakers.

After the Easter Service during his third year in college, the pastor approached him with the suggestion, "Why don't you study for the ministry?"

"I never thought of it but no! I think I want to be an engineer. The ministry never really appealed to me. I don't think that I am a good enough Christian."

The pastor asked him twice more before he graduated from college but Walt never changed his mind.

He told his father about his feelings. The older man commented, "You have known Pastor Pearlman since you were a little boy. He taught you all you know about the church. When you listen to him either in leading a service or preaching a sermon, you feel as if it is an extension of the religious education that he gave you as a young man. I think your spiritual life is wrought by your personal love/like for the man. Maybe you will meet more men who are dedicated to Jesus Christ and live the life you think a Christian should live, you'll open up and accept the inspiration that they want to impart to you. Is it one of the reasons, you never showed any interest in entering the ministry?"

A DISHONORABLE DISCHARGE

"I'm not sure." He felt uncomfortable but made no further comment. Mentally he agreed that his father's appraisal was very close to the truth.

When he was a sophomore in college, the Tommy Dorsey Band came to the University for a Dance, which was open to all students. He was unable to acquire a date and still had those memories after his basic training. He developed a fancy for jazz/big band music and wanted to attend the dance. He asked several coeds but none accepted his invitation. He could have purchased a single ticket and sat in the balcony to hear the music but since the concert was being broadcast over the University radio station, he stayed in his room writing a Physics report and listened to the music over his roommate's radio.

Artie Shaw played on the campus in 1941 and again he tried to obtain a date but was unsuccessful. His problem was that he would not ask just "any coed," he was too fussy and only asked two girls, both of whom refused. He decided to listen to the concert on the radio. When he announced his decision to stay in his room, his friends threw up their hands in despair. They felt that he should have tried harder and not just try to arrange a date with his ideal ladies.

While at home, he attended church every Sunday with his mother and sister. His father rarely joined them because he usually worked on Sundays. One Sunday, he saw Janet Moore but she avoided him and he did not even try to greet her. He was home during the Easter Holy Season and the whole family had a great holiday. Like when he was in college, he was able to attend the Tenebrae Service and the three hour Good Friday ecumenical Protestant service. He never felt strongly inspired during the services; although it gave him a sense of Christ's suffering on the cross. Generic Protestant services in either scout camp or the army bases gave him a feeling that he had kept the Sabbath Holy but were not really much more. Most of the services that he attended at St. Peter's church inspired him and that was what he looked at other church services but rarely found it, especially in the Army.

Before he left Marietta for England in early May, he attended a dinner for veterans at his church. Mr. Joseph Hector sat next to him. The older man opened the conversation: "I was in the last War. I did not belong to this church at the time. I belong to the Church of God on 8th Street. I came to St. Peter's after I came home in 1919 because there was a short Thanksgiving Service for Veterans. As I descended the stairs to the basement, I met Hazel Butterfinch. We were both waiting for a seat at the dinner. We started talking and then sat together. She belonged to the parish. When the evening came to an end, I asked to see her on Sunday afternoon. She consented and nine months later we were married. I joined the parish when we got married and have tried to be a good member. We have two girls.

"I had volunteered for the Army in the summer of 1917 and arrived in France in November. I was in the 2nd Division and entered the front in support of the French in early June, 1918. The German 6th Army had broken through. We stopped them and they never advanced again. Sometime around June 15, I was wounded! We had to cross the no-man's land and the Germans started to shell us. A shell hit about 30 feet away and I was hit by three pieces of shrapnel. One hit me in the head. Another in the chest, it broke some ribs and punctured my right lung. The third shrapnel got embedded in my right side. I was bleeding but a corpsman reached me quickly. I can't remember anything but they took me to a field hospital and the doctors operated. They operated three times while I was in the hospital. I was in terrible pain. I lost track of the time. They removed the shrapnel from my chest and side, but could not find any in my head. It had probably glanced off. I finally came home in February, 1919. I still needed rest but was otherwise good.

"I still have scars from the wounds but not much else. When I got home, I was afraid that I would not be able to work but got a job in the Nagy Insurance Agency and have been there ever since. The Army took good care of me. I want you to know that they will do the same for you, if you are wounded. My only advice is: *Tell them everything that helps them to make the right decisions.* I did and have lived quite well. I should have died on the battlefield but I cooperated with the medical people and have lived a good life."

"Oh. I did not know that you were wounded. If you arrived in France in November, why did they wait until June to send you into combat?" Asked Walt.

"General Perishing wanted the American troops to service under American commanders. It was a good decision because after we went into the line, we never lost a battle when on the offensive. We sailed from the USA with only basic training and needed more training before going into combat. Furthermore, there were insufficient American soldiers in France until late spring 1918 to do anything. We were the first to go into combat because the French need support. Before the end of the summer more than a half million Americans were in the trenches. I did not know this until I came home; much of the time, I was in too much pain to care about anything."

"I am happy that you told me. I'll try to remember your story if I get into combat," answered the captain.

Walt's sister tried to get him "fixed up" with girls in the neighborhood. A pretty girl named Marjorie Williams lived across the street in the next block. Although Abby arranged a meeting between Marjorie and Walt, he never asked her for a date. She tried a second time with a twenty year old female a few blocks away but he ignored the effort. She gave up. He spent his evenings with high school friends at the Times Square Tavern and usually drank one beer before drifting home.

He also spend time talking to his father about some of the activities at Ft. Carson. The latter politely listened but was not really interested in army training details. He stated, "We went to Denver once. We left on the bus the morning after our leave began. When we reached the city. We divided with the enlisted men going in one group and I went alone. I had a map of the city and wanted to see the historic sites. I found Horace Tabor's house where the latter lived while postmaster of the city. He lived there with Baby Doe his wife and was an excellent postmaster. After his death, Baby Doe move back to Leadville, where Horace had been a silver baron until he lost his money in the silver crash of 1893. Baby Doe lived on their claim in Leadville until her death in 1936. Even though silver and gold made Denver, I was unable to find much to show its history. I attended a Lutheran church on Sunday morning accompanied by my driver Ed Smith. The ritual was the same that I had learned in Marietta and we returned to camp very pleased with our so-journey to Denver."

Chapter 5

Laval, France

August 1944

THE four men were sent away after carrying Walt into the examining room. Along with the other three members of the patrol, they followed Nick to the Red Cross tent. Nick was flirting with the Red Cross volunteer. She was 30 years of age, 5'5" in height and had coal black hair that was pulled back into a bun at the nape of her neck. She had deep green eyes, perfectly sculptured eyebrows, ruby red lips-like a pin-up girl and touch of blush on each cheek. She had perfectly manicured nails but no nail polish. She was good looking but not what most men would call beautiful. She wore a name tag which stated, "Mrs. Jonathon Edwards."

Nick had discovered that her husband was a B-25 pilot in the Fifth Air Force and six month previously was declared missing in action in New Guinea. He was telling her the exploits of 763 recon group but she showed no enthusiasm. She had heard many GIs talk about their personal heroism and discredited half of what they imparted. As the other men joined Nick for coffee and donuts, he attempted to entice her to attend the movie with him that evening. He was persistent but she told him that she had to keep the Red Cross tent open to 2100 hours. As the other men crowded behind Nick, he gave up and sat in a folding chair in the first row of tables.

Mike Goldsmith asked, "What did you find out about her?"

"She's married. Her husband was a B-25 pilot in the 5th Air Corp and is MIA."

"Is she coming to the movies with you?"

"Naw, she has to serve coffee until after 2100." Everyone laughed. Nick was not happy that they thought it was funny but made no further comments.

Mrs. Edwards did not tell Nick that her husband's squadron leader had written, *"Every movement by aircraft involved in crossing the high mountains, some are over 13,000 feet with dense jungle extending to their top, there is a possibility of a crash. I am sorry to report that we rarely identify where the plane goes down. We often lose more planes to the jungles than in combat. About half of the crews eventually find their way out of the jungle but it can take months."* After the hopeless letter arrived, she volunteered for the Red Cross to compensate for the loss. She had also read about the Flying Dutchman, a C-47 that had crashed in New Guinea with 23 men aboard. Six had walked out of the jungle; the other seventeen died of exposure. When the rescuers finally arrived, only the chaplain was alive and succumbed within hours after being found. The story only depressed her further in regard to her spouse's loss and possible rescue. Working hard helped her to forget.

Jacob Cooper returned from the regimental headquarters fifteen minutes after the other seven men had sat down. He had reported that Walt and Ed were both wounded and that the patrol would need replacements before they could again go on a sortie. The officer in charge told him to relax and return in the morning. The men spent the next forty five minutes reviewing the conflict. It was the first time that the 763 recon group had had a serious causality. Their biggest concern was for Walt. The question was, "Would he survive the night?" Even though they only knew he had a broken arm and leg, they were afraid he might have internal injuries that could kill him. They drifted to dinner then returned at 2030 hours to see the movie, *The Miracle at Morgan Creek*, starting Betty Hutton and Eddie Bracken. Neither Ashley nor Elaine came to the movie.

The next morning immediately after breakfast, the 763 men returned together to the regimental command. The NCO in charge had the service center report on the vehicles and indicated it would be a week to ten days before they could make another patrol; he told them that at present time there were no replacements for the wounded men. He asked them to raise their hands over their head. Both Michael and William's hand trembled and the NCO stated for the unit edification, "I see that you are suffering from shell shock. Since Captain Steinberg was wounded and we have no replacement for him, you need to take a few days of R&R to calm your nerves. Don't leave the city without permission. Send someone back here each morning. If you want to go someplace beside Laval, ask at that time and I might be able to obtain passes for a day to two to some other city. We'll have a replacement for your wounded men in a few days. The damaged vehicles need a month's repair and Sgt. Smith and Capt. Steinberg might be back if you just wait for the repairs to be completed."

The men hiked to the field hospital. Ed was lying in bed. A nurse, who looked like she was only nineteen, was taking his vital signs. He tried to get her to talk but all she did was put entries on his chart and ask for medical information from him. When she was finished, she went on to the next patient without ever answering any of his remarks. Ed requested help and Jacob assisted him out of the bed to a chair. "I should be able to walk around later today and should be back with the unit by next week?"

"What can you do with an arm in a cast?"

"I can man the MG in the rear jeep and will use a .45 if we get into combat."

"I think you need to rest until the doctors give you an Okay to return to the patrol," commented Nick.

"What did they feed you last evening?" asked Jacob.

"They gave me a bowl of barley soup, bread, and milk. I asked for something else but they refused with the comment, 'You're suffering from shock and might throw up. Wait until morning and we'll get you more and better food.' For breakfast they gave me canned orange juice, bacon, and powdered eggs. The eggs were actually good. They either have a cook who know how to prepared powdered eggs or I was too hunger to care. It was much better than we were feed in Carteret. Most of the eggs they fed us there were inedible and smelled like wet gym socks. Today's eggs were edible and had no strange odors. Most of the men in the ward thought they were the best eggs that we ate since coming to France."

Nick has seen Elaine and asked her what she knew about Walt. She could not give him any information that he did not already know. She told him that Ashley had been informed about his wounds.

Nick asked Ed, "What about Walt?"

He answered, "I can't tell you much. He was back into surgery early this morning. Someone commented that his blood pressure was too low last evening so they could not operate. The doctors had to wait a few hours. I think he is in the surgery ward. Why don't you go back to see him. I'll try to make the trip as soon as I can walk possibly after lunch."

Jacob went back to the surgery area. They would not let him enter. They told him that Capt. Steinberg was resting well and might be able to see his men after lunch. He was told to return after 1300 hours.

While he was gone, Ed had set up a monopoly board and had started to play with two other slightly wounded GIs. The recon group exited the hospital and walked around the town.

After lunch Jacob returned to the surgical ward. He was told that the operation was successful and that Walt was sleeping. The nurse told him to return after dinner and she hoped that he could see his commander at that time.

Late in the afternoon, Ashley entered the ward where Walt was in traction and resting. "Elaine told me that you were wounded yesterday and that the doctors needed to operate to put your bones together. I tried to see you but they would not let me enter. How do you feel?"

"I'm in a great deal of pain. They gave me morphine but I have a few broken ribs, a broken arm, and a broken leg. It will take a day or two to suppress the pain. The doctors do not expect me to suffer any permanent damage but they needed to put a pin in the leg bone. I was also cut but they seem to have taken care of those wounds." He pointed to the bandages with his good hand.

"I don't have much time to gab right now. I will be back when I get off after dinner. At least I know that you are not permanently harmed. See you later." She blew him a kiss and exited the ward.

After Ashley left, Walt fell asleep but was awaken for dinner. He needed to be fed by an orderly, who was a German POW who volunteered to be a hospital orderly. He announced, "My name is Johann Wolfgang Becker. My father was a musician and I think he wanted me to be one. Thus I have the two Christian names of two of the greatest German composers. I was attending nursing school when I was drafted. I asked to be put into a medical unit but I was sent to an infantry battalion. I'm an Evangelical and don't like killing. I resolved to surrender as soon as possible. That happened a few weeks ago. I convinced the interrogation officer that I would be more useful as an orderly in a hospital than in a POW camp. Here I have some use; in the infantry I was useless. I usually take care of the German wounded; but today they need help here, so they sent me to help you eat."

The doctors wanted him to be totally conscience and off many of the pain drugs before they fed him solid food. The POW fed him thin beef barley soup, small pieces of bread, and apple sauce. It was the first food that he had eaten since the jeep rolled on top of him. Although it was not much, it tasted delightful. He wasn't feeling any hunger and he felt that the food was better than normal army food. Johann helped Walt with his personal need like shaving for several days but was sent to a POW hospital a week later. Walt was delight to have someone to help him with his personal needs, even if it was a POW.

Just after dinner, five of Walt's' patrol members came to see him. The doctors had taped his ribs; put a cast on his arm. Stopped all the bleeding, and had his leg in traction. He still had severe pain and was heavily sedated. He could not do much talking. His speech was slurred. The nurses asked the men to leave after ten minutes. They went to see the movie, *Swingtime John*, staring the Andrew sisters. Nick stopped at the Red Cross tent and tried to urge Mrs. Edwards to come to the movie but she evaded the question.

Ashley returned to Walt's bed at 0730 hours. She had had emergencies. An infantry battalion had been shelled and there were dozens of causalities. She was needed in the surgical rooms. She was still wearing her uniform and it had many blood stains. Since his men had left, Walt's speech had improved but was still incoherent. He stated, "We were hit by mortar fire. Two shells fell alongside of my jeep and I was thrown out of it. It rolled over an embankment into a stream and landed on top of me. I think I suffered the broken bones when the jeep hit me. Ed was also hurt but I don't know where. Did you see him?"

"Yes, he has a broken arm and a few minor cuts. He will be sent to a rehab center tomorrow or the next day. He was walking when I visited his ward. He'll be forced to take a few weeks off but he is not seriously hurt. I told him that you were here and that he could see you for a short time tomorrow before they transfer him. I'll try to see you when I have time off." She bent down and gave him a light kiss on the forehead.

The next morning, Ed came to see Walt. His arm was in a cast but all the other injuries had healed sufficiently that many did not need to be bandaged.

He told Walt, "The arm is not bad. The cast should be off in four weeks and I will return to the patrol. I walked over to the regimental HQ and asked them to send me back to the patrol—I like the 763. They told me to get well and that they were sending me to Sainte-Mère-Église to let my arm heal. I objected but no one would listen to me. I rather go to someplace more exciting but I am not sure what I can do. If you have any influence, get them to send me back to the 763. I can drive the rear jeep with one hand. I may have problems if we get into a firefight and need to use a rifle or a Thompson but I can use a pistol." He gestured with his good hand.

Walt just grunted. Ed continued, "I've been nominated for a purple heart but I don't think I deserve it. I tore up the papers that they gave

Jacob. I told them that my broken arm was due to an auto injury and did not deserve a purple heart. I told them to present it to someone who is *really wounded*!" He emphasized the words *really wounded*.

Walt was sincerely happy about his strong morale and wished him, "God Speed!" After Ed left, Walt thought about the sergeant's refusal of a Purple Heart and he wondered if should do the same. He was hurt but not because of the mortaring but because the jeep rolled over him. His injuries were due to an auto accident not really due to the shelling. If he had not fallen out of the jeep, he would not have been hurt.

The next morning, Ed was playing monopoly with the other wounded when the recon associates came to see him. They jokingly asked him if he had made any headway with the young nurse. He frowned. They went on to tell him how Nick had tried to coerce the Red Cross worker into attending the movie with him. The latter grunted loudly and they all laughed.

By the third day in the hospital, the pain had subsided sufficiently that Walt could talk almost as much as he desired. He was still in traction but enjoyed talking to the other men in the ward as well as his recon associates. He also managed to send a short note to his parents. He could not hold the pencil very well and only wrote half a page.

Ashley came for a few minutes each day and Elaine visited him several times during his first week in the hospital. When Ashley had a day off, she spend several hours with him and helped him to write longer letters to his family and friends. She usually came into the ward dressed in her khaki army uniform rather than her nurse's uniform so no one would be tempted to ask her medical questions. She helped Walt to eat and assisted him in performing the other essential things during the first two weeks after the operations.

During the fourth and fifth day following the mortar attack, the 763 men walked about the city, ate donuts, and got into a fight with some signal corps enlisted men. On the morning of the sixth day, the regimental CO approached them and announced that he was promoting Nicholas to sergeant. He also told them that he had a replacement for Walt, a new lieutenant. They were ordered to return at 1500 hours to meet the new officer and have the strips presented. Nick commented, "We're still one man short."

"Yes, I know. One of the recon groups lost an armored car and a jeep in a firefight. I'll send you a gunner from that patrol."

Jacob asked, "Will Walt and Ed return to the unit as soon as they heal?"

"I cannot verify that they will but I have no negative reasons. I suggest that you put the request in writing and I will send it to the division commander. He has to make the final decision. I have assigned Ed to the service unit here in the HQ since he made such a stink when I told him that he had to go to a recovery center. He only needs one hand to write items that recon units need either for supplies or repairs."

The men immediately sat down and wrote a note to the division commander asking him to reassign Walt and Ed to the recon group as soon as they were released by the doctors. They all signed the note and the regimental CO endorsed the note and forwarded it to the Division HQ.

At 1500 hours, the regimental CO presented Nick with his third strip and promoted Michael and Edwin to corporal. The CO congratulated the 763 group for a job well done. Then he introduced them to Lt. Graham the new CO and the new gunner, Francis Bacon. The 763 men instantaneously disliked the officer for he had no compliments for the 763 men even though the CO had praised them for their work.

Walt listened to the men in his ward reiterate their War stories. One man had been the machine gunner and assistant driver in a Sherman tank; a German 88 mm shell hit the tank and knocked the 75 mm cannon to pieces. There were five tanks in the patrol and when the other four saw the 88 mm flash they opened fire. There was no second shot from the 88 mm so they assumed that the German gunners had been either killed or wounded. Small pieces of shrapnel entered the hatch and hit the tanker in the head and shoulders. It broke some small bones and they planned to send him to England to recuperate for three months. Two other members of the crew suffered minor wounds. Except for the destroying the 75 mm cannon, the tank was only slightly damaged. The wounded man was waiting for transportation to leave Laval.

Another man in the ward told how his squad was moving forward. The company sergeant was in the lead. An artillery shell hit the sergeant directly and exploded. The sergeant's head was propelled backward and hit the speaker in the chest--breaking three ribs. He collapsed and the medics moved him to an aid station. The only thing left of the sergeant was his head and lower part of his legs. The speaker was resting for a few days until he could be moved to the recuperation center. He felt quite sore but knew that his ribs should be healed in about three weeks and he could return to his unit.

A paratrooper was hit with a rifle slug during the attempt to prevent the Germans from crossing a river. He told the men that after the initial drop in Normandy, he was struggling to remove his parachute when he discovered that it was made in his home town. The inspector had initialed the label on the chute. It was his mother's initials. He knew she worked in the parachute plant and was astonished that she had inspected his chute. He would need a further several weeks to heal even though his wound was not serious. He had not written to his family and now wanted to tell them about the parachute discovery.

The Lutheran Chaplain, Harry Weidman, stopped to see Walt at the end of his fourth day in the hospital. He asked Walt about his religious background, "Do you belong to a church?"

"Yes, I belong to St. Peter's Lutheran Church in Marietta, Ohio."

Weidman was delighted to have a fellow Lutheran under his charge. He told Walt that he also belonged to the Lutheran church. The insignia on his uniform only indicated that he was a Protestant Chaplain. He offered to bring Holy Communion to the wounded man the next morning. As he prepared to leave, he asked, "How long will you be in traction before they let you out?"

"I'm not sure. There is no permanent damage to my leg or arm. Just broken bones. They should heal in six to eight weeks. I don't think the doctors have anything else to keep me laid up."

"Will they send you to England to recuperate?"

"I hope not. Since Paris has just been liberated, I have heard that long-term patients will be sent there as soon as they have the hospitals ready for us. Will you be transferred?"

"I don't know, the rumors are not good but I have heard that most of the staff will be transferred once there are facilities. I hold services twice a week in the staff cafeteria. Once they let you move around in a wheel chair, I'll make arrangements for someone to pick you up so that you can attend the services."

"I'd like too. I will be in traction for at least another two or three day. They want to be sure that the pin has set correctly in my leg before they remove the traction equipment. At that time, the doctors may allow me to move around on crutches."

Weidman uttered, "Let us pray."

Walt bowed his head as best he could and the chaplain offered a short prayer asking God to speed the healing process. Since Walt was a Lutheran, Weidman made the sign of the cross on his forehead as he closed the prayer with a Trinitarian doxology.

Weidman came to see Walt almost every day. Two days after the Holy Communion, Walt opened the conversation, "They want to give me a Purple Heart. Ed, my driver, refused it by telling them that his injury was an auto accident rather than a wound. I think they cancelled his application. They want to give one to me, but I feel I should also refuse it. I was banged up worse than Ed but this is not a real wound." Walt patted his bad leg. "Should I refuse the Purple Heart? My driver refused the medal because 'he was injured in an auto accident.' I have been debating and think I should do the same."

"I don't think you ever gave me any details about your injuries?"

"Two mortar rounds hit the embankment besides our jeep. I was knocked out of the vehicle and it rolled on top of me. I think the broken bones occurred when the jeep hit me. The event was sort of like an auto accident."

"Hum! I see your dilemma. If Sgt. Smith had accepted the Purple Heart, you both would be in the same category. Since he refused the medal, I see that you feel you might be accused of being a medal collector. Let me think/pray about the question. I'll give you an answer tomorrow."

The next day he returned, "I think we have to look at the injuries from two points. 1) You suffered the injuries because of a mortar attack. This was a minor battle engagement but your injuries would not exist if the mortar shell had not exploded near your jeep. Thus you are eligible for the Purple Heart. 2) The injuries are not due to direct enemy fire. If you had not been knocked out of the jeep, you would not have the injuries. Thus it could be looked on as an auto accident and not eligible for a Purple Heart. I think the answer is what do you feel was the real reason that you are in the hospital, because of the mortar attack or because the jeep rolled over you. Both are valid reasons.

"I think you must resolve in your own mind about what was the cause. I feel the mortar attack is the primary reason but I leave the answer to you since you will have to live with the decision for the rest of your life."

On the fifth day, Walt told Weidman that he decided to refuse the Purple Heart even though he was going to be in the hospital for many more weeks. Weidman asked Walt if would like to have him write to his parents since his right arm was almost totally healed. He propped a clipboard on his good leg and with the chaplain's help composed a short letter.

Dear Mom and Dad,

You probably heard that I was wounded. I was not really wounded. We suffered a mortar attack and I was thrown out of the jeep which landed on top of me. I have several simple fractures on my left arm and right leg. I am in tractions but should be out tomorrow. None of the broken bones are very serious and I should be back with the recon unit within eight weeks. The Lutheran Chaplain is helping me to write this letter since I cannot sit up as yet. I'll try to write more as soon as they put a cast on my leg.

Love, Walt

"Let us pray." Weidman offered his normal prayers.

The Catholic Chaplain stopped to see Walt later on the same day. When the latter explained that he was Lutheran, the Catholic asked, "Has Chaplain Weidman been to see you?" He was delighted to know that Weidman and Walt had made acquaintances. He added, "I'm Fr. Benedict Rusinko. I come from Cleveland and I hear that you are from Marietta. I guess we can say that we are Ohio brothers." They both laughed, "If you don't mind, I will give you my blessing before I leave."

Walt was embarrassed but told the Chaplain to give the blessing. He felt that it did not hurt to have more prayers to heal his wounds. The priest finished with, "*Bénédicte vos omnipotent Deus, Pater, et Filio, et Spiritos Sanctos. Amen.*" It was the same blessing executed by Weidman but this time it was in Latin.

The next time the padre stopped, he asked, "Do you know how to play chess?"

"Yes, I was in the chess club in college. I only participated in one tournament and did rather poorly. Why do you ask?"

"There is a sergeant in the next ward that would like to play but has no partner. I'll suggest that he come to see you."

Later that day the sergeant with his arm in a sling and a bandage about his head stopped; he was carrying a chess set. Walt agreed to play. They played for 45 minutes and the game was a draw. The agreed to play again the next day and it became a late morning activity for both of them. They were evenly matched and after ten days, they were equal in wins and losses with two games a draw.

Some days Chaplain Weidman and Walt talked for fifteen or twenty minutes but most of the time the Chaplain had insufficient time to do more than give his blessing and a short prayer asking for a speedy recovery.

At the end of the second week, Elaine came to Walt. Her nails were brightly painted red so that he could see that she had stopped chewing them. He asked, "Why did you paint your nails? I thought it was inappropriate for a nurse to do so."

"I thought about your statement a few weeks ago, so I decided to try it. If I put a clear lacquer on them, I still chew them but a bright red reminds me to stop."

"It will take time until you learn to avoid the temptation. I am very glad that you stopped. You are a nice looking woman but bad nails detract from your sex appeal."

"You never told me that I had sex appeal!"

"All women have some. You are good looking. My gunner/driver, Sgt. Smith, who came to several movies and coffee with me, told me that he would like to know more about you. However, he is an enlisted man and you are an officer."

"He's a little young for me."

"Yes, but he still looked at you. I have not encouraged or forbid him to do anything. He thinks you would make some man a good wife."

"Don't encourage him."

"I won't. I just wanted to tell you not to cut yourself short." She left.

Later Ashley entered the ward and announced, "I received bad news from my family."

"Oh!"

"Here's the letter."

Dear Ashley,

Your brother Jim killed himself. He had not been good since he came home from church camp. Tuesday, he left the house late in the morning without telling anyone where he was going. I did not pay much attention to his attitude because he had gone on his own a number of times since he returned from camp. When he did not arrive for dinner, we called the police. An officer had seen him near the Mississippi River Bridge. The police started to look for him. They found his body washed up on the shore three miles south of the bridge. He is being buried in the church cemetery on Saturday.

We contacted the Red Cross and asked them to contact you but they were unable...

The rest of the letter was family news and Walt did not read it. "I'm sorry to hear about the bad news. I wonder why the Red Cross did not contact you. They could have arranged an emergency leave for you to be flown you back to the USA."

"I have not heard anything but it is only four days since the letter was sent."

"You never told me that you had a brother."

"There were three of us siblings. I am the eldest. Jim was sixteen, eight years younger than I. My younger sister is fourteen. Jim was always a problem. He would play hooky from school. One time my mother caught him hobbling down the steps towards the bus stop. She confronted him. He had a fishing rod hidden in his pants. He planned to go fishing rather than school that day. The last two summers, my parents sent him to church camp with the hope that the discipline and training might help him to configure a better attitude towards life. He apparently did not reach their goal. Jim and I never had a close relationship. I was eight when he was born. I guess I was the apple in my parents' eye. They expected him to work hard at school, like me, but he never did. He once told me, 'You are the favorite in the family. You always do what Mom and Dad ask. Did they ever spank you for doing anything wrong?' My father always found something that Jim did wrong. He felt as if he were abused. I don't think he tried to be a model son. He wanted to stretch himself and felt that everyone wanted to stop him.

"My little sister was like me. She always asked permission before doing things. Jim once screamed, 'Kathy did the same thing that I did. You did not punish her but you punished me.' My mother answered, 'Kathy always tells us where she is going. If we object, she changes her mind. You never tell us what you are going to do and sometimes it embarrasses us.' Jim just sulked after the lecture and went to his room. He did not even come down for dinner."

"Did he ever enter the Boy Scouts?"

"My father took him to a scout meeting at church. He went alone the next week but quit. His excuse was that they did silly things. He wanted more challenging adventures."

"He never gave the scouts a chance. I have been in the scouts my whole life and never stopped having adventures."

"You didn't tell me."

"I was an Eagle Scout and spend eight years in summer camp either as a boy or as a leader. My troop was always doing something or going someplace. I just never had enough time to keep up with all the activities. In fact, my first real look at Fort Harman on the east side of the Muskingum River was on a scout trip even though we only lived three miles from the park."

"Are you going back to the scouts when you get out of the army?"

"Probably, I paid my dollar registration when I was first drafted but my scoutmaster returned the money. He told me that my registration would continue as long as I was on active duty in the military. I just need to fill out the forms each year. My father is doing it for me. He knew that it was one of my best trainings in high school and college. Being an Eagle Scout helped me to avoid much of the harassment in basic training. I was made a platoon leader among the new recruits. Were you in the Girl Scouts?"

"Yes, I was a brownie and girl scout for five years. When I got to high school, I was more interested in drama than scouting and no longer could find time for both. My sister is a girl scout." Ashley left Walt's bed to finish her medical chores.

When Chaplain Weidman stopped, Walt confessed, "On one of the last patrols prior to having my leg broken, I shot a German soldier. A German scout patrol attacked us first and did some damage to our vehicles. We returned the fire with everything we had and they abandoned their position. One of the soldiers rose from his hiding place. I shot him in the head. In OTS, I was an expert marksman with the pistol. At the time that I killed the soldier, I just looked at it as eliminating a foe but as I lay here in the hospital, the event keeps moving through my mind. The soldier was in the process of retreating and would have been gone in a few minutes; he was not a real threat to me or any of my men. It was a senseless killing and now it bothers me. I snuffed out a life which was no threat to anyone."

"We don't think much of blowing people to pieces with shells or bombs. Even mowing down an advancing enemy with a machine gun does not create the trauma. Killing a man as a sniper, which is what you really did, bothers you. His only evil characteristic was that he was an avowed enemy. In your case, he wasn't even a threat in the battle. You killed him; now you are bothered by the commandment,

'Thou shall not kill.'[12] You are not alone. Many soldiers have the problem especially when they are acting out of fear for themselves or their buddies. I am not sure if I can immediately give you either a rational or a theological solution to the trauma. However, I will try to ease your mind so that it does not obstruct your officer commitment with a deep sense of guilt or when you return home. It is the trauma of War; and unless you become a conscientious objector, you must accept that it can always happen to you. Let us pray: Dear Lord, Thy servant is approaching thine altar with the difficulty of breaking one of your sacred commandments. Help him to accept the fact that he is a sinner as all men and that he broke your law. Forgive him and allow him to go forward. Amen.

"Thank you, Chaplain."

"Before I go, let me say a little about the Ten Commandments. The Lutheran Church has never distinguished between the severities of one commandment over another. It is just as much a sin to 'take the Lord's name in vain[13] as it is to 'kill a man.'[14] Remember God expelled Adam and Eve from paradise for eating an apple. However, it was God commandment that they broke not the severity of the crime. Even Jesus in his Sermon on the Mount, list all sins with the same vile status. Our society has graded sins but not the church, nor should a true Christian. What Jesus has taught us and the church has emphasized is that we must ask God to forgive us no matter what are our sins. We must pray no matter what we have done. Christ will help us to abstain from sin when we know that it is wrong.

"The Catholic Church has tried to grade sin into categories of moral sins, venial sins, et cetera. To handle this they created Purgatory where a man suffers for his sins. Protestants have never accepted this theology. All sin is wicked to a believing Protestant. There are no little sins in Protestant dogma. I think the Eastern Orthodox Churches have the same dogma but I'm not sure. It is more important to have a contrite heart and accept God's forgiveness than to consider one sin worse than another.

"I know this is hard but you must accept that you are sorry for the sin and accept God's forgiveness! I will be going and will try to return tomorrow."

---

[12] Exodus 20:13.

[13] Ibid.

[14] Ibid.

The next day he returned and asked, "How long have you been in the army?"

"Since June, 1942. My unit was selected while we were stationed in Colorado, to train new recon patrols until last May. We were one of the deception patrols in Southeast England until early July. Then we were sent to France. We were in the St. Lo breakout. The mortar attack rolled my jeep and it landed on top of me. It broke my bones. I look on it as an auto accident.

"The Krauts once missed us by less than fifty yards. We learned to run fast and I am the only serious injury in the patrol since we were organized more than two years ago. If we were not as good as we are at running, we would have been blown to Kingdom Come several times. Now I hate being here in the hospital away from my men. During our training and decoy scouting, we developed into a very efficient team but from what the men tell me; my replacement is not as good."

"I am glad that you have no permanent injuries. You are lucky. Your guardian angel must be working overtime."

"I would like to meet him!"

"It might be a her?" They both laughed.

The next morning the 763 group started a new patrol. Lt. Graham ordered Nick to take the new jeep and lead the patrol. The new lieutenant went to the jeep behind the armored car. After twenty minutes, he called a halt and walked to the lead jeep where he made a report to the regimental command post. Edwin commented after the second stop, "We're sitting duck. Walt never stopped to make a routine report unless absolutely necessary and never spent five minutes unless we really had something very important to report. One of these stops will put us into the sights of a Kraut unit and we'll be shelled. Didn't he learn anything in OTS?"

At noon on the second day, a Me 109 strafed the column; everyone drove in all directions to avoid the fighter. They fired back with the .50s but hit nothing. Lt. Graham asked why they scattered. Nick detailed, "That's the way we were taught at Ft. Carson so that a fighter could not get us in its sights! We have been strafed five times since we landed in Normandy. As yet, no one has been hurt." The lieutenant was uncomfortable with the reply but simply told the men to get back onto the road.'

Chapter 6

Paris, France

September 1944

ON August 21, while in Rennes, General Charles de Gaulle stated, "...I think it is vital to occupy Paris...with French and Allied Troops...if a disorderly situation arises, it will be difficult to get control of the city." [15] Eisenhower wanted to by-pass the city so that he would not need to feed the population. However, the F.F.I. [16] especially the Communists started to take over the city and on August 23, the French 2nd Armored Division moved into the city. The German only put up a token resistance and most of the city was not razed. By August 25, the city was liberated. The next day the 4th and 28th U.S. Infantry Division marched down the Champs Elysees in a show of force and staged a "Victory Parade." It was performed in a manner similar to the Wehrmacht parade in Paris in 1940.

On August 27, the doctors removed the traction and put a bent cast on Walt's leg. They taught him to use a wheel chair. He began to explore the area inside and immediately outside the hospital tent. He also commenced attending Chaplain Weidman's services. Very often the latter arranged for someone to assist in wheeling Walt to the service; however, he often felt that they were baby-sitting him. Once he tipped the wheel chair over while trying on his own to attend a religious service. It showed everyone that he needed assistance and he stopped being bad-tempered. Most of the services were generic military services for Protestants but occasionally Weidman took the service out of the Lutheran prayer book. When most of the attendees were Lutherans, he held Holy Communion according to the Lutheran rite. Weidman had identified almost all the Lutherans in the hospital and tried to personally categorize their needs. One of his homilies actually

---

[15] *Encyclopedia of World War II*, 1972.
[16] Forces Française de l'Intérieur (commonly called Free French Forces)

used Luther's writing on the sanctity of spirit. On another day, he expanded his theological teaching stating, "The highest expression of the dignity and vocation of man according to Christians is the divinization of man, *Agape*. [17] The Greeks surmounted all the encumbrances that pagans had accumulated on the concept of deification (Theist). They made it the fulcrum of Christian spirituality. Western Christians talk about the attainment of sanctity, i.e. *The Word became fresh*. [18] They insisted that Christ came to take away sin: the Eastern Christians insisted that He gave man the image of God through the Holy Spirit and from it divine life. I am not sure which is the correct approach but each insists on the Divinity of Christ. If true love enters the spiritual belief, the reward is eternal life."

Walt's arm healed rapidly and by the second week after the mortar attack, the cast on his arm was needed only to prevent him from using it too much. The leg healed slower. At the end of the third week, the doctors looked at the leg and decided to leave it alone for another week thus restricting Walt to using the wheel chair. He continued to play chess. The sergeant and Walt were of equal ability. There were more draws than either won. The games were a strong challenge for both men. Unfortunately, the sergeant was transferred to the divisional headquarters for final recuperation before returning to his unit. Walt found a second wounded GI, who on occasions, would play with him. The second player was not as good as the sergeant and Walt won five games for every two that the new man won. There was rarely a draw. However, both men enjoyed playing since it broke the monotony of waiting for their wounds to heal.

At the end of the fourth week, the doctors fitted Walt with a walking cast and he began to use crutches to walk. He had a great deal of difficulty because of the cast that was still on his arm but after two day, they removed the arm cast and he could easily walk about the hospital. His bandages were all gone and except for a few scabs, there was no evidence that his face and arms had been cut when the jeep hit him. Since the battle front was rapidly moving east, very few causalities were arriving at the Laval hospital and everyone was notified that it would to be closed. It was now far behind the lines and required too many staff members to be even a recuperation entity. The physicians announced that Walt would be transferred to a rehab hospital in Paris as soon as it was ready to accept patients. The Paris hospital also had a

---

[17] God's love.
[18] John 1:14.

therapy unit to assist him with his walking whereas there were no physical facilities in Laval.

Walt arrived in Paris at the American Geographic Hospital just after he started to walk and had a semi-private room. The hospital had been built in 1916 by the YMCA and the National Geographic Society to allow wounded of all nationalities to recuperate before going home or rejoining their unit. It was a civilian hospital between the Wars and the Germans used it as a military hospital after France surrender in 1940. Now it was being used almost exclusively by Americans who were recuperation before returning to their units. The seriously wounded in the Laval hospital were moved to Normandy to be sent to either England or the USA to complete their healing; the rest were sent to Paris. The day after Walt arrived in Paris, Weidman visited him. The chaplain had been transferred three days prior to Walt leaving the field hospital.

Weidman knew that Walt had been active in his church until he graduated from high school. In the army, he attended the standard Protestant service almost every Sunday. However, it was more because he wanted to please his mother, when he wrote her, than to show any real devotion. Weidman continued to take an interest in Walt, who always asked the Chaplain for a short prayer at the end of each visit. He liked the Chaplain from the first day that they met and developed a stronger attachment each time they talked.

Weidman did not make it the second day after Walt's arrival but Ashley appeared. Before closing the field hospital, Elaine had arranged for her to be transferred to Paris so that she could be near to Walt. She conceded, "Elaine knew I wanted to be near you. When you were transferred; she arranged for me to leave before most of the staff left Laval. She, more or less, assured that I'd go to the Paris hospital where you were recovering rather than another field hospital."

Walt asked, "Do you love me?"

"Yes. I think I started the day that you sent me the first bouquet of flowers."

"You are as pretty as the dawn."

"Isn't a sun set lovelier?"

"Someplace, but not in France. In Colorado, they are much prettier than the sun rises but the Rocky Mountains are known for their beautiful sunsets. While I was stationed there, there were few days that they were not really beautiful. Here in France, the sunsets are poor compared to the Rocky Mountains. But if you want me to think of you as a mountain sunset, I will! With either, you are beautiful.

"I began to love you the day that I sent you flowers. At first I thought it was just infatuation but it grew deeper each time that we met. With you as part of my nursing staff in Laval, I could exam every characteristic to help me to love you. I've seen a few women before I met you, some were prettier, some were funnier, but when they left me, they were gone. When you leave me even for a few hours, I want to chase you and be with you. Sometimes I want to cry here in the hospital because I will be alone until you return. When you walk into my room, my heart begins to flutter. I don't want you to leave me and I don't want to leave you. I guess this is love but not as I first learned it.

"Please promise that you will keeps me at the top of your heart and always in your conscious prayers. If something happens to you, I'll die."

Ashley blushed and promised, "I'll always be waiting for you. I pray we'll have a loving, playful, and deep love affair. However, even though we want to be together, I am still a hospital nurse and must care for the other patients. I'll try to say Goodbye when I get off my shift." She gave him a light kiss and continued on her duties.

The next day after Ashley arrived; the Chaplain walked through ward and saw her sitting in Walt's room. The latter introduced the two of them. The Chaplain had never met the woman in Laval. They traded a few comments and then the chaplain offered a prayer before he asked Walt, "Since you can now walk, would you like to read the scripture in a religious service?"

"Yes, I did it a few times at home but not very often."

"Good I'll bring a Bible with the scripture marked on the day before I need your assistance. If you need to sit, I will arrange a chair for you. I better see the other men that have asked for my prayers. By the way, I received a silver star for the way I have been helping patients. You are one of them and I want to thank you for your recommendation." He exited the room.

Ashley commented, "His medal is quite an honor. Also that you are being asked to read the scripture. I have never read the scriptures in my church."

"It is very common for layman to read the scripture in the Lutheran church; however, they usually ask older parishioners. I guess I am among the 'ancient' soldiers here in the hospital." They both laughed.

Ashley declared, "I like the Chaplain. I talked to him for five minutes and like his mannerism. I can see why you have an attraction for him. Steinberg is a Jewish name. Where did your ancestors come from?"

"I have also wondered. Four generations have belonged to St. Peter's Lutheran Church in Marietta. My great grandfather came to Marietta just after the Civil War. I do not know from where or if he was Lutheran before he settled in the town. My grandfather and father worked on the docks. During the riverboat days, the city was a very active site but deteriorated as the railroad became better at hauling people and freight. The docks have seen a revival since the War began. My father currently has five people working for him, before the War, he had one full time and one part time assistant."

"Is the city pretty?"

"Not particularly. It is a small industrial city. Marietta is the county seat of Washington County. The population has been flat for twenty years. It is the oldest incorporated city in Ohio having been founded in 1789. The American Army built Fort Harman on the West side of the Muskingum River in 1785 to prevent settlers from entering the Indian Territory. It was built at the mouth of the river where it empties into the Ohio River. My scout troop made visits to the reconstructed fort about once a year. It is a typical reconstructed eighteen century historic site and not very interesting. Much of the architecture in the city that dates to the riverboat days is gone. There are pretty parks on the rivers and further back from the water. My family lives in a residential section less than a mile from the docks on the Ohio River and about three miles from the Muskingum River. My father always walks to work. Electricity came to the town in the late 1880s and a building program evolved as everything was changed. However, the architecture was slapped together and is not very good. Our tourist trade is non-existent."

Ashley exited because she had duties but promised to stop the next day.

Weidman stopped to see Walt almost every day but rarely had time to say more than a prayer and a few words. Initially he was the only Chaplain in the Paris hospital which made him very busy but everyone knew that within several weeks a complete Chaplaincy staff would be present. However, until that time, he had to visit everyone regardless of their religious affiliation. A week after asking Walt to read the scriptures, he brought him a Bible with the scripture marked for the next day service. It consisted of Proverbs 7 and Romans 1:25-31. Walt agreed to practice reading the scripture and felt that he could stand as long as there was a place to prop the Bible. He told Ashley later in the day that he was reading the scripture at the religious service the next day. She told him that she would try to shift her schedule so that she could attend the service. She went to Elaine and asked to attend the church service even though it was a Thursday. Elaine asked one of the other nurses to work in Ashley's area for two hours and the nurses arranged an amiable switch in their duty hours. Ashley arrived in Walt's room almost thirty minutes before the service. Walt allowed her to assist him in navigating the corridors to the room which was being used as a chapel. Since the hospital had been built by the YMCA during WWI, there was a small chapel. It had a service table (communion table), a lectern, and three large chairs for the ministers. There were no pews, but many folding chairs which could be removed to wheel in non-ambient patients. There were sliding panels on both side walls to increase the size and accommodate three or four times the number of patients when services with large congregations were held.

The service was a generic army Protestant service and sixteen military personnel attended. Walt read the two scripture passages. To keep the service short, there was no sermon. Ashley was very proud of her boyfriend and before she had to leave to resume her duties, she had sufficient times to assist him in returning to his room. Weidman stopped later in the day and congratulated Walt on his reading. He told him that there was a Lutheran Holy Communion service on the next Sunday and would like him to read the Epistle. Walt was delighted. He agreed to practice as he had for that day's reading. The Chaplain marked the Bible that he left with the injured man.

Weidman had time to talk the next time he made his official visit, a Catholic and a Presbyterian Chaplain had come to the hospital to ease his work load. He started to talk about the early Christian church and told both Walt and Ashley things that neither had learned in Church School. Much was strongly tainted with Lutheran theology and history. One day after a Thursday morning service Ashley asked, "Why does the Lutheran Church have orders of clergy?"

"It has been that way since the beginning of Christianity."

"They aren't mentioned in the Bible."

"They are implied in Paul's letters. In his letter to Titus he wrote, '*A bishop must be the husband of one wife.*'[19] It shows the existence of bishops in his day."

---

[19] II Titus 1:7.

A DISHONORABLE DISCHARGE

"That's not a good reason."

"You're too much of a fundamentalist. I have read the literature of the anti-Nicaea fathers, i.e. the very early Church writers. There were hundreds, maybe thousands of manuscripts circulating through the church before Constantine legalized the church in the fourth century. The selection of the books in the New Testament was arbitrary: e.g. Paul's letter to Philemon is in the New Testament but his letter to the Laodiceans is not. The epistle to Philemon is Paul's request for Philemon to accept the latter's runaway slave, Onesimus, back into his household because the slave had become a Christian. The book contains nothing that is theological or of historic importance. The Epistle to the Laodicea reads like Paul's epistle to the Galatians. Laodicea is in the same geographic area in Asia Minor as Galatia and the Epistle is filled with good Christian moral theology. I feel that Philemon was accepted and Laodicea rejected because Philemon was available to the Bishops of Asia Minor and the other letter was not. The Bishops at Nicaea in 325 AD made the decision as to which scripture should be in the canon. The largest group of Bishops came from Asia Minor and Syria. And they voted for the Asian epistle."

"What does this have to do with clerical orders? Didn't God authorize the books in the New Testament?"

"No, the early Christians were still debating which books should be in the canon. When the bishops gathered in Nicaea in 325 AD, they voted on what should be in the canon and approved the current books. They rejected I Clement, the Shepherd of Hermes, and the Didactic. All of which were read and used in various churches in the second and third centuries and may predate some of the books in the present canon. Even today there is no universal agreement. Some ancient churches particularly the Armenian (the first true Christian Church founded in 301 AD), and the Chaldean Church an off shoot of the Syrian church in the fifth century have a different canon than Protestants and Catholics. Today, only scholars really argue about the books in the canon. Normal clergy and laymen just accept it. I was just showing the thinking that was used in selecting the books of the New Testament.

"Clerical orders, deacon, presbyter, and bishop are all mentioned in the First Epistle of Clement to the Corinthians —it was written about 85 AD before Johns' Gospel. Clement is believed to be the third Bishop of Rome. His Epistle is primarily a moral discussion using scriptural quotes. The majority of the quotes come from the Old Testament but all the synoptic Gospels are quoted. Only John's Gospel is missing. It probably had not been written at the time that Clement wrote and definitely was not in circulation until decades after his time. Clement did not write much about church administration but the scanty descriptions in this writing shows that traditional clerical orders were accepted in his time, the last quarter of the first century. The Lutheran Church adopted the traditional orders; we just give them different names."

"Are you saying that the Apostles created them?"

"Yes, the creation of deacons is detailed in the Book of the Acts. Over the centuries, the function of the office changed as the church administration grew. Some churches still retain deacons as helpers. In the Catholic and Orthodox Churches, they function as a minor clerical order which it was at the end of the third century. Today the Catholic Church uses it as a stepping stone to becoming a priest. We do the same in the Lutheran Church.

"Presbyter or priest came into wide existence before the last quarter of the first century. At first only bishops celebrated the Communion Service but as the church grew, the bishops could not travel to every parish and they 'licensed' presbyters to administer communion for them. Ignatius, who was Bishop of Antioch at the end of the first century,[20] wrote about sending his presbyters to the parishes in his diocese. Today we have ministers in each parish just as they did in the middle of the second century.

"Bishops have always been the head of the church and the chief clergy. James, the brother of Jesus, was Bishop of Jerusalem. Most historians believe that Mark was Bishop of Alexandria. John was Bishop of Ephesus, and Peter was Bishop of Rome before his martyrdom. Today our church leaders function as the bishops did in the early part of the second century"

"Why doesn't everyone have bishops?"

"When Luther broke from Rome in the 16th century, no bishops accompanied him. He set up his church without them. Administers were elected by the end of the 16th century and they functioned as bishops did in the third and fourth century. When Sweden broke from Rome, the bishops joined the reformation and the State Church of Sweden has bishops, so do the other Scandinavian Churches. They hold their office for life. Most other churches had no bishops in their foundation because none joined their movement. Some added them later but they don't have a historical tradition. Some Protestant

---

[20] 67-107 AD.

churches exist as autonomous parishes (churches) and only have relationships outside the parish to support missionaries or hospitals."

"I think the Baptist operate that way."

"I think you are right. I had better be making my rounds. See you
and Walt later."

Walt's recovery was slow. The doctor left the cast on his leg for six
weeks and kept his ribs taped for three. He did a lot of walking and
went to therapy several times a week but he was bored. He was lying
on the bed when the orderlies wheeled in a casualty on an operating
cart. As they moved the man onto the bed next to Walt, he thought he
recognized the man. The latter was heavily sedated and it was two
hours before he stirred. As he awoke, Walt asked, "Where have I seen
you?"

"I'm Captain George Gumbart. I was the CO of the artillery unit
at St. Margaret's in Kent. We met several times when your recon group
came to the Dover area."

"Now I remember you. You commanded the 155 mm Long Toms
that fired across the channel. Why are you here?"

"After the St. Lo breakout, the Germans moved their units away
from Pas-de-Calais. We were ordered to Portsmouth for shipment to
France. We were originally stationed near Vire during the Battle of the
Falaise pocket. I not sure we did much good. Most of the Germans
were outside of our artillery range. When the Krauts retreated, we followed. Since we had to tow our guns, we needed to set them up before
we could fight, thus when the front moved fast we did not do much.
Most of the fighting took place with the self-propelled artillery. Anyway, we set up at Leuze, just over the Belgium border; the Luftwaffe
strafed us. We did not see the planes. Three of us were either killed or
wounded. I don't remember much. I was hit twice and the medics
moved me to the field hospital. The doctors stopped the bleeding and
temporarily sewed up the holes. They moved me here to remove the
lead. Why are you here?"

"We were hit with mortars. I was knocked out of the jeep and it
rolled on top of me. The jeep broke my arm and leg. Sort of an auto
accident. I was taken to a field hospital in Laval. They moved me here
when they closed that medical facility. Everything is healing. I will
probably be back with my patrol in about six weeks. Have they told
you the seriousness of your wounds?

"No. They want to see how well I heal in the next few days. I can say that it is fortunate that the Nazis use .30 caliber slugs. If they used .50 calibers as we do, I would be pushing up daisies."

Two days later, George announced, "Well, the doctors have finally made a decision. My wounds will heal but it could take six to eight months. As soon as I can travel, they want to ship me back to the USA. They doubt if I will heal fast enough to go back to the front. I don't object to going back to the USA, but I feel that I am abandoning my men. I guess there is nothing that I can do."

"When do you think they will send you home?"

"I asked! They said that I'll be here about a week or ten days. I'll be your roommate for a few more days."

One day after Walt took a short walk, Weidman asked him, "Are you and Ashley interested in each other?"

"Yes, but we need to wait until the War is over."

"I'd like to talk to you about Christian love. I'll try to be in your room this evening if she can be there."

"I'll ask her. If she can't do it, I will get word to you."

George asked, "May I listen? I don't want to move out of the room."

"Certainly. Do you belong to a church?"

"I'm Lutheran!"

"Good. I won't need to worry about being generic in what I say."

At 1900 hours, Chaplain Weidman came to Walt's room. Ashley was sitting beside the former's bed. He began, "The English language is terrible at describing love. We have one word that supposed to cover everything. The Greeks were better; they have three, *Agape*, *Philio*, and *Eros*. *Agape* can easily be described as God's love. Jesus' sacrifice is the ultimate in *Agape* love. I don't have time now to say more about it now. If you want a more theological description, I'll give it to you but at a better time. *Philio* can easily be summarized as friendship love. In the Bible, the love between Jonathan and David is probably the best. Again I could say a lot more but do not want to take the time. *Eros* is the love between two people in love. It covers all aspects of the love process, the holding of hands, the simple kiss, the caring for each other, and sex if it comes. We have the word erotic derived from the Greek word. Since it often refers to pornography, it has a bad connotation. True *Eros* is found in a loving pair—the love between a man and a woman like between Jacob and Rebecca. I don't read Greek well enough but I suppose it is used to describe their love. Some people be-

106   A DISHONORABLE DISCHARGE

lieve that it means you want to go to bed with the other person but this is not true. When you feel that way, it is not *Eros* in the religious sense but *Eros* in a pornographic sense. As *Eros* deepens and you want the best that God can give to a person that you love, not just sexual love, it can become *Agape*--particularly with the inclusion of God into the love affair. *Eros* then becomes a merger with *Philio* and *Agape* love. It commences when the couple wants to exchange affection but it may only be holding hands or defending you partner from verbal abuse by someone else. It is tenderness, and fortitude, with the focus on doing the right thing for yourself and your loved one. *Eros* can involve God or not involve God; however, if you expect God to protect your partner, you must include Him in your daily life and the love merges with *Agape.* I don't know either of you sufficiently to know if God is part of your love affair; however, you give me the feeling that if He is not, He will become a quintessence part.

"There are many love stories in the scripture and in the secular literature. I personally feel that one of the greatest love stories is the medieval love between Abélard and Héloïse. Abélard was a philosopher. She was a brilliant scholar of Latin, Greek, and Hebrew, and had the reputation for intelligence and insight. He wrote that she was most renowned for her gift of reading and writing. Not a great deal is known about her immediate family except that in her letters, she implies that she came from a lower social standing than Abélard. He was originally from nobility, though he had rejected knighthood to be a philosopher.

"Héloïse had an uncle, a canon in Paris, named Fulbert. As a teenager, she was renowned throughout Western Europe for her scholarship, and she was a student of Pierre Abélard (Peter Abélard), who was one of the most popular teachers and philosophers in Paris. Abélard tells the story of his seduction of Héloïse and their subsequent illicit relationship. It continued until Héloïse bore him a son, whom Héloïse named Astrolabius (Astrolabe). Abélard secretly married Héloïse, but both of them tried to conceal this fact in order not to damage Abélard's career. Fulbert's ensuing violence against Héloïse caused Abélard to place her in the convent of Argenteuil. Fulbert believed Abélard had abandoned Héloïse, and, in his anger, wreaked vengeance upon Abélard by having him attacked in his sleep and castrated. After the castration Abélard becomes a monk.

"At the convent of Argenteuil, Héloïse took the habit and eventually became the prioress. She and the other nuns were turned out of the convent when it was taken over by the abbey in which Abélard had first taken his monastic vows. At this point Abêlard arranged for them to enter the Oratory of the Paraclete, an abbey he had established. Hêloïse became the abbess.

"At this time the correspondence commenced between the two former lovers. After Abêlard's left the Paraclete, fleeing persecution, he wrote his Historia Calamitatum, explaining his tribulations both in his youth, as a philosopher, and subsequently as a monk.

"Hêloïse responded, both on behalf of the Paraclete Abbey and herself. In the letters that followed, Hêloïse expressed dismay at the problems that Abêlard faced. Since Abêlard was still wed to Hêloïse, she scolded him for years of silence following the academic attack upon him.

"Thus began their correspondence both passionate and erudite. Hêloïse encouraged Abêlard in his philosophical work and he dedicated his profession of faith to her. Ultimately, after telling Hêloïse of the instance where he had abused her and forced sex, he insisted that he had never truly loved her, but only lusted after her and their relationship was a sin against God. He then recommended that she turn her attention toward the only one whoever truly loved her, Jesus Christ, and to consecrate herself fully to him. He encouraged her to throw all her human effort into her religious vocation.

"In this writing, some scholars believe that Abêlard was attempting to spare Hêloïse the damage to his hormones and psyche. From this point on, their correspondence focuses on professional subjects rather than their romantic saga. Hêloïse's problems appear in four papers in a collection of theological questions directed to Abêlard at the time when she was Abbess at the Paraclete. His answers are found in her writings.

"Hêloïse's place of burial is uncertain. According to the records at the Pere-Lachaise cemetery here in Paris, the remains of both lovers were transferred from the Oratory of the Paraclete in the early 19th century and were reburied in the famous crypt at the Paris cemetery. I would like to see their grave(s).

"I know this is a long story but I think it is a model for love between two individuals who are restricted by their environment. You are basically restricted because you are under army rules. They may be dumb but they still control all of our lives. Since neither of you have ever been disciplined, I assume you have learned to live under those rules."

George clapped, "I am happy that I was able to hear your appraisal. It will be helpful to me. I had never heard about Abélard and Héloïse but I can see how they have come to be a model. Thank you!"

A DISHONORABLE DISCHARGE

Chapter 7

Paris, France

October 1944

T HE new second lieutenant, appointed to the 763 recon unit during Walt's recovery, was disliked by all of the patrol members. Almost every week, a member of the patrol received a few days leave and came to the hospital to see Walt. They complained about Lt. Graham. The always asked when the former CO would return so the new officer could be removed. The new man would not ask opinions and one jeep was destroyed because he ordered it to go in the wrong direction during a firefight. The armored car was also hit and had lost a wheel. Morale was low because the men began to fear that some of them would be seriously wounded or killed due to the lieutenants' ineptness. Fortunately, none of the men were seriously wounded or killed and the patrol was back at the front two days after the appalling firefight. They were issued new vehicles to replace the damaged the jeep and armored car. However, the men as a group complained to the regimental CO about the lieutenant errors. They petitioned the CO for Walt's return; however, he had not sufficiently healed, to even walk, much less consider returning to the patrol. The regimental CO called Lt. Graham into his office and ordered an inquiry into why he lost a jeep. Hearing the facts, he reprimanded the lieutenant, and then told him that if there were any more losses to the recon patrol that were due to his orders and not agreed upon by the entire group, he would be dismissed and be busted. Morale was still low but the patrol stopped complaining to the CO after Graham was forced to use the tricks that the 763 patrol had developed during their training.

Major Glenn Miller came to Paris at the end of September. Walt heard about the band leader's visit and asked if he could attend the concert. The hospital personnel discovered that there was to be a special concert for wounded GIs. They arranged for Walt to go in his wheel chair and sit in the front row. Miller played *Stardust*, *Dispy Doo-dle*, *What do you do in the Infantry*, *Tuxedo Junction*, the *Victory Polka*, and many more popular songs. After the concert Miller consented to meet with the enlisted men and Ray McKinley agreed to meet with the officers. Walt manipulated his wheel chair into the officer crowd and moved it near the front of the group. From his front row position he could adequately hear the entertainer.

McKinley enlightened them, "I obtained my musical start with lo-cal bands in the Dallas/Fort Worth area. I joined Smith Ballew in 1929 where I met Glenn Miller. Miller and I joined the Dorsey Brothers in 1934. They split in 1935; Glenn went with Tommy; I remained with Jimmy Dorsey until 1939. In 1942 I formed my own band, which was recording for Capital Records. However, the band was short-lived. When it broke up, I joined Miller's Army Air Corps band. I have been with it for two years. Jerry Gray does much of our arranging. He gives me many of my special pieces like those that you heard today. I have also been a co-leader of the band." He had a fifteen minute talk but Walt did not listen too much of it for he knew most of the biographic data.

Walt spent most of his time reading and writing to his family. He told them about attending to the Miller Concert. He contrasted the Paris concert with the ones in Kent and Normandy. He was well pleased that he could not really say that one concert was better than another. He had developed a strong interest in the arrangements that Miller used. He expressed hope that he could learn more when he re-turned home.

He became very well acquainted with the librarian in the hospital. She was French but knew English extremely well and helped him search for books. He read Dostoevsky's *The Brothers Karamazov* and liked the book so well that he read *Crime and Punishment* and the *The Idiot*. He never read anything by Russian novelists until confined in the Paris hospital. He asked about other authors. The librarian sug-gested Tolstoy's *War and Peace* and *Anna Karenina*. Since the only copy of *War and Peace* in the library was over 900 pages, he chose *An-na Karenina*. He told Ashley about his new likes and she found an abridged version of *War and Peace* with less than 400 pages in a Paris shop on the left bank of the Loire. Walt attempted to read it but never finished it before he was released from the hospital.

Four weeks after he arrived in Paris, the doctors took the cast off his leg. He was allowed to walk about the hospital on crutches. He ribs were totally healed but he still had minor pain when he exercised too much. One day he was outside alone and fell. He was not able to hoist himself off the ground. He laid for fifteen minutes before a man entering the hospital saw him and helped him back on his feet. When Ashley heard about the fall, she made him promise that he would never go outside alone until he was released by the doctors. He had hoped to be discharged in two or three weeks and return to his unit, however, the fall demonstrated that he was still not able to maneuver on his own. He continued to walk outside of the hospital with the crutches but only in the company of other patients, friends, or Ashley.

Ten days after the cast was removed, the therapist told him that he could move about; however, he was to stop if he grew tired or had any pain. When Ashley finished her duties, she would come to his room and both would go walking inside and outside of the hospital. Often she agreed to meet him but was forced to cancel because she was needed in the surgery room or had to assist patients moving from the recovery room to their "permanent hospital quarters." The hospital was very short of staff. Walt and Ashley wanted to see the city. As Walt improved, they ventured farther and farther from the hospital. Walt usually wore his parade uniform with all the ribbons that he had earned. He walked with his crutches because he could not put all his weight on his bad leg. It improved each day. The couple discovered every side street within six blocks of the hospital, drank sufficient wine to get tipsy, and started to seriously show their love for each other. Ashley did not like to be seen drinking in her nurse uniform, so she would change into her army parade uniform before exiting the building. She would stop to tell Walt that she was off duty, then go to her room, change into her tan uniform, powder her face, and put on fresh lipstick.

They discover a little café on a dead-end street, rather an alley, three blocks from the hospital. The café had the name *Jean du Arc*. Their first visit occurred on October 23. The waiter recognized the uniforms and addressed them in English. He asked their unit numbers. Walt explained that he was the CO of a recon patrol 763 and Ashley explained that she was a nurse but preferred to stroll the streets in her parade uniform since it attracted less attention. The waiter, Antonio, an Italian who came to France after World War I because he hated Mussolini, went back to the kitchen and returned within a few minutes with the owner. The owner, Serge, did not speak English but was delighted to have Walt and Ashley as patrons. He presented them with a small bottle of red wine, a piece of fried rabbit, and a large slice of French bread. He charged Walt two Francs ($0.08) and refused to accept any further remuneration. Through the waiter, he explained that the Germans stole food from his café and he had a hard time surviving during the occupation. He speculated that the Germans targeted him because he was Serbian. He never had any complications with Americans. Because Walt was wounded, he wanted to show his appreciated for the security that American Army provided for him.

Ashley and Walt kept returning every few days, Antonio gave then wine and bread before they even requested it. He stated, "In the summer of 1915, I entered the Italian infantry and was sent to the front near Trento but I never saw action. When the British and French sent troops to support the Italian Army in 1916, I was needed to drive supply vehicles which I did until the Armistice." Ashley queried Antonio how he learned his English. He expounded, "I went to Canada for two years in 1933-35. I did not want to be confused as a French Canadian, so I learned to speak exclusively English. When I returned to France, I toiled in a restaurant that catered primarily to American and English tourists. But I did not like the attitude of either the owners or the patrons. Shortly before the outbreak of the War, I procured the post at *Jean du Arc* and had been here for five years. I liked everything and stayed throughout the War.

"How old are you?

"Forty nine but I never married. I don't think I would be a good husband and am not sure I ever earned sufficient funds to support a wife and family. I like just being a waiter."

The trips to the little café became a great joy to both Americans. Since they were usually there in the late afternoon, they were frequently the only customers. They held hands, joked, and exchanged little kisses. The time together allowed them to explore their feelings. It was evident that they had fallen deeply in love but did not know what to do. Antonio was always obliging and encouraged their little affections.

Sometimes the owner joined them and the four "friends" had good time drinking wine and laughing. When this occurred, Serge only charged Walt, his cost of the food, and Antonio refused to accept a tip. He stated, "The fun I have had in your company/love is more compensation than the small gratuity that you might give to me. Let's just enjoy the afternoon and pray that it will help the Captain to get better."

When they reached the café late one Tuesday afternoon, Ashley handed Walt a short note,

> *"My dear friend, I'm in love with you and as long as we keep making these little trips, my affection will grow. You are a very nice man. You have a nice looking body and you always dress well. I never see anything amiss. You are a good Christian even if you are occasional cynical about some of the statements in the Bible. I was brought up a fundamentalist but never could believe everything just because it was written in the Bible. You taught me that principles are more important than words and I am learning to adopt your philosophy. Chaplain Weidman has tried to teach us love and his assistance has made me look beyond simple appearances. I'm not sure if I want to be your wife but I hope our* Philio *friendship will last until we die.*
>
> *Affectionately, Ashley."*

Walt read the note, folded it, but was embarrassed. He did not know how to answer it. He vaguely stated, "I don't know what to say."

"Why don't you think about what I wrote and when you are comfortable, tell me how you feel?"

Walt showed a big broad smile and the twosome laughed. Antonio saw the change in the couple from a sober concentration to a joyous encounter. He asked, "May I join in the fun?"

Walt handed him the note and he slowly read it. "Congratulation Captain. I could have told you this two weeks ago. I am very delighted that you two are going to be a single couple. Why don't we go to Mass together to celebrate the happy occasion?"

"When?"

"There is a Mass at seven every morning in the chapel in the next street. I am on good terms with the priest. I'll get him to give you his blessing. He's a nice guy and treats non-Catholic as all Christian should be treated. Can you make it some morning?"

"Yes but we need to check our schedules. May we phone you here in the café?"

"Yes, let me give you the number."

The couple walked over to the chapel in the next street. It had sufficient pews for sixty people and was a typical small Catholic church with plaster statues and Stations of the Cross. It was not an important church and remained open because the local parishioners used it and paid its bills. The priest like the parish and stayed even after being offered another location.

Thursday morning Walt and Ashley joined Antonio and Serge at the Mass and the priest blessed the couple even though Antonio was the only parishioner at the service to take communion. When they exited the church and walked back to the hospital, Serge admitted that he was Greek Orthodox.[21]

Walt asked Ashley, "Are you going back to school when you get out of the army?"

"I guess I will but I am uncertain if I want to. If I want to teach nursing either in a hospital or in a university, I will need degrees. However, I am not very interested in teaching. I really prefer to work for a doctor in private practice. The hours are a little better than in a hospital or even teaching. Furthermore, I would like to raise a family and this requires established hours so that I can plan about caring for my family."

"Am I a possible husband?"

"I think I indicated that in the note; however, we need to wait until the War is over before we seriously think about marriage and a family."

"I agree. I just wanted to know if I would fit into your plans."

"I think I had better get back to my duties at the hospital."

"Are you sidestepping the discussion?"

"Yes, but I do have work that needs to be done. We have been gone a long time. We can continue the dialogue during our next trip into the city."

Two days later, they were back at *Jean du Arc* café. Walt opened the conversation about love. "I have reread your note. I feel that I am also in love with you. I've had an attraction for you since we first met. When the men talk about women, they talk about sex. I have never been sexually excited when looking at you or when we move about together. Even when I kissed you, I did not become excited. I just want to be with you. I love the little snacks that we have with Antonio and Serge. I feel good when I am with you and feel depressed when you leave me. I hate the walks back to the hospital after visiting the café because I will lose your presence. I want to be with you always and live with you where I always know that you will be here."

---

[21] All Orthodox in Western Europe are known as *Greek Orthodox*.

"I think you have a very mature attitude in your 'love' for me. When people let their hormones govern their attractions, the love is deep but has very little substance. They lose their love as fast as or faster than it was initiated. I think we ought to talk to Pastor Weidman about our attraction."

"He gave us a dissertation on 'love' a few weeks back but I'm not sure I paid as much attention as I should have to his lesson."

"Maybe we should go back and have further discourses with him. He has been very supportive in abetting our courtship."

The next day Ashley saw the Chaplain and asked him to talk to them again. He agreed to meet them in his office at 1930 hours that day. Walt and Ashley were there before he could return from seeing the wounded. When he arrived at 1946 hours, he asked, "What bring the two of you to see me?"

Ashley stated, "We have been talking about love. We think we are in love and need some pastoral advice. We want to eventually get married. At the moment, we want to express our love but in a Christian environment. We thought you might help."

"You're both in your mid-twenties. I'm only five years older than you. I took courses in seminary but let me tell you something about myself. Between the second and third year in seminary, I had a clinical internship at a parish in Bucks County, Pennsylvania. While there I met my wife Penelope. She was the oldest daughter of my intern church pastor. We found that we had a number of similar feelings. After I graduated from seminary, we got married in the parish in Western Pennsylvania where I was the assistant in training. Six months after the wedding, I accepted a call to the parish in Winerfield, Missouri. I was in Winerfield just over a year before I entered the army. Even though I'm only five years older than you, I think I can talk as a pastor even if my experience is limited.

"You must think about what Christ would want you to do. Paul stated, '*I consider everything as complete loss for the sake of what is so much more valuable, the knowledge of Christ Jesus.*[22] He goes on further in the Epistle, '*They are going to hell, because their god is their bodily desires. They are proud of what they should be ashamed of.*[23] I think these two passages must be considered if you really want a Christian courtship and not one governed purely by hormones. You must be proud to stand before Christ and confess that you love and want to be loved in

---

[22] Philippians 3:8.
[23] Ibid., 3:19.

the way that He desires you to exhibit the emotion. I am not going to tell you what you should or should not do. I think you should ask Christ how He wants you to show your love to each other (*Agape* and *Philio)*. If you feel that what you are doing is acceptable to Christ, I am sure your love will be true and lasting. If you hesitate because you think that Christ would disapprove, then you need to cease, maybe swallow the pride, and not see each other. If you consider Christ in every act, you will have a God loving relationship. A further passage *'Put into practice what you learned from both words and action.'*[24] I hope these scriptural passages will help you with your decisions. I think you should read the entire epistle before you arrive at the way you want to live your life."

"We have talked and sex does not seem to be our main yearning. Our main craving is to be with each other and try to help each other. I think you listed this type of feeling as *Philo* love."

"Yes. It also shows that your affection is much more mature than your ages. I am delighted that I can be of assistance. Let us pray: 'O Christ bless this couple and lead them by their love for each other to you. Keep them under your wing and help them to perform acts that will serve you.' Our Father which art in heaven..."

When the couple had more than a few hours, they traveled all over Paris, visiting museums, cabarets, and started to chat about what they would do when the War came to an end. On one of their trips, they walked on a back street more than a mile from the hospital. They found St. John Chrysostom's Orthodox Church; it had three gold plated onion domes but showed the lack of maintenance because of the War. They entered into the church. It smelled of incense. As they approached the front of the church, a man in his fifties stepped up to them and asked in English, "Can you smell the myrrh?"

"Myrrh? I thought it was incense!" stated Walt.

"No. it is myrrh that flows from the weeping icon."

"Weeping icon?" asked Ashley.

"Yes. Here let me show you." He went to the right side of the iconostas.[25] A framed icon of the Virgin and Child stood on a stand. The bottom was lined with cotton and a tear hung on the Virgin's right eye. Walt bent over and smelled the strong scent of myrrh. Ash-

---

[24] Ibid., 4:9.
[25] The panels of holy pictures in front of all Orthodox Churches

ley did the same. "Our priest anoints everyone with myrrh at the end of each service."

"Where did the icon come from?"

"We call it the *Theotokos* or *Our Lady of Mt. Athos*. It was painted at one of the monasteries at Mt. Athos. A parishioner bought it ten years ago and hung it in his bedroom. A year ago it started to weep and he brought it to the church. Some days the myrrh pours out of the eyes of the Virgin and Child, other days nothing happens. When the Battle of Paris was raging, it stopped crying. When the city was declared liberated, myrrh stated to flow heavily. There does not seem to be good reason for it to cry. There are many crying icons. Some secrete water, some tears, and a few like, this one, myrrh. No one understands *why*?"

Ashley asked, "Where is Mt. Athos?"

"It is on a peninsula that sticks into the Aegean Sea north of Salonika, Greece. You may know it as Thessaloniki; like St. Paul's epistle. There are twenty monasteries on the Peninsula. I have never been there but would like to go. Maybe when the War is over, I can make the trip. If you come back tomorrow evening at 1800 hours, Fr. Basil will anoint you."

The couple exited the church and proceeded to a small café in the next block. Ashley stated, "I have never heard about crying icons!"

"I saw an article in Time Magazine but only read the first paragraph. I guess I was skeptical and never read the whole article. Now I wish I could find it. I'll write my parents and see what they can tell me."

In his next letter, he told is parents about his experience with the crying Theotokos. When they answered the letter, they said nothing about the apparition.

Ashley was not free the next evening but Walt found his way to the church. The priest was celebrating Vespers. The whole service was in Slavonic and Walt did not understand a single word. The icon was in the center of the church and a slow stream of tears flowed from the eyes. The church was full of the myrrh odor. When the service came to an end, everyone, including Walt, went forward to kiss the icon, and to be anointed with the tears. He did not see the man with whom he had talked to him the previous day. He exited rapidly after the anointing and rushed back to the hospital because he was embarrassed.

The next time that Walt and Ashley talked to Chaplain Weidman, they confronted him with the minor miracle that they saw. He answered, "I don't talk about Jesus miracles. It would be a transgression of my ordination vows. I must believe in them to avoid controversy but let's talk about other miracles. As you commented, even *Time Magazine* commented on crying icons. The icon is just a board with a painting on it. It is a sacred subject but only in the sense of the believer. It is a picture to a non-believer and I doubt if it would cry for them. The myrrh was created out of nothing and poured from the eyes of the images. That means that God is creating the myrrh or transferring it from some other source. I tend to believe in the latter. Einstein's theory basically says that matter cannot be created or destroyed but can be converted into energy. I believe that the myrrh arose someplace in the world, was converted to energy, and then transported at the speed of light to the back street in Paris. Energy (light) moves at 186,000 mph in a straight line. I think the frequency and speed varies and because it varies we cannot measure it. It was converted back to matter as tears on the icon. It was God's power that reconverted the energy. The faithful concentrated on the icon and the tears freely flowed. No one understands why God produces miracles. They are not rational, at least to men. Miracles are a one-time event and unless you believe in them at the time that they occur, you cannot prove or disapprove that they occurred. They do not lead to scientific verification because they are gone and only exist in the mind of those who saw it. To them it remains a visible and true experience. Since God changes the frequency and speed of the movement of mass/energy, the proof of a miracle cannot be obtained since our instruments require that the same event must continue to occur. Maybe something interfered with the energy waves during the Battle of Paris, when the liberation was declared, the interference stopped, and the icon began to cry again. Do I believe in it? I don't know. I need more information and it does not exist."

Neither Walt nor Ashley had anything to say. They promised to go back to the church but never did. The next time they visited *Jean du Arc*, they asked Serge about the crying icon, he stated, "I have heard about them but have never been in a church where one cried. You say it is nearby and has three onion domes?"

"Yes."

"It must be Russian. I'll try to visit it."

He never made any further comments about the icon to neither Ashley nor Walt. They do not know whether he ever visited the church or saw the icon.

By the middle of November, Walt no longer needed crutches but still used a cane. He asked if could spend a night away from the hospital; the attending physicians did not see a problem. That afternoon, he told Ashly, I have permission to leave the hospital for a few days to test my ability to move around without medical assistance. I would like to make a short trip. Will you go with me?"

"Yes and no! I will need to know when you can go and where you want to go. I will talk to Elaine and see if she can give me a night or two away from the hospital."

"I think I can leave almost any time that I desire to go. I just need to make preparations. I thought of going to Senlis; it's a small town about thirty miles north of Paris. It was the home for early French kings and sounds interesting. Why don't you ask Elaine for time off?"

"I will try."

The next day, Ashley had coffee with Elaine. She stated, "Walt is going to spend a few days away from the hospital to test his ability to move around without medical assistance. He wants to go to Senlis and asked me to go with him. May I arrange a few days' leave to join him?"

"Your affair with Walt is becoming very serious. I am not sure that I approve of you going way with him for a few days. Can I trust you?"

"I hope so! I am in love with him but do not want to jeopardize my nursing career. Can you arrange the leave?"

"I'll look at the schedule. If possible, I will give you two full days away from the hospital. Can Walt arrange his departure in order to match your leave time?"

"He told me that he could go anytime. Please see what you can do."

Five days later, Ashley was given two days leave. Walt made arrangements to go to Senlis, a small village on the Nonette River thirty miles north of Paris. She met him a block from the hospital on Tuesday afternoon. She was dressed in her khaki uniform and appeared the prettiest that Walt could remember seeing her. She had even borrowed a pair of pumps with two inch heels from another nurse. They took the trolley to the RR station. Since one of the other nurses with whom Ashley worked was on the trolley, Ashley sat with her colleague and Walt sat by himself. The nurse left the trolley a block before the station and couple entered the station arm in arm. They took the train to Senlis. When they reached their compartment, no one was there and they engaged in intimate talk. Ashley had polished her nails a fashionable red and Walt asked, "Why did you paint your nails today, you never did it before?"

"Red nails are considered to be non-professional for a nurse. I know that you like them because you talked Elaine into polishing her nails. It seems to have worked at stopping her from chewing them. However, I secretly think there was more in your suggestion than getting her to control her bad habit. I think you like it. Some of the other nurses have painted their nails for special occasions. No one ever say anything if they don't remove the polish before they get to work. I may do the same. They gave me a two day pass so I can do things that I normally would not do for time off. Note: I borrowed a pair of shoes which are a little more feminine than army boots. I do have my white nurse's shoes in my bag and can wear them when I return to the hospital. I can also remove the polish if I think that it is too unprofessional early in the morning."

"Are you trying to seduce me?"

"Would you like me to do so? I guess that is a leading question. Elaine was a little loath to give me time to exit the city with you. I think she is afraid that we might do something that would get me into trouble. I ensured her that I would not do anything to jeopardize my nursing position."

"Let's enjoy the trip."

"Good."

Ashley changed the subject and described much of the work that she had recently performed in the hospital. She did not feel it was appropriate to talk about hospital problems when she saw Walt in his room because there were always other patients or staff near-by. "The hours are long. The doctors labor fourteen to sixteen hours almost every day. We could use ten more nurses in my area. Elaine tries to prevent the scheduler from assigning us more than twelve hours a day or more than six days a week. But when we get a lot of causalities, we must work until they either die or we move them into rehabitation. Elaine devotes more time to obtain rest for us than anything else. I have more patients here in Paris than I had in Laval or Domfront. Even in Sicily, we had additional staff. You got approval to leave the hospital more than a week ago. I asked Elaine for a weekend but she had to pull strings to get me two days off in the middle of the week. I just hope she did not have to have one of the other nurses do a double shift for me. Oh! Have you noticed; I was promoted to First Lieutenant on Tuesday? There was no ceremony, Elaine, Dr. Russell, whom I work with in surgery, and two other floor nurses were present. The doctor pinned the bar on my uniform and gave me a little kiss on my cheek. I have been working so hard that I forgot to tell you. What do you do during the day?"

"I read a lot of books and play chess. In the past week, I read *Anthony's Adverse*, a novel on 18th century England published about seven years ago. I think they have made a movie form it, but I never saw it. I also read Ernie Pyle's "*Here is Your War*." It's about the North African Campaign. He talks about the duties of soldiers and rarely mentions the senior staff. His writings appear in the *Stars and Stripes* several times a week. I always read the articles. We get the *Stars and Stripes* each day in the hospital and I read almost everything. I like Bill Mauldin's cartoons. I think every crazy idea of Willie and Joe fits something I have experience in the Army. Mauldin makes them funny. However, I don't think I chuckled when the incidents occurred. I like the *Stars and Stripes* but when I was on patrol, I rarely see it. When I do it, it is several days old."

Walt and Ashley found a small tourist home two blocks from the Senlis RR station. The two Americans walked around the town viewing the historic buildings. The French kings resided in the town in the late Middle Ages. It possessed a 12/13th century Gothic cathedral. There were some Gallic and Roman towers in the town as well as medieval ramparts and bastions. The biggest industry in the town was a wood processing plant. Since the war did not affect the plant, the people did not suffer like in other towns that Walt and Ashley had visited in western France. The couple entered the cathedral. It was a beautiful Gothic Cathedral with two tall towers on the west side and an ornate entrance in the southwest. It had a twenty foot six-segmented circular rose window above the main entrance. The stone work was typical of French churches of the era and reminded them of Notre Dame in Paris. When they entered, Walt commented, "I didn't know that they built such large churches in small town."

"I think I read someplace that the French built 300 cathedrals in the twelve to the fourteenth centuries."

"It was in Henry Adams's' book, *Mount St Michele to Chartres*. I read it a few weeks ago."

"Yes, a year ago, I read the book on the boat to Sicily."

"Why?"

"I was bored and the book was in the ship's library. There were nice line drawings in the book but I had never heard of Henry Adams."

"He was a congregational minister who traveled in Europe at the beginning of the century. I think he was a descendent of John Adams, the second president. I don't know any more."

They found a nice café near the cathedral and had an excellent dinner. They had chicken, potatoes, boiled greens with peach pie for dessert. They drank two bottle of red wine and even had a cordial after the meal. The bill was 200 Francs, more than either had spent on a meal since they had left the USA. It was dark by the time they left the café and walked to the tourist home. The owner did not speak any English and made no comment when they returned from the sightseeing walk. After they entered their room, Walt began to passionately kiss Ashley. She responded. However, when he started to remove her clothing, she objected and sat on the bed.

Walt asked, "Is your reluctance to make love because you do not want to jeopardize your position?"

"No. I just think you are going a little too fast. Did you ever make love to a woman before?"

"No. No women ever showed any interest in me."

"I think you need to be taught how to act with a woman. You have a nice body and even Elaine remarked that she thought you were an attractive man. We need to talk a while and give signals that we want more than small talk."

"Oh! I had no idea."

"I know." They talked and giggled for the next forty minutes then undressed and crawled into the bed. Because of his injuries, Walt was unable to take the lead in making love. However, Ashley showed her sexual expertise and helped him. He positioned himself on the bottom and she climbed on top. They did not have an organism within a few minutes and fell asleep.

When they awoke, Ashley asked, "Are we going to try and make love again sometime."

"Yes, if you will help me. I cannot do my share. It will be up to you. My injuries just make it impossible. I did not realize that my broken bones interfered with any sexual activity that I might to want to perform."

"I am sure that I can help you. Let's enjoy the day and worry about making love later."

They rose had their breakfast in the tourist home where they were served boiled rice with milk and cut apples. The meal demonstrated that there was still rationing in France since none of the items were on the rationing list. They went to see the rest of the city. They found remnants of the Roman Constructions and other interesting sights. They had lunch in a café. It consisted of noodles covered with a cheese sauce, bread, and red wine.

By mid-afternoon, Walt needed to retire to the tourist home to rest. Ashley suggested that they try to make love. Walt was unable to obtain an erection and fell asleep even though she tried to stir some fervor in him. He awoke in time for an evening sojourn into the town. They had the dinner and two bottles of red wine. They were both a little tipsy as they returned to the room for the night. They scanned the radio stations and found an Armed Forces Radio broadcast which played music by Harry James and Frank Sinatra. The latter sang his version of *Let's Get Away from It All*. They thought it was very appropriate for their escape from the War. The next tune was the Andrews Sisters singing *Don't Sit Under the Apple Tree with Anyone but Me*. Again, they thought the popular love song fit their feelings.

Even though it was only 2130 hours, they quit for the evening and went to bed. They had a successful love making session. Walt was more aggressive than in the two previous attempts and noticed that Ashley's toe nails were painted the same red as her finger nails. He asked, "I see you polished your toe nails."

"Yes, but I did not think you would be that adventurous to see them."

"Isn't painting your nails a lot of work?"

"Not really! I don't mind the work if it pleases you. It adds little special adventures to our love making. We have kissed and done a few things but never to the point where either of us have shown special attraction to each other. I wanted this trip to be special."

"It is. I never felt that I could ever love a woman. You have shown me that I can be as manly as other men. Like you said—I just don't have any experience."

Walt kissed her on the shoulders and ran his hands over her whole body. He kissed her red finger nails and toes nails. When she asked, "Why did you kiss my nails?"

He answered, "Because they show that you want me to love you. I want to love you like I never loved anyone. Do you love me?"

"Yes!'

"Have you ever read Ernest Hemingway's book, *A Farewell to Arms*? He also wrote *For Whom the Bells Toll*; the movie for the latter novel was shown in one of the Signal Corps movies."

"No! I took my nursing training in a hospital. They never assigned fiction for us to read. If we had any free time, they expected us to read nursing journals. I have heard of the books but know nothing about them. Tell me about them."

"*For Whom the Bells Toll* is a story about the Spanish Civil War. Hemingway served as a reporter with the Republican Army early in the War. The hero in the book is sent behind the Fascist lines to blow a bridge that will be used to bring up armor during the Republican offense. He has a love affair with a gypsy young girl who lives with other gypsies whose support he needs to blow the bridge. There are many unforeseen problems but he blows the bridge by putting hand grenades in with the explosives. He is wounded during the attempt to escape and stays behind to stop the "Fascists from catching the other saboteurs." The book leaves the story hanging in the air. You assume he was shot by the Fascists.

"Hemingway served as an ambulance driver in the Italian Army during the Great War. The book, *A Farewell to Arms*, has some autobiography about his time in Italy. The plot is basically a love and death story during the Piave Campaign in Northern Italy. The hero, Frederick Henry, an American ambulance driver, falls in love with Katherine Barkley, a British nurse, whose fiancé was blown to bits during the Battle of the Somme. He meets Katherine in an air raid through an Italian doctor, Captain Rinaldi. He sees her several times. The Austrians shell Fred's aid station. He is wounded. Rinaldi sends him to Milan to recuperate and Katherine becomes his nurse, where they made love and she discovered the hero was an alcoholic.

The head nurse discovered him with more than a dozen empty liquor bottles under his bed, and he is sent back to the front without being able to say *Good-Bye* to Katherine. She is pregnant and is kicked out of the army. She flees to Switzerland. Fred goes back to the front but deserts during the Austrian/German assault on the Isonzo front in 1918. He escapes to Milan but Katherine is gone. He tries to find her and finally Rinaldi tells him that she is in Bissago, Switzerland. Since Fred is a deserter, he cannot cross the border legally but sneaks across the border at night. He finds Katherine just as she is going to the hospital to give birth to their son. She and the boy both die during childbirth. You ought to read the book."

"Are you saying that we are doing the same as Hemingway describes it?"

"I hope not. I hope you don't get pregnant. If you do, I will try my best to be with you to the end unlike Frederick in the book. However, if the Army determines that you are pregnant, they will send you home and I'll lose you. I will really miss you"

"I would miss you too but I hope you would find me at the end of the War!"

"That could be soon. I know you live in Memphis so I know where to look. Oh! Many soldiers are predicting that the War in Europe will be over by Christmas but I am not sure. The attempt by Montgomery to cross the Rhine in September was a dismal failure and no one else has issued much good news in the past few weeks. The *Stars and Stripes* only talks about the little successes and failures. The big advances in August are not being repeated and we are still hundreds of miles from the Rhine. I have my doubts that the War will end in eight to ten weeks. Do you hear anything?"

"I've heard a little from the wounded GIs. They talk about the difficulty in advances. We had had a number of wounded from the Third Army that is stuck at Metz. None of their talking indicates that anything really good is happening. I guess they are having too much trouble breaking the German defenses."

"That is basically what I read and hear." They went to sleep.

They needed to rise at 0530 hours so that Ashley could get back to the hospital for her shift at 0800.

Ten days later, he asked for another leave and was granted it. He was given permission to be gone for three days in order to prepare for the return to his unit. Elaine had difficulty getting a leave for Ashley. By scheduling her overtimes and rearranging the schedule of two other nurses, she was able to give Ashley two days off. She was late leaving the ward and could not change her clothing or primp before leaving the hospital. She met Walt at the train station. When they reached their compartment, she was able to shed her white uniform and put on her khakis. Walt complimented her on her beauty but she was not happy; she did not have time to even put on fresh lipstick before she boarded the train. She commented, "You just want to make me to feel good. I did not have time to do anything. I even came in my nursing uniform."

"Love is blind. I see you as I want to see you and you are the beautiful girl to whom I want to show my love."

Ashley knew she could not convince him that she could look prettier and changed the subject, "Do you know when you will return to your unit?"

"Yes. I am ready to leave as soon as the doctors give me the papers. I should get them when I return in three days. They are a little slow. They reminded me that I did fall and wanted to be certain that I function without help."

He and Ashley traveled to Senlis and rented the same room that they had used previously. Since Walt no longer needed his cane; he was much more aggressive than during the previous escapade. They make love and went to sleep. Ashley only had two nights and had to return to the hospital to fulfill her duties. He promised to return to Paris when he received more than a one day leave.

He told her, "After I return to my unit, I'll need about a week's training before I can really take command."

Ashley repeated an earlier request, "Have they told you when you will return to your unit?"

"Not for certain. I acquired three days away so that I can test moving. I cannot do this in the hospital. I'm not sure where the unit is stationed. The last time Corporal Livingston came to see me; he told me that the unit was on the Luxemburg border. They move all the time so that I am not sure if they are still there. I do want to return as soon as possible because the men hate the lieutenant that replaced me. However, I'd rather stay here where I can be close to you. I guess I could duplicate Hemingway's' hero and desert so that you and I can get married."

"That would not solve anything."

"I know but I can think about it."

"You need to be cooperative. You duty is to return to your unit as soon as the doctors will release you. You won't get my respect by doing otherwise."

Walt answered, "I suspected that you would feel that way. Thank you for telling me. Will you marry me?"

"I would marry you now, but I don't think we can get permission to do so. We need to wait until we know what is going to happen in this War. After all, you might not be so lucky next time. I might find you in a military cemetery. There is also the possibility that the Krauts will bomb my hospital and I will be killed."

"I'll spend the rest of my life lamenting the lost."

The rest of the two days was similar to the earlier visit except that Walt was able to take the initiative in everything. They caught the train back to Paris.

When he returned from the three days in Senlis, he was interviewed and told that he could return to his unit the next Monday. He told Ashley that he was going back to his unit in a few days. She wished him, "God Speed!"

Chapter 8

Luxemburg

December 1944

DURING Walt's absence, the patrol sought German installations in NE France. After the regimental CO reprimanded Graham for the stupid handling of the air attack, he changed his tactics. When the group shouted run, everyone turned the jeeps and armored car around the raced as fast as possible to safety. They participated in a few firefights, but often the German's saw them first and opened fire before they were really within range. In one small firefight, they were racked by machine gun fire. Peter received a nasty gash before they escaped. However, except for superficial bleeding, he was not seriously wounded. He returned to the patrol two days later with a small bandage on his head. In another incident, the Germans opened with artillery while the patrol was more than two miles away. They ran as fast as they could but a shell exploded behind the last jeep and Edwin was hit in the shoulder by a piece of shrapnel. No bones were broken but he needed ten days of rest to allow the wound to heal. They were still attached to the same regiment that they had been since they advanced across France after the St. Lo Breakout. Most of the patrols were routine. They were often stationed one to three miles in front of a motorized battalion. If they found Nazi defenses, they called for air support and/or armor. In many of these patrols, since the division was trying to annihilate German resistance, they were actually seeking Germans for the battalions to fight. They often had to approach closer than they would if following routine patrol procedure as they learned at Fort Carson.

The 763 patrol was stationed in northeast France near the Luxemburg border when Walt returned to them. The men were jubilant. After Walt returned, Lieutenant Graham stayed for two days to instruct him in the exploits of the unit during the twelve weeks that the injured man was gone. The men continued to demonstrate their dislike for

Graham by going to Walt for every order and information session. Sometimes when the whole group went into a discussion, Graham was totally ignored. Everyone was happy, including Graham, when the regimental CO ordered him to the regimental headquarters. They were now essential the same group of men even if some were wounded that had trained at Fort Carson.

Shortly after Walt returned to the patrol, the regiment was transferred to eastern Luxemburg. Aero reconnaissance showed no real German activity and everyone assumed that the real fighting had stopped until the weather turned more suitable for ground movements later in the winter or early spring. Basically the routine patrols were dull. During the race across France, Walt normally sent his reports by radio or delivered them by hand at the end of each day. Usually the regimental CO used Walt's recommendations for sending tanks, infantry, or artillery to where the 763 patrol observed German activity. Now Walt sat for an hour at the end of each patrol with the CO looked at one or more maps before making a decision, Most of the time, because of supply problems, they were negative.

The Germans were either in stationary defenses behind natural barriers like small rivers, steep hills, or easy to fortify villages with heavy tree cover. They fired on the recon patrol but often the latter was out of range and could not return the fire. There were cat and mouse engagements with neither side accomplishing much of anything. Most days the regiment could not enter the firefight because there was insufficient ammo and fuel. The men of the 763 unit were frustrated but until the allocations people could deliver more provisions to the front there was not much they could do.

After one patrol, the unit had to wait until the following morning before they could acquire any supplies. Fuel was scarce and the search missions were often short in both time and distance due to the gasoline shortages. They looked for German concentrations but did not discover many. The weather was also terrible with low overcast skies and just enough rain to keep everyone wet and uncomfortable.

Walt was frustrated just like everyone else. Sometimes he did not always watch what he wrote in his letters even though he knew the censors might not let his comments stay and would strike them out. He stated in a letter to Ashley,

> *"We have stayed here for three days. There is no fuel or ammo for vehicles. Each day, the supply people tell me that they would meet our needs tomorrow. When we go back, they tell us that there*

were more essential needs with other units. The men are edgy because there is nothing for them to do. I wish the supply personnel would solve the problem and put us back on the road. It would make everything easier. I complain but no one listens. Mike Goldsmith says that it was worse during the Market Garden fiasco in September; however, Graham did not bitch to the higher authorities as much as I have. I could lose a promotion but we are frustrated."

In his letters to his father, he basically wrote the same thing but toned down the criticism. To his surprise most of his letters went with the derogatory comments through without a censor's black mark. His father explained that the problems that Walt indicated were detailed in the newspaper or in the weekly issue of *Life Magazine*.

The British had captured the port of Antwerp on September 4 before the German could destroy any of the facilities. Next to Hamburg, it was the largest port in Western Europe and the only one captured by the Allies that had not been extensively damaged. However, the Germans controlled the Scheldt estuary. The port could not be used until the estuary was cleared of defenders and mines. Unfortunately Eisenhower allowed Montgomery to waste men, supplies, and fuel trying to capture a bridge at Arnhem (Operation Market Garden). The Dutch had condemned the strategy. When Market Garden maneuver failed, Montgomery sent the Canadian First Army to clear the Germans from the approaches to Antwerp. The Germans had fortified their holding and flooded the lowland during the three week lull. The Canadians were not militarily strong enough for the fighting and Bradley had to send the 7th Armored and 104 Infantry Division to support the Canadian attacks. It was a day by day slugging match but by November 9 the mine sweepers could finally enter the bay and start to clear the estuary. On November 28, the first convoy berthed at Antwerp and the supply problems disappeared in the next few weeks.

By the end of the first week in December, fuel, ammo, and other supplies shortages started to disappear as the Allied/American ships unloaded at Antwerp. It still took a day for trains to reach Luxemburg city and another half day to deliver the fuel, ammo, and food to the regimental depot. Since the railroad was in good shape, after a few days there were more than sufficient quantities of everything. With the change in resources, the regiment started to operate against German installations; however, the latter moved east and were now hiding behind the Moselle River whose bridges had been destroyed. Furthermore, the dreadful weather raised the water level in the river a foot or a foot and a half so that amphibian type attacks were necessary before the American Army could move eastward.

During the long hours and days just waiting, Walt wrote love letters to Ashley as often as possible. She returned them within a few days. He was very discrete and tried not to show too much of his love so that the censors would not flag his letters. However, at times he just did not care and wrote what he felt, "*I want nothing in life but for you to be forever with me. I want to love no one but you with all the passion on earth.*" She was not sure what to say and only commented, "*I set forth my thoughts in the note that I gave you before we separated a few weeks ago.*"

She kissed a letter and left a lipstick mark. Walt was astonished that the censors just sent the letter without any restriction but it was only a two day interval for mail service between Paris and Luxemburg. If there was nothing military in the letter, it was delivered without any censor marks. Walt wrote in his return letter, "*I kissed your signature to show that my love is like the passion inside the popular song 'Love Letters'.*"[26]

Ashley told Elaine after one of the letters arrived, "His voice is soft but has authority. His speech is slow but catches my imagination. I think I am stricken with an arrow as it strikes the bull's eye. It is ridiculous about how I feel; but I fell in love with him during his second visit to Domfront. He wanted to kiss me and we made silly jokes. He persisted and I gave him a light peck. He came back for more in the next few weeks and conveyed flowers on most of the visits. I knew we were in love. I guess Chaplain Weidman would call it *Eros* in the finest sense."

"I'm concerned that you are spending too much time idolizing the man. Your work is not suffering from you infatuation but with the slightest advance on his side you could be doing things that will get you into trouble with the army. I wish you both would back off until the end of the War."

Ashley shrugged her shoulders and kept answering the love letters to Walt. After receiving a letter one day, Walt told Ed, "What a woman, I can give her my whole heart and body and not be satisfied. I hint-

---

[26] *Love Letters* is a popular 1945 **song** with music by Victor Young and lyrics by Edward Heyman. The **song** appeared, without lyrics, in the movie of the same name.

A DISHONORABLE DISCHARGE

ed that we should get married but she delayed the real proposal. There is a geographic separation but that only make me want to go back to her. Unfortunately we need to wait until the end of the War before we do anything serious."

Ed remarked, "I think you're spending too much time thinking about her! It could interfere with your decisions concerning the safety of the patrol. I can't really complain; you are so much better than Graham that I never have any fear concerning the execution of your commands."

Each day the patrol would rise before dawn, eat a cold breakfast, usually C rations, and drive the river road along the west branch of the Moselle river looking for any German activity that might have occurred during the past 24 hours. The section of the river was difficult to maneuver. The road was set eighteen feet above the water which put it above the flood plain. The bank on the east side had a very steep slope and was actually below the flood plain. The river itself was six to twenty feet deep and moved at four to six mph in a narrow gorge. All the bridges had been destroyed and much of the piling. Both sides of the river had heavy forests and only a few very narrow roads existed where the bridges had stood. The bank on the west side of the river was fifteen to eighty feet high and it would take a well-equipped engineering group to rebuild any of the bridges. It was obvious that the access roads had been constructed decades previous and any ferries that had plied the river were long gone.

The 763 patrol rarely saw anyone. If the Germans exposed themselves, they racked the area with .50 caliber machine gun fire. The Germans occasional returned the fire but not often. The territory was terrible and it was obvious that the Germans had concentrated their forces in the north where movement was easier. Furthermore, there was an armored and infantry division in Thionville about was thirty miles to the south. The latter could easily move north if any real enemy activity occurred. Everyone was certain that the German intelligence knew about the American firepower in Thionville and did not want to challenge it.

Although the Battle of the Bulge started on December 16 and went bad for the American First Army, the 763 patrol operated the first four days of the battle without seeing any activity along the Southern Luxemburg border. They pulled into a small orchard 300 yards from the river at the end of December 20. A small hill separated their site from the river; from the top they could see the east side of the river and anyone on the east side could see them. They pitched their pup tents out of sight of the river. They set a guard schedule with each man including Walt standing guard for one hour. As the eastern sky began to get light the next morning, Ed woke everyone and they packed their gear. Walt pulled a couple boxes of grenades from his jeep and used them as seats and tables while Nicholas started a small fire to heat water. By 0830 hours everyone had drank coffee and eaten warm C-rations. As they started to congregate to start their patrol, a company of 155 mm Long Toms pulled into the orchard. The Lt. Colonel in charge of the artillery platoon walked over to Walt who was still sitting on the grenades and drinking coffee. Walt opened the conversation, "Would you like a cup of coffee. We just made it."

"No. We have been told to set up an artillery battery in this spot. Where is the front line?"

"You're standing on it."

"You must be crazy. We're supposed to be six to ten miles behind the front."

"Nope, the Nazi patrols are just over the crest of the small hill but on the other side of the river. We have not seen much." Walt pointed to the fifteen foot hill that lay between the patrol and the river. By this time all of the members of the patrol were standing around listening to the officers.

"Something must be wrong. I'm getting on the radio."

"We need to start our patrol. Would you like us to wait a few minutes so that you can check your position?"

"Yeah."

The Lt. Colonel went to the radio and argued with the regimental headquarters. After five minutes of fruitless discussion, he returned to the patrol and announced, "They insist that they are correct and we are to set up in this orchard. Can you stay a little longer?"

"We should not! If the Krauts tried to bridge the stream last night, we need to find it before they finish. We must progress over the road or we may all be in trouble." He waved his men into their vehicles and they moved to the crest of the hill. Nicholas stopped far enough back from the crest so that Walt could scan the east bank with only his head above the crest. He saw nothing and the patrol moved over the summit onto the river road. They move at 30 mph in the hope that they could hide if anyone shot at them. They traveled a mile before a rifleman fired at them. The bullet went over the top of the third jeep and everyone moved their guns to try to determine the source of the single shot. They couldn't see anything and moved further north along the

A DISHONORABLE DISCHARGE

river. There were no further conflicts with the enemy. They pulled off the road at the end of their patrol and moved over the crest of the river bank. As soon as they were safe, Walt stopped the column, wheeled his jeep in a 180 degree movement, and walked back to the crest to scan the east bank. He saw nothing, after thirty minutes the patrol moved west to the fuel dump five miles back from the river.

Fifteen minutes later, they entered the storage area. There were no vehicles there and they rapidly top off their fuel tanks. Ed went to the mail area and pick up the mail for the men in the recon unit. There were three letters for Walt from Ashley. He ignored the service personnel appraisal of what needed to be done with the vehicles and read the letters. When asked what to do about the servicing, he stuttered and then told Nicholas to see that they were properly serviced. When the servicing was completed, everyone climbed into the vehicles and they drove the six miles to the regimental HQ to make a report. Ed complained that Walt was spending too much time reading the letters from Ashley and not watching the patrol. He grunted and said nothing. Since nothing had happened except for the single sniper shot, they were ordered back to the river and asked to make another run before nightfall. They did as they were ordered and moved north to south. Walt concentrated on his duties and men were happy. Again they saw nothing.

When the patrol pulled into the orchard that they had left early in the morning, they discovered that the artillery platoon has set up a nice defense. They had positioned six of the Long Toms so that they could each cover a 75 ° angle of the hill crest with the huge guns overlapping their fire. They had situated the remaining four guns so that they could fire their shells five to ten miles across the river. Walt stopped long enough to talk to the Lt. Colonel. Walt asked, "Has anything occurred since we left this morning?"

"No, we have not seen or hear anything. Are you going to spend the night here?"

"No, we still have 90 minutes of daylight. We are going to drive to the other end of our patrol area and set up camp there. I think you should station a few men on the crest of the hill and if anything occurs, radio regimental headquarters immediately."

"That's a good idea. How long have you been patrolling this area?"

"Five days and we have not been fired upon by anything but a few rifles. I don't think the Krauts have anything on the other side of the river. They probably moved everything up north in the area around

St. Vith. The approaches on both sides of the river required a large engineering battalion to build a crossing. The banks are extremely steep and the river runs swift and deep. If you go thirty miles north of here, the river is easy to cross either with or without special equipment. I assume it is the reason the Krauts launched their attack in that area rather than in these forests."

"I think you are right."

With that statement, the patrol progressed over the crest of the hill and headed north. Long shadows fell on the river and they could not see very much, but they were also hidden from eyes on the east side of the river. They made an uninteresting patrol and located an abandoned farm house about half a mile from the river. They dragged their equipment into the house and searched for a way to get comfortable. They posted a single guard, as the previous night.

The next morning, they arose early. The temperature was 33° F and the snow had become soggy. When the patrol had entered the house that they occupied the previous evening, ice and snow hung on all the trees. Now it was rapidly melting and cold droplets of water was coating everything. It only got worse as the day matured. It was miserable and everyone prayed that the sun would come out and make life a little better.

They drove south. After two miles, they discovered that the road had been destroyed by mortars. There were holes too deep to drive through and would require shoveling to level the dirt. Walt suspected an ambush and ordered the patrol to retreat half a mile. He called the regimental headquarters and reported his observation. They asked, "Is the artillery group still there?"

"Yes. We left them last evening."

"Go back and explain your problem to them. Ask them for support; then go to where you think there is an ambush and direct their fire into the area where the Krauts could have set up the mortars. Under fire, you should be able to repair the road. I'll look for a report in an hour. I will also alert the infantry in Thionville."

"Roger."

Using a back road, the patrol drove back to the artillery unit. With a map of the area, Walt conferred with the Lt. Colonel in regard to the road destruction. The Colonel ordered his men to drop four shells into the woods on the east side of the river. Walt positioned his radio to the artillery unit's frequency and gave details to the Colonel as they advanced on the road. Half a mile south of the destruction, he asked for more shells to be dropped on the east side of the river. The 155 mm guns fired eight more rounds. The patrol carefully moved to the destruction. As the drivers shoveled dirt back into the holes, Vladimir stood at the 37 mm cannon pointing into the woods and other men stood by the .50 calibers. Walt kept talking to the Colonel. No one fired on the men and after an hour; they had the holes filled sufficiently that they could continue their patrol.

The patrol reached the end of their run, turned around, and moved back south. It was quiet. When they pulled into the orchard where the artillery was located, the Colonel walked over to Walt and stated, "Did the shelling help?"

"I don't know. Nothing happened! The mortar destruction could have been a fluke or the Krauts might not have been willing to challenge your artillery fire. We'll make another run before dusk. I'll keep in contact with you on the radio. One of us should report to the regimental headquarters."

"Good. I will not change the coordinates on our guns until you give the OK or something more serious occurs." The patrol progressed north and observed nothing; they lodged in the same abandon farm house where they resided the previous evening. Walt wrote his report.

At daylight the next morning, they returned to the road and drove south. Again they saw nothing and exited the river road where the artillery unit was setup. The Long Toms were still there but the Colonel told Walt, "I finally convinced the CO that we were wasting our time here. He promised to get us moved by noon. I don't expect to be here when you return. We received no orders and never used our artillery to fire a single shot except the shells that we discharged to support your movements on the river road. I guess this is part of the army stupidity. Dig in, wait, wait and if nothing happens wait some more,"

Walt had no comment and headed over the crest for another patrol along the river.

On the morning of December 23, the 763 recon group pulled into the service depot for fuel, ammo, and other supplies. They had only fired twelve 37 mm shells and less than two hundred rounds of machine gun ammo but decided they wanted to have full vehicles in case they should be induced into a firefight. As they pulled into the depot, an MP approached them carrying a clip board. He announced, "A cease fire has been negotiated from 1800 on Christmas Eve until 0600 on St. Stephen's Day (December 26) for the SE section of Luxemburg. We need to know who wants to attend the Midnight Mass in the church in Ramiche. A meal will be served after the Mass. There is limited seating in the church and if all the American personal attend the

Mass, there will be no seats for the parishioners. We need to know who wishes to attend. If you are not on the list, we will not allow you to enter."

"How do we know if we are on the list?"

"It will be posted at 1800 hours tomorrow."

Walt, Ed, Nick, Edwin Yavorski, and Edwin Scalise signed the sheet. The other members of the patrol were either Protestants who did not want to go to a Catholic service or preferred to attend services on Christmas morning. The service in the church was the primary discussion throughout the next 24 hours. During one of the rest stops, Edwin Scalise told a story of going to Mass when he was nine years old. "We did not have an automobile when I was a kid and the church was a mile and a half from our home. We walked and rarely attended when the weather was bad. I was not an altar boy because I could not guarantee that I would be at the services. I did sing in the youth choir when I was in high school but I wasn't very good--no one cared. When I was nine, my mother and father felt that we children were old enough to walk to the church for the Christmas Eve Mass. We had a traditional Christmas Eve meal of fish, potatoes, and greens at 7 PM. We opened half of our Christmas presents and at 9:30 my father had us put on our best clothing. At 10:15 we left for the church. It snowed that afternoon and there was two inches of snow on the ground. No one had shoveled their sidewalks so we hiked through the streets. The moon came out when we were about half way to the church. It was beautiful in the moonlight with the twinkling of the Christmas lights on trees and shrubbery. I was cold by the time we reached the church but I'll remember that night until I die. The church was full of the aromas of pine and candle wax. There were trees, pine boughs, and candles all over the front of the church and in the windows. It surpassed any Christmas card I ever saw. The Mass opened with the singing of the *Asperges* in Latin. I followed every word in my prayer book. The plain song was truly beautiful. During the reading of the Gossip, a ninety year old parishioner placed the Baby Jesus in the manger. During the Elevation of the Host, I felt as if angels were singing the responses. I looked about the church expecting a miracle. At the end of the service we all kneeled in adoration at the Nativity crèche. I was cold on entering the church but did not notice the wind or cold while we walked home. It was the first time that I attended a Midnight Mass but it was the most joyous experience in my childhood. I attended more Midnight Masses in the past fifteen years but none gave me the feeling that I experienced at the first one."

Jacob Cooper told his story. "I'm Moravian and we tried to go to the Christmas Eve Love Feast at the Central Moravian Church in Bethlehem, Pennsylvania each year. My father did not own a car but my uncle did. We normally took the bus to church on Sundays but they stopped running on Christmas Eve. I was twelve; my father wanted me to wear a cap but I refused. He told me that I would regret it and I did. My uncle picked us up. We all crowded into his car. We drove through a light rain and arrived at the church at 7:15 for the Love Feast. The Moravian church does not allow many decorations but there were two huge pine trees on either side of the pulpit. They must have been ten feet tall. Just before the service began, two men lit the candles attached to the end of the branches. It was the first time that I saw real candles on a Christmas tree. In the Moravian Church, we sing a lot of hymns and read numerous scripture passages. The hymns and other music were traditional and I have heard them count-less times but they were most beautiful that night. Like Edwin, I thought angels were in the choir loft singing the hymns. We serve cof-fee and rolls at a Love Feast. The coffee was delivered on big trays and had lots of milk and sugar. Some people did not like it because it was so sweet but I loved it. It was one of the few times that my parents let me drink coffee as a kid. The serving women were dressed in colonial outfits. My mother was never a server but my sister became one in high school. After we drank our coffee, all the lights were turned off. It was dark when they brought in the candles near the end of the ser-vice. The ushers passed out lighted beeswax candles. As each parishion-er received his candle the light spread through the church. Some years later, I sat in the church loft and watched the candle light spread across the church. It was beautiful. The pastor rose and asked us all to raise our candles. He ended his short talk by asking us to take our light out of the church and show people that Jesus was the true light of the world. I did not want to put out my candle at the end of the service but my father snuffed it out for me. He did it to prevent a possible fire. We went home and had a big Christmas dinner. It was midnight by the time we went to bed. I never wanted to get up the next morning but my sister dragged me out of bed. She wanted to open her presents and our parents would not allow us to open any presents until everyone had enter the living room. I am sure I have had other nice Christmases but this is the one that I remember most of all."

Ed stated, "I'm a Methodist. We had a candlelight service on Christmas Eve. Everyone was given a candle as we entered the church. There were little Christmas trees on either side of the altar. They were covered with lights. It was the only light in the church as we entered. The service opened with a tradition Christmas carol. The ushers walked down the aisles lighting each person's candle. Then the pastor read the Gospel according to St. Luke. We sang more carols. The pastor read a short Christmas story like *The Littlest Angel* or an abbreviated version of *The Fourth Wise Man*. We sang more carols and closed with a blessing. We walked out of the church with our lighted candles and only extinguished them after we had exited the main door. We usually went to bed early, rose early on Christmas morning to open our presents, and prepared a big dinner. I usually went ice skating on Christmas afternoon if there was any ice. I didn't have the deep feeling that Edwin and Jacob had. I never felt that angels were guiding our Birthday Celebration of the Savior; but I always came away from church elated and was proud that I was a Methodist."

"Walt you have not said anything!"

"As you know, I'm a Lutheran. We never did much on Christmas Eve. When I was young, we had a Communion Service at dawn on Christmas day. I hated to rise in the cold dark morning but did it anyway. When I became an acolyte, I did not mind the early rising. I think I liked people watching me and complimenting me at the end of the service. The service was taken out of the Service Book and was the same that was used six times a year. There were trees and candles but I do not remember much about them. We went home after the service, opened our presents, and had a big dinner. In the afternoon, we walked along the river. It was a Marietta custom and thousands of people were out to walk in the late Christmas afternoon. In the evening, my father led us on a walk about the neighborhood to see the Christmas decorations. He always knew where the best displays were exhibited. There was a religious tone to the observation but I think most people thought of it as a typical American Christmas."

Mike Goldberg stated, "I'm an Episcopalian. Our Christmas Eves were more or less a combination of what the rest of you have described. We always had a Communion Service which started at 11:00 PM with special Christmas music. We had a large choir, more than thirty members; they sang both hymns which the congregation could sing and special music, like a Bach cantata or a Mozart piece. The service opened with a Christmas carol. During the singing, the altar boys lite the candles attached to the end of each pew. Once they were lite, the ushers extinguished all the light except in the chancel and the safety lights at the ends of the pews. At 12:00 midnight, the clergy and servers processed into the church as we sang, *Oh Come All ye Faithful*. The service came directly out of the Prayer Book but the choir sang the most beautiful setting for the service that I have ever heard. Some of the canticles were sung in Plain Song. After the creed, the pastor always preached a Christmas message. Sometimes it was a regular homily but one year he spent more than twenty minutes reading about St. Francis' creation of the first crèche. Francis put live oxen and asses in his crèche.

Peter interrupted, "There were no ox or ass at the first Nativity. In fact, Jesus was born during the summer."

Walt commanded, "We are not here to debate when Jesus was born. We're telling stories about what was pleasing to us. Now let Mike finish his story."

Mike continued, "I've read other versions since that Christmas but I think our pastor did a better job of telling the story than any book that I have read. My father was on the vestry so after the service we went to the rectory where the priest served coffee, cake, and cookies. Then we went to the home of the town's bank president. He served alcoholic drinks to visitors over 21 years of age. My parents usually let me drink a small glass of wine during the reception. After an hour, we finally went home. It was about 3 AM when we went to bed. We usually slept to 10 the next morning then opened presents. We ate a big dinner in the afternoon, and then visited neighbors. In the evening we often drove about the town looking at the decorations. The day was always very full."

The others told stories similar to those that had already been told.

The patrol arrived back in Ramiche at 1700 hours on Christmas Eve. All those that had signed the list were on it. The signal corps prepared mimeograph copies of the service in English. Every seat was taken with about half of the attendees being military. The parish church was beautifully decorated with greens and candles in all the windows and poinsettias on the altar. The choir sang Bach's *Magnificent* before the service. The Mass began at exactly midnight. During the communion, a tenor sang Schubert's *Ave Maria* then after the choir returned to their pews, they sang Mozart's' *Ave Verum Corpus*. Walt was familiar with all the music but had never heard most of it in Latin. The choir also sang *Christus Natus Est*, *Hodie Christus Natus Est*, and a number of plain songs pieces. The Mass was beautiful.

During the service at the point where special prayers were offered, a colonel rose and led the Americans in prayers for the embattled 101 Airborne Division in Bastogne.

He then asked everyone to pray St. Francis' prayer for peace that was printed on the mimeographed sheet:

"Lord make me an instrument of Thy peace; where there is hatred, let me bring love; where there is injury, pardon; where there is doubt, faith; where there is despair, hope; where there is darkness, light: and where there is sadness, joy.

"Oh divine Master let be not so much be consoled as to console; let me not be understood as to understand; let me not so much be loved as to love; for it is in giving that we receive, it is in pardoning that we are pardoned, and it is in dying that we are born to eternal life."

Since the prayer was Catholic, Walt had never heard it. Some of the other men started to say the prayer from memory but quickly turned to reading it after they discovered that the words were not exactly as they had memorized them.

After the dismissal at the end of the Mass, a large number of attendees both parishioners and service men, went to the Nativity crèche in the front of the church to kneel and pray. Walt followed Edwin and did as the others did. The Nativity was a set of wood carvings about 14 inches tall. There were Mary, Joseph, the Babe, sheep, goats, three shepherds, a cow, and an ass. In his church, no one knelt or made separate devotions to the Holy Family but he was feeling good and felt that he needed to present a special thanksgiving because his injuries had healed so well. He knelt for less than ten minutes then went to the basement of the church to enjoy the dinner. He sat with a parishioner who spoke English. He asked, "Where did the crèche come from? It's beautiful."

The man answered, "It's been in the parish for more than a hundred years. Legend says we received it from Emperor Frederick Barbarossa. However, I don't think it is that old. Someone probably bought it in Italy at the end of the 18th Century and gave it to the church. This is the first time; it has been on display since the War came to Luxemburg. We were afraid that the Nazis might steal it because it is so old. It was hid behind a false wall in the basement. Legend had it that the wall was built during the Napoleonic Wars to hide the chalices and other valuables. Again it is legend. The wall was probably built during World War I to hide valuables. Almost all the parishioners know about the wall, so if the "enemy" really thought there was something of extreme value in the parish, they could probably find were the wall is located.

"For the last four years, we set up the small crèche that is in the front of this room." Walt had not noticed it but now as the man described the crèche; the American looked at the six inch plaster figurines in the front of the room.

The meal after the Mass was a typical Christmas dinner with turkey, cranberry sauce, dressing, mashed potatoes, peas, and fruit cake for dessert. Almost all the parishioners attended the dinner and those that spoke English kept a conversation going with the servicemen.

During the dinner, Walt asked a parishioner, "Where did you acquire the poinsettias?"

"They come from Spain or Portugal."

"Do they grow them?"

"No. Portugal and Spain are neutral countries and their merchant ships freely sail across the Atlantic. No one bothers them as long as they only carry essential food or flowers. They always load a ship with poinsettias in Mexico and bring them to Europe. Again most of the trains from those countries come through because everyone knows that they only carry flowers or holiday food. We have brought flowers throughout the whole War. Sometimes they are expensive but they have always been available."

Everyone went home at 0300 hours. The 763 recon group camped outside of the town and those men who attended the Mass slept to 1100 hours. The other attended services held by the chaplains during the morning hours. Late in the afternoon, the patrol drove back to the Moselle River to start their patrol the next morning.

The next day, Walt thought he heard artillery fire; the front up north had been too quiet. They had patrolled for several weeks and except for the damaged road and a few rifle shots, they had neither seen nor heard anything. He was nervous but there was not much he could do but keep on patrolling.

While waiting to make their patrol, Walt wrote to Chaplain Weidman, "On Christmas Eve, we had a minor disagreement about when Jesus was born. I stopped the discussion because it was Christmas Eve, but now I want to know if there is any real knowledge about Jesus's birth."

The patrol returned to driving the river road. They stopped at an empty house. It only contained a table and two broken chairs. They tuned the radio to the Jack Benny Christmas program on the Armed Forces Radio network. As they made camp in the evening of December 26, the BBC announced that the 4th Armored Division had entered Bastogne to relieve the encircled 101 Airborne Division. The shell fire continued throughout most of the next morning; however, no one was able to identify exactly where it originated or could see anything. Walt wondered if the shell fire came from the armored units attempt to enter the Belgium city. However, everyone felt he was being ridicules since Bastogne was more than fifty mile away.

The recon group arrived back at the supply depot in Ramiche on New year Eve. The men had hoped to get the day off but no permission was granted for anything except to continue their monotonous patrols. A message was waiting for Walt on January 1, he was ordered to report to regimental HQ. He and Ed drove as fast as possible to the HQ. The major in the intelligence section explained, "Now that Bastogne is relieved and the Nazis are on retreat, we want to cross the Moselle River. As soon as we have nice weather, we will call for fighter bombers to attack the Krauts on the east side of the river south of your patrol area. When the planes leave, we will shell everything that moves; we hope by noon to start to build a pontoon bridge and be finished before nightfall. We'll send two battalions of infantry across the bridge as soon as it is finished. We need you to scout ahead. I will radio the code word, *New York Yankees*. I want you to start moving as soon as you get the code words."

"Why don't you build the bridge across the river in our area? There doesn't seem to be any Germans on the east side of the river?"

"A bridge in your area might take days to build. The river is too swift and rough. We'll lose our surprise and be forced to fight a pitching battle. Below here, we can be across the river before the Krauts know we're trying. Tell your men to be ready to move and nothing else. It could be five or six days until we have the type of weather that we need."

On January 1st, the Germans attacked British and American bases in Northern France and Belgium. They destroyed over 200 Allied planes, most on the ground. There were only 16 Allied causalities. The Germans returned to their bases but flew over a rocket testing site. No-one had notified the AA people at the site about the sorties. The German gunners shot down about 200 planes and caused about 180 casualties. One of the worst disasters for the Nazis in the whole War.

Four days later, the 763 patrol received the code words and moved south to where the bridge was being built. They crossed the Bailey

A DISHONORABLE DISCHARGE

bridge with the initial infantry movement and positioned themselves on the east side of the river. The next morning, they moved out in front of a company of tanks.

The 763 recon unit cautiously moved along the road east of the Moselle River. There were many small German defenses. They all had small artillery pieces and were well stocked with supplies. Walt's patrol avoided most of the firefights but gave the location and strength of the defenses to the regimental HQ who sent infantry/armor to destroy the Nazi strongholds.

On the second day, they were driving on a heavily damaged macadam road. There was a solid cloud cover at 7000 feet. It was a nasty day. The temperature was just above freezing and the snow on the road turned to slush. The snow by the side of the road was four inches deep. Visibility was less than 1500 feet and the men were very tense. It was an excellent condition for an ambush. Since the patrol was now in Germany, there was no possible assistance from the native population. They ran into a German defense near a farmhouse. They spotted the enemy before being seen and carefully watched the German company of soldiers. Walt notified HQ. He sat for an hour until six P-47s broke out of the clouds and dove on the Germans positions. They dropped six 500 pound bombs then circled and came back firing all forty eight machine guns. They kept strafing the defense for twenty minutes then flew west. Walt felt certain that they needed ammo. During the attack, he could see anti-aircraft fire but it diminished as the fighters strafed the Nazi position. He assumed that the men assigned to man the guns were killed. The German infantry did not have anything except light machine guns. Before the planes were out of sight, a battalion of infantry came roaring down the road in armored personal carriers. They moved on the German defense. There was a lot of noise but no one could determine what was happening. A few Germans surrendered and the infantry move throughout all the nearby building to see that no one was hiding. It was a big conflict but the patrol personnel had no knowledge what had really happened. They never fired a shot.

Walt radioed the regiment HQ. They told him to retreat and move north to the next east-west road and scout it. They reached a road junction and turned north but ran into German defenses in a small ravine. Again they radioed HQ. Within fifteen minutes eight tanks and a company of infantry were plowing into the weak German defenses. The battle was over in fifteen minutes. Walt waved "Good-bye" to the tank commander and drove to the road where he had been ordered to scout. As they moved east on the road, a plane emerged from the clouds. Everyone drove into the ditches. As they stopped, they saw two parachutes open and the white star on a B-17. There was fire coming out of the #4 engine and the plane was so punctured with bullet holes, it looked like a sieve. As the patrol arranged their vehicles back on the road, Walt ordered Edwin and Peter to drive ahead and try to find the parachutists. He ordered Ed and the armored car to move back west. Before he finished his orders, they heard the plane crash and saw a large ball of fire rise from the damaged plane. They drove as fast as possible towards the wreck. As they entered the field, four airman came running towards them. The airman pulled their revolvers but then realized that it was an American patrol. Walt pulled up to the pilot who shouted, "I'm Lt. Glenn Ford in the 100th bomb group. We were shot up by a bunch of Nazi fighters as we left out target."

"Where is the rest of your crew?"

"Five bailed out. The radio operator is dead. He was hit in the neck by a 20 mm shell."

As they shouted at each other, the men could hear a machine gun. Walt rapidly asserted, "That's my men. I can tell that fire comes from our .50 calibers. We saw a ball of fire, what happened?"

"We hit a tree as we crashed. It tore off the wing and separated the burning engine from the plane. I assume a great deal of fuel came out of the wing tanks and the ball of fire was the fuel rapidly burning away."

"Jump into the jeep and we'll see if we can find the rest of your crew. Let the three other men stay here. We should be back for them in thirty minutes." The Lieutenant jumped into Walt's jeep and the two vehicles raced down the road. Walt was 400 yards in the lead when he saw the other two jeeps of the patrol. He drove off the road and rapidly approached the idle vehicles. Two airman were standing alongside of the jeeps. "What happened?"

"Nazi infantry were approaching the flyers as we entered the field. We opened up with the MG and the Krauts fled. I do not know if we hit any!"

"Load up the crew members and let's get out of here!'

The patrol returned to the road and drove west. Just as they lost sight of where they had picked up the flyers, Nick shouted, "I think I saw an armored vehicle emerge from the woods, but I can't see anything now."

Ten minutes later they were at the point where the plane crashed. The fire was almost out. The three crew members were standing by the body of the dead radio operator. Glenn Ford asked, "Where are we?"

"In Western Germany. We are about twelve miles from the Moselle River. We crossed the river three days ago and were moving east towards the Rhine. If you had crashed two miles to the east, you would be in German held territory. Your other crew members probably landed in Nazi Germany and are POWs. Let me contact regimental headquarter and see what they want me to do."

Walt talked with the regimental intelligence officer and explained the whole situation. As he was talking, Ed came back and signaled to Walt that they were low on fuel and .50 ammo. The regimental officer told them to try to reach a service depot. The men tied the dead airman to the back of the armored car and the other six air corps personnel found room in the jeeps. An hour and a half later, they reach the service sector near the river. An MP was waiting for them, "I'll see that the airmen are secured. They can talk to an interrogator and get back to their unit as soon as possible."

The next day, the patrol ran into a German anti-tank unit. The Nazis fired a number of 75 mm shells. One hit the armored car at the right front. It tore off the wheel and Vladimir was hit by shrapnel. Another exploded just behind the 4931 jeep and it upset. Two more shells landed close to the patrol vehicles but did not do any material damage. Walt ordered a retreat. The three movable vehicles drove into the ditch where there was some protection. The armored car could move a little on five wheels and it went in the ditch head first.

Fortunately, there was a company of tanks half a mile behind the patrol. They began to fire upon the German defenses as soon as they saw the 75 mm flash. The tanks rushed forward, shelled, and machine gunned the antitank defenses. One of the tanks was hit by a 75 mm shell and was set on fire; however, the Germans did not have any infantry or other units and in twenty minutes, the tanks had silenced the 75 mm anti-tank gun. The few Germans that could still run disappeared before anyone could determine how many or where they were going. The CO, a major, of the tank company walking nearby trying to determine who were causalities in his destroyed tank; one man was wounded the other four were dead. He then approached the 763 patrol. Walt had not appraised the damage so the two officers walked among the vehicles, Vladimir's wounds were not serious. He had been hit by a piece of shrapnel and it was sticking out of his shoulder but only oozed a tiny stream of blood. He had very little pain. The jeep that had been upset was damaged beyond simple repairs. The armored car needed to go to the repair shop for major repairs. A tank came up to the armored car, attached a tow, and pulled it back onto the road. It could still move at twenty miles per hour or less. Walt stated, "I guess this puts us out of action for a few days. I'll order the patrol to retreat as best as possible to the service unit near the river."

Vladimir climbed into Walt's jeep, he had three other minor wound which needed to be bandaged. No one wanted to try and remove the shrapnel for fear that it might really start to bleed. It took more than an hour to reach the service area. Vladimir was talking incoherently and suffering from shock when he was put in an ambulance that took him to field hospital on the west bank of the river. The service personnel inspected the vehicles. They estimated that they could fix the damaged jeep and the armored car in less than three days. The service personnel were also sure that they could find a third jeep for the group. They took directions on where the knocked out jeep had been ditched and hoped to bring it into the service repair area within a day. While the men headed to the Red Cross tent, Walt walked to the regimental HQ and made his report. He was told to rest until the vehicles were ready to move. He joined his men for coffee. None of the Red Cross women interested the men. Ed and Walt later appraised the lack of interest as due to the horrible day's action that they had led to the firefight that they lost. Everyone was tired and suffered from shock. Young women did not appeal to the men because they were just feeling bad.

The Red Cross tent was nice, like the one in Laval. It was also warm with a small coal stove behind the table where the women served coffee and donuts. Ed went looking for a place to stay until the vehicles were repaired. He returned twenty minutes later telling everyone that he had laid claim to a wall tent behind the service repair area. It only had eight cots but he was sure they could find a ninth. Walt suggested he try to find an officer billet but men wanted him to stay with them. They ambled back to the service area; pick up what equipment had not been damaged and deposited it inside the wall tent. They even found warm dry sleeping bags for the night. They dragged a cot from another tent and made a bed for Walt. There was a field kitchen in the service area and they had a hot meal. They all ate together and did not pay attention to the signs designating enlisted men and officer sections. The food tasted good but no one could determine if the food was really good or that they had not had a hot meal since they crossed the Moselle River. They figured that it actually might have been the lack of hot food that just made them hungry. After din-

A DISHONORABLE DISCHARGE

ner they went looking to see if a movie was being shown. They could not find one so they returned to the Red Cross tent to drink coffee and talk about the patrol by candle light.

The next morning they obtained a brand new jeep from the service staff and four of the men drove to the field hospital on the west side of the Moselle to see Vladimir. He was in good shape. He had a number of bandages and was complaining that he needed to return to his recon unit. He stopped talking as soon as he saw his colleagues. They asked him how bad the injuries were. He hedged the statement that they were nothing and he would be back with the unit as soon as he could find a pair of pants. Walt told him to stay in bed. There would be no immediate patrols. He continued, "We got a new command jeep this morning but it needs to be outfitted; furthermore, the other three vehicles need some repairs. It will be at least three days before they can be put on the road. As I listen to you, I assume the wounds are not serious?"

"No, I was suffering from shock when they brought me here. The shrapnel came out easy without serious bleeding. One nice thing about this hospital is that the food is good and they even gave me a small dish of ice cream before I went to sleep last evening. Did they give you ice cream in the hospital in Paris?"

"Yes, but only two or three time. It was very good."

"So was this. I wonder if I can get another dish later today."

"If they keep feeding you like that; we'll never get you back on another patrol." Everyone roared with laughter. In fact they were so loud that one of the nurses came to determine what the noise source was of and asked the patrol to be a little quieter.

Edwin asked, "Captain did you experience shock when we put you in the hospital in August?"

"I was in terrible pain. I don't remember anything except the pain for first two days. Like Vladimir, I wanted to get out of bed at the end of the first week and I would have returned to the patrol at least three weeks before the doctors released me. They kept telling me I was not healed but it did not mean anything to me until the day that I fell and could not get up. However, that is now history. Vladimir, I'll try keeping your position open until you return. A group of us will come to see you each day and let you know how the repairs are progressing. Keep your chin up and God bless you."

While waiting for the vehicles to be repaired, Walt received a letter from Chaplain Weidman. He answered Walt's question,

"I asked the other chaplains about Jesus' birth during a meeting with all the ministers here in the hospital. No one had an immediate answer but everyone thought they had seen something in one of their church journals. I was given the following story the next time we met. It came from a church publication but no one has identified it. I think it is the best answer that I have ever seen.

"Jesus was NOT born on December 25! Our Christmas is the observation of the Roman Saturnalia Feast which was observed during the winter solstice. At the end of the fourth century, Italian bishops, especially the Bishop of Rome, complained about the revelry and drunkenness of the Saturnalia holiday. They moved the Nativity Mass to December 25 (the Winter Solstice at that time) in order to force Christians to forgo the pagan feast. The Christian Church imposed a fast period for forty days prior to the feast. It was successful for about 1000 years. In the 12th Century, the RC church reduced the length of the fast by only including the four Sundays (and week days) prior to Christmas. The Eastern Churches still observes the forty day fast. About 200 years ago the fasts were modified and in practice are not well observed. The eastern Roman Empire, the Byzantine Church, continued to observe Christmas on January 6 unto the sixth century (Justinian time) partly because the pagan feast was not a serious problem in the Hellenistic portion of the Empire. Our current observation is derived from a pagan feast. Its secular nature came about because the Italian bishops complained about the Roman feast in the fourth century. A number of theological justifications have been written since the fifth century but they have neither scientific nor historical validity.

"Our scriptural knowledge of Jesus' birth is based upon the first two chapters of Mathew's and Luke's Gospels. We also have historical and scientific studies put together since the 17th century. Luke's Gospel was written about sixty years after Jesus' birth. Tradition tells us that Luke received his stories from Mary who must have died many years before the Gospel was written. The Gospel is based upon Luke's recollection of what he could remember. There is no good traditions about the source of Matthew's Gospel. It is believed that it consisted of what he could remember as an apostle and was written a decade after Luke's Gospel, likely in Antioch. Christian Traditions about the Nativity began about 180 AD and have few historic or scientific basis.

"Jesus' Birth is tied to the Birth of John the Baptist, a cousin. Unfortunately, we know little about the family relationships except that Elizabeth and Mary were cousins (some recent translations list them as relatives[27]); the Greek text is not clear.

"Zechariah was of the priestly order of Abijah and Elizabeth was of the line of Aaron.[28] Traditionally Zechariah and Elizabeth lived in present day Ain Karem, a village about five miles west of Jerusalem. This is a good hypothesis since Zechariah was a priest and would easily reach the Temple in about an hour and a half walk on any day that he needed to serve at the altar. Currently the Church of St. John the Baptist stands on the traditional site of John's birth.

"When the angel appeared to Zechariah, he refuted the angel's message with the statement, 'I am an old man and my wife Elizabeth is getting on in years.'[29] In their time, Jewish girls were bestowed to a young man when they were about 13-15 years of age. The male was usually 15-17 years of age. They were married as soon as the male member of the family had completed his apprenticeship and could support a family. There was no consideration of love between the young couple. Marriages were arranged to begat children and preserve the family line. Zechariah was a priest so he could have been as old as 21 before the marriage took place, old enough to be employed as a cleric and support a wife and children. The marriage between two important people in the village, which they must have been, was a large village social affair with lots of food, beer, and wine and lasted for days.

Elizabeth and Zechariah followed the normal Jewish custom. However, they begat no children, even though they were in the prime of their lives. They probably worked at inducing Elizabeth to become pregnant for 15-20 years and then gave up since the purpose of sex in those days was to begat children; it is possible that they stopped having sex when there were no children after more than fifteen years. By the time the angel appeared to him, Zechariah was in his mid to late thirties. We do not think of this as old but most men in his time died before age 32 so that more than 50% of the male population in the village was 15-20 years younger than he. Elizabeth would have been 30-35. Most women stopped bearing

---

[27] Luke 1:5.
[28] Ibid.
[29] Ibid., a:18

children in their late twenties and were dead by 32. Elizabeth was barren at the time the angel appeared to Zechariah. [30] In their society, Zechariah and Elizabeth were likely in the elderly 20% of the village population and no one expected a couple of their age to bring forth a child. There are a number of stories in the Bible concerning elderly couples bearing children. [31] Careful analysis of the passage indicates that they were in their mid-thirties to early forties. (Today we know couples can begat children at this age. However, few did in the ancient world.)

"Zechariah was selected to officiate at the Altar of Incense in the Holy of Holy of the Temple while the congregation prayed outside. The Altar of Incense was located near but not in the holiest part of the Temple. The angel appeared at the right of the altar and told Zechariah that he would begat a son. He refuted the angel and was struck mute. [32] When he emerged from the sanctuary, he was dumb and the people believed that he had seen a vision. [33] This was not unusual! Most Jews believed that angels protected the inner portion of the Temple and appeared to select individuals. Even though Zechariah could not speak, he still served at the altar for a time. [34] The end of his tenure probably occurred at the end of the Jewish New Year holidays in late September or early October, 4 BC.

"The medieval writers invented the story that Zechariah went home and Elizabeth became pregnant the same day that the angel appeared. This is not likely; [35] God works within his created domain. Scientist today predict that it takes an average of forty love making sessions for the average woman to become pregnant. For people in their late thirties or early forties, it could likely take longer. Elizabeth probably became pregnant sometime between November, 4 BC and January 3 BC and remained in seclusion for five months. [36] Miscarriages were common among older women, and she likely did not want the gossip if she did not bare the son. She likely wrote to her relatives and Mary was a prime receiver of

---

[30] Ibid., 1:36.
[31] Judges 13:3.
[32] Luke 1:26.
[33] Ibid., 1:22.
[34] Ibid., 1:18-25.
[35] Ibid., 1:4-25.
[36] Ibid., 1:24.

the letters. The latter came to assist her cousin after the Annunciation.

"When John was born, the neighbors and relatives rejoiced.[37]
There was now a son to carry on the family line and produce a future priest in the family. On the eighth day the baby was circumcised and given the name John.[38] As soon as the naming was official, Zechariah regained his speech.[39]

"The angel told Zechariah that John would live the life of a
Nazarene (no beer or wine).[40] The prediction may not have been
made by the angel but since it magnified the importance of John's
mission, it could have been added by Luke when he composed the
Gospel sixty years later. Tradition tells us that Zechariah and Elizabeth died while John was a teenager. He was not destined to follow his father into the priesthood. Today most scholars interpret
the statement that he lived in the wilderness[41] as meaning that he
joined the Essene community near the Dead Sea until he emerged
in his late twenties to become the prophet recorded in the scriptures.[42]

"Mary was of the line of David. There are two genealogies in
the scriptures but neither agrees on the exact number of ancestors.
Since there was a great deal of intermarriage, especially after the
Babylonian exile, any Jewish family had three of four lines to trace
their ancestors back to important people. Mary was likely 13 or 14
years of age when the angel appeared to her[43] and was already bestowed to Joseph, who likely came to Nazareth from Bethlehem to
set up his carpenter shop. Neither Matthew nor Luke gives any in-
dications that Joseph was a native of Nazareth. He was probably in
his early to mid-twenties when the couple was married. There are
some Christian traditions that make him an old man, over 45, but
these stories probably arose to account for Jesus' brothers and sisters
and have little validity (see end of the letter).

---

[37] Ibid., 1:58.
[38] Ibid., 1:60.
[39] Ibid., 1:64.
[40] Ibid., 1:15.
[41] Ibid., 1:80.
[42] Mark 1:4ff.
[43] Luke 1:26.

"In the sixth month, the Angel Gabriel appeared to Mary.[44] Medieval writers put it when Elizabeth was six month pregnant; however, Luke was a Greco/Roman and he probably meant the sixth month of the year. Since the Roman calendar started in March; it was likely that the Angel appeared in August or September. The word September in Latin means seven. The Angel tells Mary that Elizabeth was six month pregnant but six months in the first century meant an extended period of time and cannot be looked upon as a fixed time period. It only meant that Elizabeth had reached an advanced period in her pregnancy. The infancy Gospel has the Angel appearing to Mary while she was drawing water for her parents at the well in Nazareth. This is as good as any tradition.

'We do not know if Mary told her parents about the Angel before her "announcement" that she was traveling to Ain Karem to visit her Cousin Elizabeth.[45] However, it is a good hypothesis that she left Nazareth a day or two after the Annunciation. Ain Karem is a four day trip from Nazareth if Mary traveled through Samaria. This is unlikely, since "good" Jews did not travel through Samaria. It is more likely that she followed the caravan route east of the Jordan River to Jericho. This is the traditional route used by Mary, Joseph, and Jesus when he was twelve years of age;[46] she then took the Jericho road to Jerusalem and from there to Ain Karem. She could have spent seven or eight days on the road.

"Since there is no indication that Mary had a companion, it is likely that her father, Joachim,[47] took her to the caravan route, less than a two hour walk from Nazareth, and arranged for a caravan/pilgrim group to take her to Jerusalem. This would have cost about one silver coin, about $0.25. Mary stayed with Elizabeth until her child was born.[48] This was likely four to six weeks if the scientific approach to the story is used. She returned to Nazareth in October or November 3 BC and married Joseph.[49]

---

[44] Juke 1:26.
[45] Luke 1:39.
[46] Ibid.., 2:41.
[47] Traditional name for Mary's father.
[48] Luke 1:39ff.
[49] Matthew 1:19-25.

"Luke writes that a decree went out when Cyrenius was governor of Syria.[50] Neither Cyrenius' reign nor the empire wide taxation gives us the correct date for Jesus' birth. Luke wrote his Gospel sixty years after the event. While Augustus' taxations and Cyrenius' reign were still well known by many living in the Middle East at the time of the writing, the events correspond to the approximate date, if not the exact date. It is like asking someone to tell us what happened during the Coolidge presidency. Most cannot give you the years or events but can give details about Lincoln's presidency for events and dates of the thirtieth president were forgotten. The time frame as given in Luke is close—not just accurate, like comparing the two presidents.

"Joseph most likely came from Bethlehem. They set out for the village when Mary was about seven months pregnant. It would have been in the spring of 2 BC. Tradition tells us that Mary rode on a donkey, most likely the animal that Joseph used in his carpenter trade. He needed an animal to haul wood, tools, etc. from job to job. He likely made the decision to be in Jerusalem for the Passover in the spring of 2 BC and meet his political obligations (enrollment) at the same time. They likely joined a Passover pilgrimage. Since Bethlehem is only five miles from Jerusalem, or an hour's fast walk, they probably turned off the main road on their initial travels but could go to the Temple for the holy feast at any time that they desired. Since Joseph came from Bethlehem, the Holy family likely stayed with relatives; Joseph's parents if they were still alive.

"In the first century, Bethlehem was a village of about 300 people (one historian commented, they must of have also been counting the cats and dogs). It was a "farming" community, with no major roads and no industry. It probably did not have a commercial inn. The Greek word for inn used by Luke actually refers to the living portion of a building that housed a family living quarters in the front facing the road. The rear of the building was a stable where the animals were kept during the winter or severely inclement weather. The rear portion of the building was usually below ground level with stone walls whereas the front of the building had a loft, was above ground level, and many portions were likely built of wood. A stone manger was often constructed under

---

[50] Luke 2:2.

the loft where the family lived. There are still buildings like this in Palestine and some are 2000 years old. Today, none are located in the Bethlehem area. Since it was the Passover season when Mary and Joseph arrived, relatives and friends occupied the loft and there was "No room in the inn." The animals would have been in pastures and the building was scrupulously cleaned as dictated for Passover by the Torah. Thus when Mary and Joseph arrived, there was no room in the family portion of the house, but lots of room in the clean stable. They likely used the stable for their lodging by spreading clean straw and blankets on the floor.

"The shepherds were keeping watch over their flocks by night.[51] This occurred normally during lambing time in spring or later in the summer season. The men were in the fields from late spring (Passover) until October or November except during severe weather. During the long winter evening, the animals were moved to the stable at dusk to protect them from predators and avoid the necessity for the men to spend the night in the field during cold or inclement weather. During lambing, wolfs, lions, etc., were menaces to the animals. After lambing time, the predators were less of a problem but the herds still required protection (guards).

"The Angel appeared to the shepherds while they were tending their flock with the announcement of Christ's birth.[52] After the Angels went back into heaven, some of the shepherds went to Bethlehem to observe the miracle.[53] Some stayed to watch the sheep and likely went later. All Jews in Jesus's time looked forward to the Messiah's birth and the announcement would be something for them to behold even if they had some doubts about its meaning. It is possible that one of Joseph's relatives was a shepherd in the field and led the men directly to the stable where Mary, Joseph, and the Babe were housed. Even so, Bethlehem was so small that Joseph's and Mary's presence would be known to everyone. Most families did not know how to care for a woman in labor, thus Joseph probably asked a midwife, to come to assist Mary. One early Nativity story talks about the midwife and records her name, Salome.[54],[55] Since Jesus was born in the stable portion of the house, it would

---

[51] Ibid., 2:8ff.
[52] Ibid., 2:10.
[53] Ibid., 2:15.
[54] Protevangelion 14:14.
[55] Sarah.

have been convenient to lay him in the "stone" manger under the loft after he had been wrapped in fresh clothing (swaddling cloth).

"On the eighth day, Jesus was circumcised as required by the Law. It was likely performed by a priest, possibly Zechariah since he could perform the rite in the Temple. However, there is so much intermarriage that one of Joseph's relatives could have been a priest. A party was probably held in honor of the new man child. However, very few extensive parties were held by anyone when a child was first born because about 50% of the babies died before they reached the forty day feast of purification. After that time, the survival rate increased. On the fortieth day, the Holy family traveled to Jerusalem to make the ritual offering of two turtle doves in the Temple. [56] Since it was about an hour's walk, the trip and its return could be accomplished in the same day.

"After Jesus was circumcised, Mary and Joseph made the decision to remain in Bethlehem and be near Joseph's family. It is also possible, that being a few hours walk to Zechariah and Elizabeth's home in Ain Karem, that it might also have affected their decision. Joseph knew that he needed his carpenter tools in order to provide a living for his family. He likely left Mary in care of his family or with Elizabeth, took the donkey that they had used to travel to Bethlehem, and returned to Nazareth for his tools and cart. The tools were originally left behind because the original trip was only temporary. It took him a week or ten days to make the round trip to Nazareth and return. It could have been accomplished during the forty days prior to the purification.

"Either Mary arranged for a house/shop while Joseph was gone or they quickly found one after he returned. The house may have been built by Joseph's relatives or rented from them. They were likely in the new house by the middle of June, 2 BC. The house could have been a typical farm house with a stable in the rear and living quarters in the front; like the house where Jesus was born. The stable would have become Joseph's carpenter shop. The donkey may have been kept by Joseph's agrarian family and used to assist Joseph in his trade.

"The next few months were uneventful except for the normal work required of all families. It appears that the Holy family did little but visits Zechariah and Elizabeth. They likely made the trip

---

[56] Luke 2:22.

on Friday before dusk and returned to Bethlehem on Sunday thus honoring the Sabbath Day prohibition for a long walk.

"The Magi were astrologers who lived in Babylon. They might have been Jews who did not return to Palestine after the Persians destroyed the Babylonian empire in the 6th Century BC. This speculation is based on their knowledge of a "King of the Jews," who would not have been important to most near eastern astrologers.

"The star was most likely a convergent of the four visible planets, Mercury, Venus, Mars, and Jupiter; the moving stars of the ancient world. In the spring of 2 BC, the four planets came together into a single "star," about the time that Jesus was born (see above). The planets separated but repeated the convergence in the autumn of 2 BC in the constellation Pisces, which in Babylonian astrology was a symbol of Judah or an assumption likely made by Jewish astrologers. Thus when a second convergent occurred, the astrologers would realize that this was a very unusual event (it only occurs every 800 years) and they felt that they needed to investigate the phenomenon. The magi set out for Jerusalem for they believed that the King of the Jews should be born in the capital.

"The magi were wealthy astrologers and likely assembled a small traveling group. This likely included a few armed members for protection. When they reached the border of the Roman Empire, the guards were probably forced to return to Mesopotamia and the Magi either joined a caravan which was guarded by Roman soldiers or paid a small tribute to have Roman soldiers escort them to Jericho. The Magi probably arrived in Jerusalem in December 2 BC. When they reached Jerusalem, they requested an audience with Herod. The Bible indicated that they saw Herod immediately[57] but it was probably days or even weeks before they met with the King. They presented their astronomic observations and were told that the messiah would be born in Bethlehem.[58] They took the road to Bethlehem about five miles south of Jerusalem. The Bible tells us that they saw the star again.[59] Legend has them seeing the star in Jacob's well about half way to Bethlehem. On the night of January 6, 1 BC the planets converged for the last time. The star would appear as if it was directly above Bethlehem and would have been visible if the moon was full. The planets separated before

---

[57] Matthew 2:1ff.

[58] Matthew 2:6.

[59] Matthew 2:9.

A DISHONORABLE DISCHARGE

dawn and would not converge for 800 year. They again merged about 1600 when Johannes Kepler, the German astronomer, made observations and calculated that it was the star in the Christmas story.

"The Magi inquired where Jesus was housed. [60] *Since everyone in the village knew of the angel's apparition to the shepherds, anyone could direct them to the house occupied by the Holy Family. They presented their gifts of gold, frankincense, and myrrh; the gifts likely consisted of two or three gold coins, a small pot of frankincense, and a small pot of myrrh. However, the value of these gifts was greater than what most peasants saw in their entire life. When the Magi indicated that they would return to Herod to report their finding of the young child, Joseph's family strongly objected because they knew that Herod could not be trusted. The Magi agreed to wait until the next day. While they slept, an angel appeared to them in a dream* [61]*—it must be remembered that the seeds of the dream had been planted by Joseph's family. The next morning they took the road to Jericho and from there, home without returning to Jerusalem.*

"In days following the Magi visit, word traveled that Herod was very angry. Since the Temple priests were the first to hear imperial gossip, it is likely that Zechariah was one of the first to know that Herod would seek Jesus's life. He immediately made a trip to Bethlehem to warn Joseph. However, members of the Bethlehem community frequently traveled to Jerusalem and might have returned with the feeling that Herod was angry and that he wanted to kill all the boy children in Bethlehem. Because of the fear for Joseph and his family, they likely urged him to flee. Joseph likely went to sleep worried about the warnings, and then an angel confirmed the warning in a dream. [62] *He immediately arose and told Mary that they had to flee. Since Herod controlled all of Palestine, there was no place to hide, even in Nazareth. They chose Egypt because it was a different Roman province where Herod had no jurisdiction. In the first century, Alexandria had the largest Jewish*

---

[60] Tradition says that the myrrh was used to anoint Jesus after being removed from the cross. In a practical sense it was probably used to anoint Joseph's body when he died or even earlier when Mary's parents succumbed. It is unlikely that it was kept for thirty years.

[61] Matthew 2:12.

[62] Ibid.., 2:13.

population in the world, in excess of 60,000 Jews, about 10% of the city. It is also very likely that either Joseph or Mary had relatives in the city. Since the flight into Egypt was considered a permanent move, Joseph loaded his tools in the cart and Mary gather all the food and clothing that they could carry. They left at night and took the road to Gaza. It probably took more than eighteen hours to reach the city and they could have arrived near dusk the next evening. Gaza was a busy trading city and had many accommodations. With the Magi's gold, it would have been easy to find a suitable lodging and have a good night's rest. The Holy family likely set out the following morning and arrived in Alexandria about a week after they left Bethlehem. They easily became part of the Jewish ghetto and Joseph continued to support his family as a carpenter.

"Herod in his anger sent his soldiers to Bethlehem to kill the young babies. Since the population was only about 300, they would have been less than ten babies under two; and half would be females. Since the families were warned, it also likely that some of the boys were successfully hid from Herod's soldiers. At most only three or four male children were killed. The soldiers were probably satisfied with a death of a few boys and returned to Jerusalem with praise to Herod that they had killed all the male babies. Medieval Christians set the number at 20-30,000. For this number to have meaning, the town would have had more than half a million people or be equal in size to Antioch or Alexandria. These are invented numbers! The killing of two or three babies was not much more than occurred on a foraging trip by soldiers with few scruples. It would not warrant a recording except by those who lost a son!

The Holy family returned to Bethlehem after Herod's death. However, since his son was on the throne, they chose to move to Nazareth where Mary's parents live.

"Since Mary and Joseph knew the scriptures very well and also the legend that the mother of the Messiah was to be an ever virgin, they probably abstained from sex to fulfill the legends. By the middle of the second century, the Christian church was preaching that Mary was an ever virgin. However, the scriptures contradicted these statements.[63] Nazareth was about twice the size of Bethlehem, about 600 inhabitants. Since more than half the population died for one reason or another by the time they were 32-35 years of age,

---

[63] Brothers and sisters.

A Dishonorable Discharge

there were at least six to eight new orphans entering the streets of the town each years. If there was no money in the family, the orphans became street urchins and probably succumbed to exposure within three or four year. Since Joseph and Mary were comfortable middle class citizens, they likely adopted orphans. If the proper legal forms were filed, the adopted children under both Jewish and Roman laws had the same status as natural children (consider the relationship between Julius and Augustus Caesar). It is likely that Jesus had six or eight brothers and sisters, of whom about half lived to adulthood. This theory would account for James, the brother of Jesus, who became the leader of the Christian church (ruling bishop) after the death of James the son of Zebedee in 44 AD. Brother James ruled the church, not only in Palestine but throughout the entire Near East until his death in 62 AD. [64] He could be called the first pope. He oversaw the Council of Jerusalem in 49 AD.

"Mary and Joseph adopted children would also account for Eusebius' statement that Jude, the brother of Jesus, ruled as Bishop of Jerusalem after James' death. He would have been about 50 years of age if the orphan theory is accepted but over 80 if the medieval stories are believed. Not likely in the first century. However, Jude never had James's power. Within a few years after he became the leader of the church; he was forced to flee with the entire Christian community into Jordan during the Jewish revolution (67-71 AD). When peace returned to Palestine, the power of the church had shifted to Antioch and Alexandria. There are no records of any further Christian Bishops that were in the Mary and Joseph lineage.

"When was Jesus born? It appeared to occur early in May, 2 BC plus or minus ten days. Not in December but within a year of the date normally accepted.

"This is a long dissertation on what may have occurred at the time of Jesus' birth. I hope it will give you the information that you were seeking.

"Lovingly, Henry Weidman.

---

[64] Josephus.

Chapter 9

Paris

February 1945

RECON group 763 was relieved on January 31 because the vehicles needed to be served and repaired. They had been on the front line for two months with the only break during the Christmas truce and when the vehicles required extensive servicing. The men were granted a fortnight leave to have freedom and calm their nerves; the patrol had experienced many traumatic events since they had crossed into Germany in the early part of the month. Every house, every hill, every stream could be an ambush and extreme care was needed to move everywhere. The vehicles needed oil every day and the guns needed new firing pins.

Walt was delighted to have the furlough because he wanted to see Ashley. They had exchanged many letters but he had not seen her since he was discharged from the hospital in November. They had expressed their love in the letters but it wasn't much compared to being together. He sent her a note as soon as he knew he would have a leave. She actually answered the letter before he left the vehicles for service in Remich. When notified that the leave would originate in Luxemburg city, everyone bought a ticket on the train to Paris that left immediately after the leave started. They reached the Paris RR station on the morning of February 2nd. Walt phoned the hospital. However, he was informed that Ashley was on duty and could not answer the phone. The operator agreed to notify her that Walt had arrived as soon as the operator could find someone to take the message to the surgical unit where his girlfriend was working. Walt and Ed caught a trolley to the hospital. They arrived at noon. There was a note for him in the reception area, "I get off at 1500 hours. Please meet me in the reception area at that time. Love, Ashley." The two soldiers left a message that they would return at that time and then walked to *Jean du Arc* for lunch.

Ed would have preferred to visit a small café nearer to the hospital but Walt persisted and they hiked the six blocks. The day was beautiful but chilly (45°F). There were more than a dozen people in the café. There was a lot of smoke in the building and neither American liked a smoke filled room. They decided to sit in the outdoor eating area. They preferred the better atmosphere. Since food was still rationed, they ordered omelets, fresh bread, and red wine. As they finished the last of the wine, Antonio brought the men French pastries and a cup of very bad coffee; he told them, "This is a gift from Serge." The meal was Okay, but not as good as Walt had during the autumn visits. Food was actually even shorter now than in the autumn even though merchant ships from the USA and Africa were docking in French ports. There were many more mouths to feed than four months previous and the European harvest was worse in 1944 than normal.

Both GIs felt that they could have done better in an army cafeteria but it was too late to do anything about it. It was almost 1430 hours when they finished eating so they paid their bill and walked back to the hospital. As they crossed the reception area, Ashley emerged trough the double doors that led to the wards. She was a little early but announced, "I'm finished until seven tomorrow morning, unless we get a large number of casualties." She was 5'4" in height but looked shorter in her white nursing uniform and low heeled white shoes. There were a few small red smudges on her uniform, either from blood or medicine that she spilled while caring for her patients. Her hair was short but hung almost to the base of her neck. She wore a white peaked hat with a small red insignia, which indicated that she had graduated from South Central Hospital. She had taken a few minutes to powder her face, put on mascara, and fresh red lipstick before entering the reception area. She was good looking but not beautiful. She looked like a nurse who cared about her appearance but was not trying to look like a *glamour girl*. Her attire was very practical for her job. Walt had seen her look better but realized that she had finished a hard day's work

Walt rushed towards her with the intension of kissing her but she eluted him. She stated, "Let's go to a café and have a glass of wine."

Sergeant Smith interrupted, "I think you two want to be along."

Walt answered, "I'll see you tomorrow at noon." With that statement, Ed disappeared out a side door.

Walt stated, "Ed and I ate lunch at *Jean du Arc*. It was not very good. Anyway let's go to a café nearer the hospital." They went to a small café in the next block.

As they sat down and before the waiter came to the table, Ashley opened the conversation, "I think you should know that I am pregnant! I guess we are living a *Farewell to Arms*; I have read the book while you were gone. I found a copy among the Red Cross books that are available for the wounded."

"Wow! Why didn't you tell me about the pregnancy in one of your letters?"

"It was too early to be certain. I did not know if you would return. Something could always happen to you. Furthermore, you had other things to demand your attention."

"We need to get married. Can you get permission?" asked Walt.

"There is a great deal of red tape. I'm not sure it is the best procedure. Let's ask Chaplain Weidman. I would want him to perform the ceremony if we do get married."

"Have you seen him in recent weeks?"

"I saw him this morning; he is still at the hospital. He was visiting the men in my surgical ward. He might not have left the hospital. Let's go back and see if we can find him?"

They left the café without ordering their wine and walked back to the hospital. Ashley went to the house phone and made a call. She returned in a few minutes, "Chaplain Weidman told me that he will meet with us in his office as soon as he can get there. It's down the hallway. It's the same one that he had when you were a patient." She pointed to the door to the ward that she exited when she greeted Walt. The twosome walked to the end of the building and found the Chaplain's office off the main corridor.

They had just sat down when the padre entered the room. "Hello Captain Steinberg. I did not know that you were returning to Paris. Ashley told me that you were up on the Luxemburg border and I was surprised when she called me a few minutes ago."

"As you know, we fell in love when I was recuperating from my injuries last November. Because she is the first and only woman that I ever loved, I came back to see her. We want to get married."

"Hum! That could take time. The army has all kinds of regulations about marriage between officers. Since you are both officers, that will not be a major problem but it will still take at least three weeks to get permissions. How long is your leave?"

"Fourteen days but I have used some of the time already. My patrol left our vehicles in Remich a city near Luxemburg. We need to be back there by the 15th. I have no idea where they will send us. The regiment has been stationed in Remich but it moved east and we have been scouting in Western Germany. We were hit hard a week ago and needed extensive repairs before we can go back to our scouting. They gave us leave until the vehicles are repaired. My men, all have frayed nerves and needed a rest"

"We can start the army paper work and maybe everything will be approved for the marriage by the time you get your next leave.'

Ashley comment, "I don't think we can wait that long. I'm pregnant."

The Lutheran minister rubbed his chin and commented. "That complicates the administration. You know that there will be screams if they find out about your condition?"

"I thought about telling Captain Shook but then I received the note that Walt was coming to Paris within a few days. I decided to wait for his arrival."

"Ashley do you belong to a church? I know you are not Lutheran."

"Yes. I belong to the Southern Baptist Church in Memphis. However, I have not attended any services since I entered the army."

Weidman responded, "I can always marry you. The army will not recognize the ceremony but the Lutheran Church will. I will be in a lot of trouble if the army discovers that I performed the ceremony without approval. You just need to keep the papers safe and any Protestant Church will re-administer the rite when the War is over. You'll need to obtain a county marriage license but that is no problem. The Roman Catholic Church does not recognize Protestant marriages and require that a ceremony be held by a priest. They require you to get a marriage license from the county before they will perform the ceremony and make it a sacrament. Every county will issue a license; just don't tell them why you need it. Oh! If Walt is killed, the army will give you his insurance if you show them the certificate that I will give to you. You know that if the army discovers that you are pregnant, they will give you a Dishonorable Discharge?"

"Yes, that is why I need to talk to Captain Shook. I'm not due to have my yearly physical until July but by that time everyone will know that I am carrying a baby."

"Let's get the paper work started. I have the forms. Since both of you are officers, rank should not be an issue. Red tape will be the real problem. The commandant always puts these papers in the bottom of the pile and it could take weeks before anyone reads them. It is not an important request to a division commander and he won't expedite the approval. I have never seen one come through in less than three weeks. However, we can try."

Walt and Ashley filled out the forms and Weidman mailed them to the respective administrative authority.

The couple exited the office and went back to the café where they had previously talked about getting married. They had a dish of fried rice and a bottle of red wine. Ashley stated, "Did you know that Glenn Miller was killed?"

"Yes. *The Stars and Stripes* indicated that his plane had disappeared on a routine flight from London to Paris but nothing more. There are hundreds of rumors; some have been created by my men. They don't have any basis. Do your people have any facts?"

"No, just rumors. There is circulating a rumor that a U-boat shot down the plane and he is a POW. That is stupid. No U-boats have been in UK waters for the last two years. Furthermore, how could a U-boat shoot down a plane flying at thousands of feet? They can't hit slow patrol planes flying at a few hundred feet. When I was stationed in England, I never had a flight patient that had been wounded by a U-boat. All my naval patients and I had lots, resulted from torpedo attacks in the North Atlantic. The probability of that rumor is too remote to even consider."

"Let's go and see the cemetery where Abélard and Héloïse are buried."

"Good idea. I'm finished at noon on Thursday. Why don't we try? I have a city map. Maybe I can locate the cemetery and find a direct route."

"There's an officer pool. Maybe I can get a vehicle for the afternoon. I'll tell you tomorrow."

The twosome had dinner at *Jean du Arc* the next evening and made arrangements for the Thursday date. The meal was much better than the snack that Walt and Ed had eaten on Tuesday. Antonio was not there but Serge saw the couple and came over to the table to greet them. His English was improving but not sufficiently to hold a conversation. Furthermore, it was dinner time and he was needed in the kitchen.

Walt was allowed to have a jeep from noon to 1900 hours on Thursday. He picked up Ashley at noon and with her map they found the St. Pere-Lachaise cemetery. Since it was February the cemetery did not have a nice appearance; furthermore, it showed a great deal of deterioration because of four years of neglect during the German occupation. The couple was astonished at the date when the monuments to the medieval lovers were constructed.[65] It was a tourist site and not much more. After walking about the cemetery, they drove out to Versailles but could not get into the buildings because they had become SHEAF headquarters. They went to a nearby officer's mess for dinner and then returned the jeep.

The next few days, the couple visited tourist sites in Paris whenever Ashley had time off from work. Since she worked twelve hours most days, their movement was quite limited. Furthermore, she was often tried from the long days. Since they did not hear anything about their request, even an acknowledgement that it had been received, they approached Weidman at the end of the week about getting married, he stated, "I can't legally marry you but will do it anyway. One of the Catholic priests married a couple without approval and just gave them a certificate that priest's issue when the marriage is not a sacrament. He told them to get a church wedding when possible. No one made a comment even though I am sure the colonel knew it. I will do the same."

"When can the ceremony be held?"

"I'll check. There is a small chapel four blocks from the hospital that the chaplains use for services that cannot be held in the hospital—like requiems or memorial services for relatives of service men who died in the USA. I'll try to get it for Saturday afternoon. I'll let you know tomorrow. Ashley, you will need to get off work Saturday afternoon to Monday morning. That might be difficult. Talk to Captain Shook. You'll need a bride's maid. Walt, you'll need a best man."

Elaine promised to give Ashley off Saturday until late on Monday morning. She also agreed to be the bride's maid. Walt asked Ed to be the best man with the understanding that the wedding must be kept a secret. The couple told Antonio about the secret marriage. He agreed to attend and asked Serge to come along.

Everyone was at the chapel at 1445 hours. Weidman was decked out in his vestments. Walt and Ed wore their best parade uniform. Elaine wore her khaki dress uniform. Ashley had taken two hours to dress for the ceremony. She had borrowed a nice "Sunday" dress and a pair of heels from other nurses in the hospital. She had expertly made up her face and polished her nails. To Walt, she looked the prettiest that he had ever seen her. Weidman read the standard Lutheran marriage ceremony, the service lasted thirty minutes. At the end,

---

[65] 1933.

Weidman congratulated the couple and had everyone sign a standard Lutheran marriage certificate and told them to have a real church ceremony when the War was over. There was no reception and all guests returned to their responsibilities.

The newly married couple took the train to Senile and stayed in the same bed and breakfast that they stayed in November. They only had Sunday as a real day for a honeymoon but made the most of it. At dinner on Sunday evening Walt stated, "It would be nice to have candle light for our dinner."

"This is a rather simple dinner."

"It could be romantic even if the food is not as good as the Army chow. It is our honeymoon. Anything that makes it nice so that I can admire you in the flicker of a candle. Back in Paris, we never had a romantic setting. You spent your time looking pretty for the weekend. I'd like to see you in a manner that will stay with me until we die."

Ashley blushed. Walt could see the flush in her face. "I did not mean to embarrass you; I just wanted to show my love by admiring you. I get little time to say—I love you. You are light as an early spring bird singing to show your desire to show off your traits. Like the bird, you are at the height of your beauty and like a bird seeking a mate, I need to show that you are what I desire—be near to you in everything we do and anticipate the beauty of the spring."

Ashley blushed even more. Walt stated, "I'll change the subject but let me admire you even if it has to be in silence. At Christmas we attended the Catholic Church in Remich. It was beautiful. The whole service was in Latin but because there were about a hundred Americans at the service, the signal corps provided us with an English translation of everything. I had never heard *O Come all ye Faithful* in Latin. They sang Mozart's' *Ave Verum Corpus* for an anthem. A Colonel asked us to pray for the men at Bastogne and also to pray St. Francis' Peace Prayer. I had never heard the prayer before that Mass and was really impressed with its beauty. Have you ever heard it?'

"No."

"I recommend that you look for it since it is beautiful! The service lasted two hours. After the service, the mess people served a traditional Christmas dinner in the undercroft of the church. Everyone including the parishioners was invited. A few days later, I heard an officer comment that, 'Since we had disrupted the town many times in the last two months, we can serve the civilians a turkey dinner. They had probably never seen one.' There were many Catholic and Protestant services the next day, but I did not attend any. We needed to return to our patrol after the evening meal on Christmas Day. My patrol talked a lot about Christmas traditions at home. What did you do?"

"I'm a Baptist. We don't observe Christmas."

"Oh! Don't you miss a lot?"

"No. Our neighbors were either Baptists or Seven Day Adventists. Until I left home, I never knew what Christmas celebration could be."

"What did you do this year?"

"I went to Pastor Weidman's service here in the hospital."

"What did you think?"

"It was very pretty but I was not use to all that ritual. He even wore Eucharistic Vestments like he did for our wedding. I have never seen him wear them at the normal services in the hospital. If we go to a Lutheran Church after we get back to the USA, I'll have to learn a lot that I have never experienced. I feel more satisfied in the Lutheran services that I felt for many years in the Baptist churches. If you become an active member in a Lutheran church now that we are married, I will join you."

"By the way, your hair looks very good. I see that it is longer than when I first met you."

"Thank you. I can say the same for you but I don't think you changed your style."

"I have not. It is too much work. Oh! I saw a 'Kilroy was here' sign painted on a fence on a patrol. Someone beat us to the town."

Ashley was back at work on Monday morning as if nothing had happened. Elaine asked, "Did everything go well?"

"Yes, it was nice to show our love. Walt leaves on Wednesday to go back to his patrol. I hope to see him in about a month."

Three weeks after the wedding, Ashley saw Walt for two hours. She announced, "I have decided to leave the Army and go back to the USA. I have heard nothing about our request for permission to get married. I am beginning to feel the baby. I develop tensions. One day because of the hard work, I asked Elaine to go to my room to rest for a few hours. I think it would be best that I leave the Army rather than to try to hide the pregnancy. I'll talk to Elaine and see what can be done. I don't want to be discovered and be given a Dishonorable Discharge."

"I also have heard nothing about the request. I don't want you to go home for I will not be able to see you. Oh, why were we so dumb to make love? It would have been better to wait so that we could be near to each other for the rest of the War.

"We're in love. Two people in love don't always make the best decisions. When do you have to be back with your unit?"

"Tomorrow. I only have sufficient time to see you before I take the train to Luxemburg. I knew that I did not have time to do much except to spend a few hours with you but I wanted very much! I don't know when I will have even a few hours. The regiment is due to move forward and we could be on the Rhine within a week or two. The Germans are putting up a stiff resistance and we will be in firefights. Some of my men and I could be killed. Do you know where you will go when you get back to the states?"

"No. I cannot go home to Memphis. My parents will not accept me."

"I told my parents that I wanted to marry you. You can go and live with them in Marietta."

"I might but I would rather go someplace else and work as a nurse. The work is easier in a U.S. hospital or even a doctor's office than working for the military. Here we have long hours, in the U.S. I will only work 40 hours a week. You can write to me at my parents' home. They will know where I am and will forward the letters before I can send you an address. I will write to you as soon as I get established."

"Let's go to see Chaplain Weidman. Did you talk to him about leaving the army?"

"No. Let's see if we can find him."

Walt and Ashley were in luck. The Chaplain was in his office filling out papers when they arrived. He also had the notes for his Sunday sermon on his desk.

Ashley talked first, "Chaplain, I want to leave the Army. I am starting to have problems because of the long hours that I need to work. I may have to disclose that I am pregnant to set sent back to the US but I will only have more problems in the coming weeks. I have not talked to Captain Shook as yet, but will do so in the morning. I cannot go home and Walt has suggested that I go to live with his parents but I would rather not do so. Do you have a suggestion?"

"I grew up in Western Pennsylvania and went to seminary in Gettysburg, PA. When I was ordained, I worked for six months in a large parish in PA, and then went to Winerfield, Missouri, to be the pastor of the parish. I was there less than two years before I entered the military. Winerfield is north of St. Louis and there are lots of jobs in the St. Louis area. Furthermore, there are a number of church homes for unwed mothers in the big city. I am not sure what you want but the city is a good place to live. Are you going to try and hide the pregnancy?"

"I don't know. I will talk to Captain Shook and do as she recommends. I will make more permanent decisions when I get back to the USA."

"Good luck. If I can do anything for you, let me know!"

They left the office. Walt kissed Ashley goodbye and caught a trolley to the train station.

Ashley talked to Elaine the next morning. She told the senior officer everything. The Captain commented, "I shall try to get you discharged. It may not be honorable. I will try to tell the senior officers that you are having mental problems and maybe I can get a discharge without telling him the truth. I am not sure that they will cooperate. As you know, we are short of staff but they have granted another nurse a leave because she was exhausted. I recorded your half day off last week because of nerves. Maybe I can push it further and get you sent home."

Elaine caught Ashley late in the afternoon of the next day. "I talked with the colonel in charge. He does not want to discharge you because of staff problems. I told him that you are becoming unsafe because you are suffering from exhaustion. He was not happy. He suggested that I give you two weeks leave but I told him that it was not enough. He grumbled but told me that he might be able to arrange a General Discharge. It is less than honorable but better than a Dishonorable Discharge. If I can arrange it, are you interested?"

"Yes, I cannot continue at this pace. I am exhausted after six to eight hours and our days are rarely that short."

Two days later, Elaine stopped to see Ashley. "I have asked for you to be released from the Army. They are not happy but will give you a General Discharge. However, it will have conditions that will only make it slightly better than a Dishonorable Discharge. You are free to leave next Monday. I suggested that you be put on a hospital ship and work your way back to the USA. They are just as short of nurses on the ships as we are here in this hospital. They were a little happier about letting you go after I made the suggestion. You'll need to take a hospital train to Antwerp and they will put you on a ship. You can leave Monday and should be in the USA in about three weeks. Since I have listed your problems as nerves, don't let them overwork you on the ship. When you are too tired, ask to rest for a day or two. I don't need to read that you had a miscarriage because you were over worked on the ship. I wish you luck and let me know where you settle in the USA. I will write as soon as I have your address."

Monday morning Ashley accompanied six ambulances that carried wounded to the RR station. It took eight hours for the train to reach Antwerp. She had no rest periods and was exhausted when she finally arrived at the hospital ship. Her speech was slurred. The head nurse told her to go to her cabin and sleep until she woke the next morning. At the evening high tide, the ship moved out of port. Ashley's record showed that she was having nervous problems from exhaustion and she never worked more than eight hours/day during the trip back to the USA.

Chapter 10

Missouri

April 1945

SINCE Ashley felt that she could not return to her home in Memphis, she decided to go to Winerfield, MO, where Chaplain Weidman's former parish was located. He had been the pastor for less than two years and had told her that Winerfield was a very nice Midwestern town, where everyone knew everyone else's business but were extremely friendly and helpful. The town shut down on Sundays, everyone went to church in the morning, and to the park in the afternoon. In warm weather, the park was jammed with picnickers. It could become very hot in the summer and sometimes the winter temperatures hung near zero for days. Ashley knew what Memphis was like in the summer and assumed that nothing could be much worse. When Weidman entered the army in 1942, a retired Lutheran minister, Josiah Schubert, took over his parish for the duration of the War. Weidman had told Ashley that she could easily find employment in the St. Louis area and that there were several church homes for unwed mothers if she did not want to raise the child.

Ashley took the train from Norfolk, where her General Discharge was issued, to St. Louis. She arrived at 2:30 AM and decided to stay in the terminal until she could catch a bus to Winerfield later in the morning. The latter was a typical mid-western town with two main streets, a square at their junction, and a number of churches within walking distance of the square. She walked about the small town and found St. John's Evangelical Lutheran Church, Weidman's former parish. As she walked back from the church to the center of the town, she passed a doctor's office. Dr. Paul Oven, M.D. was written on the door. She entered to see if he needed a nurse. There was one man about sixty years of age in the waiting room. She sat down and after five minutes, the doctor entered from the examining room. When he saw her, he asked, "What can I do for you?"

"I just came to town and wonder if you could use a nurse?"

"Definitely, let me take care of Mr. Green and I will talk to you."

The two men entered the examining room and after ten minutes they emerged. Dr. Oven told Mr. Green, "Fill the prescription at O'Dell's pharmacy and come back to see me on Thursday." Turning to Ashley, he asked, "What's your name?"

"Ashley Miller. I received my RN from South Central Hospital in Memphis in 1941. I was discharged from the Army just a few days ago. I've spent the last two and half years caring for wounded in Europe."

"What brings you to Winerfield?"

"Pastor Weidman was the Army Chaplain in my hospital; he married Walter Steinberg and me. I still use my maiden name because as yet none of the records have been changed. Weidman talked about Winerfield. Since I did not want to go home, I decided to look at the town."

"Oh, yes! I attend St. John's Church but I really did not know Pastor Weidman very well; he left for the army four months after I arrived in Winerfield. A Reverent Schubert is the pastor until Weidman can return. I opened this office but never had a full time nurse. The military grabbed all the young nurses and the big hospitals recruited the older women; thus I have been without a nurse throughout most of my stay here in Winerfield. I need assistance with the routine medical chores, with the administration, and someone who can accompany me on emergency visits. I assume you did all of this?"

"Yes, I worked in a small hospital in Memphis before I entered the army."

"Winerfield is a small town. I am afraid I cannot pay you what you might receive in a big city. I need help from noon to 9 PM Monday till Saturday. I can only give you $30/week to start but if you want the job, it is yours."

"Thank you, I will take it. I only arrived this morning and need to find a place to live. I have a nurse's uniform in my bag and could start immediately."

"Mrs. MacDonald runs a boarding house on the next street, Spruce Avenue. Let me call her and see if she can take an extra boarder." The doctor made the call and Mrs. MacDonald told Ashley to come right over. When Oven saw that Ashley had a place to stay, he asked, "Can you start this evening at six?'

"Yes. You really need a nurse don't you!"

"I have a great many patients in the evening and can use help. Return at six in your uniform and we'll see if the job is right for both of us."

Ashley found Mrs. MacDonald's boarding house which was located on a small one way street two blocks for the doctor's office. The house was a large six bedroom Victorian house with a large kitchen, a dining room, and a living room on the first floor. It had a porch that ran half way around the house with lots of fancy woodwork. A typical house built at the end of the 19th century. Including Ashley, there were four boarders.

Ashley retrieved her bag from the bus depot, took a bath, ate a light supper, and returned to Dr. Oven's office at six. There were four patients sitting in the waiting room. She knocked on the examining room door. When Paul opened it, he stated, "Take their names. You'll find the charts in alphabetical order in the file along the wall. Find out why they are here, take their temperatures, and blood pressure if you think I can use it."

Paul Oven was 5'10" tall. He was slender constructed with bony hands. Both his shirt and his pants were baggy. Ashley could not determine if the poor dress was because he did not care about how he looked or that he had problems buying clothing because of the War. His face was long and slender, his nose was very narrow, and had a lump in the middle as seen with men who broke it early in life; and never had it fixed. His hair was still blond but prematurely thinning. He had a very pleasant baritone voice; he was not good looking but had an interesting appearance and a nice smile.

Ashley determined the order in which the patients had arrived, their infirmities, found the charts of those that that previously visited the office, and made a chart for the one new patient. She finished the first patient's temperature as Oven came for him. Patients kept arriving all evening. At 8:30, Paul told her to lock the door and send anyone away who was not an emergency case. Shortly after nine, they sent the last patient home. Both medical personnel were tired! Oven commended, "A cleaning lady comes at seven in the morning and will straighten up the place. Let's go to the *Hole in Wall Café* down on the square for a cup of coffee. I need to know more about you."

"Okay!"

Oven called his wife and told her that he would be late because he had just hired a new nurse. The twosome walked the block and a half to the café. It matched its name. It had a front door, a small door in the rear, was twelve feet wide, and thirty feet long. On the left side was a bar and grill and on the right side six very tiny booths which would only sit two people. At the back of the café were eight larger booths, they could tightly sit six people. Flower print linoleum was on the floor, counter tops, and booths. Oven sat in booth halfway to the rear and Ashley took the seat opposite him. The waitress knew him by name. He ordered coffee and a piece of apple pie for both of them. She shook her head negatively to the pie. Oven opened the conversation, "You started very well. I can see that you have training in the routine work required in a medical facility. You have the type of expertise that I need. Now why did you leave the army?"

"Pastor Weidman married Walt Steinberg and me. I got pregnant and the Army sent me home. Since we both liked Pastor Weidman, I came here to Winerfield. My parents are stout Southern Baptists and would not approval of my marrying without their consent."

"I understand. There is one other doctor in Winerfield but he is in his mid-sixties. He closes his doors some days and refuses to see patients. When he does, I work eighteen hours! I really need assistance and with the War, I cannot hire anyone. Even a receptionist would help but I have been unable to keep one. There is a large poultry complex just north of town and they hire everyone who knocks on their door. I can't compete with them." He finished his pie and stated, "I think we should be going. I need to start my calls before nine and I will see you at noon."

"How do you pronounce you name?"

"O-o-oven with a long O."

Ashley was too tired to do anything but go to sleep that evening. Late the next morning she wrote letters to Walt and her parents. She told her parents that she had met a very nice Lutheran Pastor and since Walt was a Lutheran, she decided to settle in his hometown. She did not mention either the marriage or the pregnancy. She had previously written from France that she was going to marry Walt. She indicated that she was applying for a General Discharge because the work was too hard and was bothering her in many ways.

Mrs. MacDonald woke her at 8:30 and told her to come to the kitchen in her house coat for some breakfast of hot cereal, rolls, and tea. She explained that coffee was very difficult to procure because of the War and that tea was served except on Sundays. Ashley was at the table less than five minutes before Mrs. MacDonald told her that the other three boarders worked in the poultry plant and needed to leave before seven in the morning. They talked about the house and the work schedules. She agreed to provide a light lunch of soup and a sandwich at 11:30 so that Ashley could be at Oven's office at noon. Dinner would be served at 5:30 because the poultry workers needed to go to bed early. It also meant that Ashley would be back at the office shortly after six. At eleven Ashley put on her uniform and fixed her face. She was at Oven's office at noon. Since there were no patients, he gave her keys to the office and they talked about the setup that they would use to run the office. Their first patient entered at 12:25 and one or two patients were always in the waiting room until after five. Twice Oven stopped for coffee and asked Ashley to join him for the beverage in the examining room. They talked about patients. After dinner at Mrs. MacDonald's, Ashley was back at six but Oven had not returned from his dinner. The evening was not as hectic as the previous day. Because there were no further patients, they closed the doors at 8:45 PM.

Dr. Oven had a full practice and Ashley worked more than the 48 hours/week that she agreed to work when hired. At the end of the first full week, to show his satisfaction, Oven announced that he was increasing her salary to $32.50/week. Paul was a good physician and was very sympathetic towards his patients. Every day he spent a few minutes discussing the maladies with Ashley who told him a second time that she was pregnant. He suggested that they start prenatal care so that he baby would be as healthy as possible. On her first Sunday in Winerfield, she attended the Lutheran church and was very pleased with the service. She decided to join the parish sometime in the near future. She took time to talk to Reverent Schubert after attending the second service and told him about Weidman marrying her to Walt. He invited her to call him for any reason and suggested that she stop at his office on the Tuesday morning during her third week in the town. He introduced her to several parishioners. She began to talk to a parishioner, named Charles Richer, who was a gunner on a B-25 in New Guinea. He had been wounded and given a medical discharge. He still walked with a limp and was missing two fingers on his left hand. They were severed when a 20 mm shell exploded inside his plane. When he heard that she was married to Captain Steinberg, he wanted to hear more about what Walt was doing on his patrols. Ashley agreed to meet with him in the future. They had coffee together two weeks later and she told him about her marriage to Walt.

Ashley wrote to Chaplain Weidman informing him that she was attending his parish in Winerfield.

At the end of the second week, Oven's wife Margaret came to the office to see Ashley. She had blond streaks in her brown hair and it was tied in a knot behind her head. Her hair was pulled so tightly that it gave a stretched look to her forehead. She was wearing pink rouge and very dark red lipstick. He shoulders were deeply rounded and she walked with a twist in her left foot. Her dress was as poor a fit as her husband's suit. They talked for a few minutes before Mrs. Oven invited Ashley for dinner after church on the next Sunday so that they could get to know each other.

Tuesday she was in the Pastor's office at 9:30. He opened the conversation, "You indicated that Chaplain Weidman married you in France."

"Yes. I was Walter Steinberg's nurse when he was recuperating from his wounds in my hospital. We fell in love and Weidman married us. I became pregnant and the Army sent me home. I like Weidman and came to live in Winerfield until my husband is discharged."

"We'll need to get you on the church mailing list. Are you Lutheran?" He wrote her address on a 3x5 card as she gave him the information. "Since you're a Baptist, we need to get you confirmed if you want to be a full member of this parish. I'll start an instruction class in September but if you prefer, I can give you private instruction over the next six to eight weeks? I'll write to Chaplain Weidman."

"I've already written to him."

"Good! Do you wish to have private instruction or wait until September?"

"Let's wait until September. My husband might be home by that time."

"Excellent. I hope to see you next Sunday."

"You will." She exited the office and prepared for her afternoon work. She liked Schubert almost as much as Weidman.

Ashley asked if she could take off a weekend to see you parents in Memphis. Oven agreed to give her off from Friday to Monday on any weekend that she could arrange the trip to Memphis; however, he told her that he would deduct $5 from her paycheck on the week that she was gone. She wrote to her parents to arrange a time to make the trip. They suggested early May. After they responded, she wrote and told them that a Lutheran chaplain had married her to Walt and that she was given a discharge because she was pregnant.

Walt first letter stated,

> "Since I last saw you, we have been scouting for the regiment. The German defensive positions are everywhere. There are not

many men in the defenses but they fire at everything and only stop when they are either killed or they run out of ammunition. Most of the time, the regiment does not arrive before they surrender to us. We show much more caution in our scouting patrols than we did in France. I guess the changes are due to the fact that the Germans soldiers have no place to retreat or have no means to do it. Furthermore, they are on their own territory and local population usually informs them that we have entered the town.

"Yesterday, we entered a village. There were white flags hanging on most of the building and we ignored them. We passed through most of the village when a woman ran out of the door of a house waving a Nazi flag. She drew a revolver and Edwin shot her. She slowly collapsed and the flag draped over her body like a shroud. We were afraid other citizens might attack us, so we left as fast as possible and outside of the town I radioed a report to the regimental HG. I have heard nothing. It is things like this that scare us."

Walt was in the armored car when it was hit by a 50 mm antitank shell. Jacob was killed instantaneously when the shell fragment hit him in the head. Bill Johnson suffered scalp wounds. Walt was wounded when a piece of shrapnel hit him in the groin. The bleeding was not serious. He stopped it by putting pressure over the area. He managed to crawl out of the car. The jeeps had opened fire with their fifties before the Germans could load a second shell. The jeeps moved left and right and sprayed the enemy position with more than a thousand rounds of ammo. As they neared the enemy line, almost two hundred enemy troops ran away from the defensive position. The jeeps turned around and retreated to where they could take shelter behind the armored car. The men assisted Walt and Bill as best they could and removed Jacob's body. A half mile behind the recon unit was an armored infantry battalion; they rapidly closed on the Germans and were alongside the jeeps by the time the latter had found shelter behind the armored car. Two tanks moved in the fields on either side of the armored car and two truckloads of infantry move ahead of the recon group. The tanks lobed shells in the retreating Germans and the infantry fired indiscriminately at anything that moved. More infantry and amour moved forward. When the firefight ended, no one could determine what had happened. The field where the German defense occurred was littered with bodies and six German soldiers surrender to the infantry. The whole fight was over in thirty minutes. Bill was unconscious. Walt lay on a stretcher and the corpsman bandaged his wound and gave him a shoot of morphine. Both of the wounded men were loaded into an ambulance that had followed the second infantry unit along with two other wounded infantry men. The wounded were moved to a field hospital twenty five miles to the rear. Walt fell asleep as soon as he was loaded in the ambulance and did not wake until they arrived at the hospital. Bill's wounds were not serious but the wound would take weeks or months to heal. Walt's wound was permanent. Ed followed the ambulance leading the other three jeeps. The armored car was abandoned. The jeeps had not been hit but were low on fuel and ammo and needed to go to a service depot.

The next morning the seven unhurt men came to see Walt and Bill who were in the same ward. They were only suffering from mild pain but could not tell if it was the sedation or if they were still in shock. Ed told the two wounded men that the 487 regiment had crossed the Remagen Bridge and had a beachhead on the east side of the Rhine. He had no idea what the regiment would do with the seven men since they needed replacements before they could make any scouting trip. Everyone felt that it was unlikely that either Walt or Bill would ever return to the unit.

The next day, the regimental CO came to see Walt to inquire about his wound and to promote him to Major. He pinned the oak leaf on his hospital gown. He told Walt that the promotion had been approved the previous Monday but that he did not have an opportunity to announce the advancement in rank. He expressed sorrow that Walt would not be able to return to scouting since he felt that the new Major had the best recon unit in the regiment.

During the second day in the hospital Walt wrote to Ashley and Weidman. He sent basically the same letter to both.

"*I'm back in the hospital again. We had moved south and were approaching the Rhine when we hit a strong defense. I was manning the cannon in the armored car. A sniper had hit Vladimir and he needed an easy job until the wound healed, I took over the cannon and he operated the radio. They fired first. An antitank shell hit the car and killed Jacob. Shrapnel hit Bill and me. Neither of us was injured too badly but we are likely out of the War. Neither of the wounds is significant; however, I lost my testes. The doctors have not told me what if anything can be done. It will take at least two weeks before they can tell me anything. A number of men*

A DISHONORABLE DISCHARGE

have suffered the same wound from land mines but I don't know what they do.

"Ed told me that they fired over a thousand rounds of ammunition after the armored car had been hit. They found three dead Krauts but did not know how many more were in the ambush. An infantry and armored battalion were very close behind us and destroyed the German position. Ed also told me that the First Army has crossed the Rhine; however, it looks like I shall never see the river. I will be sent to a rehab hospital tomorrow or the next day, as soon as, they have a place to send me. The CO came to see me yesterday. I have been promoted to Major but it means nothing to me because I will probably never go back into action. I may heal fast enough to do something but I don't have much hope.

"I'm having problems seeing and reading. The doctors think it is shock and I should see well in a week or ten days. I may need glasses but will need to wait for an eye exam to determine if it was the wound or just shock.

"Take care of the baby, it will be the only one that we will ever have.

"Love, Walt"

Ashley wrote to Chaplain Weidman immediately after she received Walt's letter. Weidman received Walt's note on the same day as her letter. He wrote back that he had asked to go to the recuperation hospital to see Walt but had not yet received permission. He promised to write as soon as he returned from the trip. He wrote,

"I had heard that Walt Steinburg had been wounded again. He is in western Germany and I am still in Paris; thus I don't hear much unless someone writes to me. I did get a letter from Walt and he told me that he lost his genital organs. The adrenal glands produce testosterone and some of the men who lost their organs produce sufficient hormones to still make love. They are sterile. His lost need not stop your love life. He may need injections but wait and see what goes.

"If you are in love, as much as you professed to me in February, I feel certain something can be done to help you have a satisfying love life. I know you cannot have any more children but you can adopt them. There are several good Lutheran orphanages in the St. Louis area. Before I left Winerfield, I have assisted couples with the church adoptions.

"I'm extremely delighted that you are attending my old parish. Now that the War is almost over in Europe, I expect to be home in the next three to six months. Chaplains are still needed in the hospitals but the number of patients is decreasing. They are being sent home as soon as they can be moved to the coast. I estimate that I will be out of a job by September.

"Oh! I received a letter from Pastors Schubert. I recommend that he prepares you for confirmation. I used to hold the ceremony on the last Saturday in October, Reformation Sunday. I might be home by that time.

"Faithfully, Henry Weidman"

Five days after Walt was moved to a recuperation hospital, Chaplain Weidman enter Walt's ward. He announced, "Ashley told me that you were wounded again and I made arrangements to come here as fast as possible."

"Thank you; I never expected you to travel all the way from Paris to see me!"

"That's a chaplain's job to visit the wounded especially if they know them well. Ashley wrote me but did not give details."

"I don't think I gave them to her. I wrote to her, as soon as, I reached the hospital but did not say much except that I was not seriously hurt.

"I was wounded again. I was in the armored car because Sgt. Livingston had been hit by a rifle bullet and could not operate the 37 mm cannon until the wound healed. We were hit by a 50 mm antitank shell. It killed Corporal Cooper and wounded Corporal Johnson and I. A piece of shrapnel hit me between the legs and I lost my testes. Otherwise, I was not seriously hurt. We stopped the bleeding by applying pressure to the wound. I feel as if I can return to the unit already.

"They tell me that I need a few more days rest than I can go back to my patrol. We are short of experienced recon units. I know the War is coming to an end but there are still many small fanatical units. We need to wipe them out and my unit has received a number of regimental awards for our job at scouting."

Weidman responded, "A large number of GIs lost their sex organs from land mines. I have met a number of men. The doctors told them that the adrenal glands produce testosterone and some have sufficient hormones to function sexual. The others need shots if they want to have sex. Women obtain their testosterone from the adrenal glands; it assists them to build strength in their muscles. I have counseled the wounded and let them know that all is not lost. They will not be able to sire children, but they can operate as a normal male. They just need to plan their sexual activities. Because we have been so close, I came to see you. Now I know the problem and will help you as best that I can. What are you going to do?"

"I'll heal in about a week and I plan to be back on my patrol. They have come to depend upon me. I can function as an officer which is my real duty. As I mentioned, I was in worse shape last September. I'll see what the doctors can do when the War comes to an end."

"You're a very courage man."

"Not really. I need to live with the wound. The sooner I go back to my duties, the sooner that I will learn to live with the problem. When discharged, I'll go to live in Winerfield—your hometown. Ashley is already there."

"Yes, I know. What did you family do in Marietta?"

"My father worked on the docks and was responsible for determining, when, where, and how riverboats would tie up at the piers. He normally worked five days from 7 to 3:30, but had to go in at odd times especially if a ship hit the dock or ran aground. Even though the position sounds like a very important managerial position, the pay was not very good because Marietta is only a small local distributor and manufacturer. Since it was cheaper to move cargo by barges than by rail, there is a railroad dock where twice a week barges transferred full railroad cars in and out of Marietta. However, it was not under my father's authority but controlled by the RR. During summer a passenger riverboat docked twice a week, my father had to check the passenger list when it docked and arrange for help at the docks. I worked part time. The pay was poor, only $0.20/hour. I rarely tried to get a summer job because I felt I could save more money by working in scout camp.

"Oh! I was promoted to major."

Weidman thanked him for the information and promised to write to him. However, neither man ever sent the letters before the War came to an end.

The colonel recommended that Walt be given a purple heart. This time he did not put up any objections. It was presented two days after the recommendation was approved. They attached two stars because they felt he should have received the award after the first wound even if he considered it an automobile accident rather than a mortar wound.

When Walt moved back to the patrol, he answered some of Ashley's letters. He wrote,

> "*I sent several letters since you left the army but most of them went to your parent's home. I think the War is coming to an end. I have sat on the Czech border for the last few days. No one has any orders for us.*
>
> "*The men are still lamenting Jacob's death. He was well liked; we feel it was unfair that he was killed so close to the end of the War. He has not been replaced and there is almost nothing for us to do.*
>
> "*The doctors have not told me anything about my wound. They want me to come back in a few weeks.*
>
> "*With all my love, Walt*"

Six days later, Ashley received another letter from him,

> "*I am still sitting with the patrol. We have no orders. We scout for Germans but usually have nothing to report. In fact, most of our patrols are a waste of time and fuel. We visit towns that had a large concentration of Nazis but on the whole everyone ignores us unless we have food to distribute. We transport some from our supply dumps. Some of the people are emaciated from the lack of a full diet, especially children. We could carry more food if we could remove the machine guns from the jeeps but last week another patrol met a Wehrmacht pocket and only escaped by using all their firepower. For this reason, we are afraid to remove the guns even if it assists in enhancing our humanitarian operations.*
>
> "*I have started to tell people that we are married. My men knew it in February but discretely said nothing. Since you are back in the USA, I don't see any reason to hide the fact. Ed is the only member to ask me what I will do with the wound when I get back to the USA. I have not given him a good answer.*"

At the end of June, the enlisted members of the patrol were given another stripe.

Chapter 11

Missouri

December 1945

THE War in Europe officially came to an end with the signing of the German surrender on May 8, 1945. Some units did not surrender until May 10 but on the whole the fighting came to an end on May 8th. Since Hitler was dead, the SS, and other Nazi units had no reason to continue fighting. A few fanatical Nazis believed that Hitler had escaped during the waning days of the defense of Berlin and formed pockets of resistance. Although small, they continued to fight until totally subdued. These small pockets either died fighting or finally surrendered later in May. During May, the 763 recon unit drove through dozens of towns looking for fanatics. Since they had few weapons besides rifles, pistols and submachine guns, the firefights were heavily tilted in favor of the patrol. However, the fanatics often mined the roads into the villages where they put up a defense and the 763 patrol lost three jeeps to mines. Although none of the men were killed, five were wounded. The worse was Jacob Cooper who took a piece of shrapnel in his shoulder, was put in the hospital, and was sent back to the USA rather than returning to the unit. During the cleanup, there were almost as many causalities as during the previous year.

The 763 patrol had few duties after the last of the Wehrmacht surrendered. They looked into the killings by a few fanatical Nazis. On the whole, the problems were handled by the local police who often shot the fanatics before the recon patrol arrived. By the middle of June, they removed the .50 calibers from the vehicles to decrease the possibility of accidents. The rest of the summer was a bore; their main duty was delivering food to the starving German civilians. The Allied bombing had completely destroyed the transportation system and there was little means to move food from the supply dumps to the population. Furthermore, the firebombing in the last few weeks of the War left thousands of unburied dead and this needed to be reported to the senior commanders. On July 10, the food problem in Germany was temporary resolved when the Allies-American, British, and Soviets agreed upon a program to feed the Germans in their occupation zones.

In the middle of June, Walt wrote,

"*I read an interesting article in* The Stars and Stripes. *I checked some newspapers. Apparently a C-47 crashed 150 miles west of Hollandia, New Guinea. Twenty one of the twenty four passengers in the plane were killed. The three survivors were a WAC corporal, a lieutenant, and a sergeant. On June 8, parachutists landed in the valley called Shangri La, named for the village in James Hilton's book* Lost Horizons. *They hoped to bring out the survivors by glider. If you see any articles, let me know what happens.*"

Walt continued to write to Ashley. He did not mention his lost sex organs but wrote love letters in the hope that she would still want him as a husband. They were all vague without any discussion concerning physically making love to her. He had a number of visits with the doctors who worked with other soldiers who had the same injury. They explained that he could still have sex. He needed to schedule his love making activities and take a shot of testosterone thirty to sixty minutes prior to the activity. They told him that he could compensate for the lack of testosterone but they always let him know that he could never have any children.

Ashley began to show her pregnancy early in June. By the middle of June, she officially changed her name to Mrs. Walter Steinberg. No one asked why she waited so long to change her name nor did anyone ask to see the marriage certificate. Dr. Oven estimated that the baby would be born at the end of August. In the middle of July, Ashley was having problems with her work and cut her hours in half. During the last week in August because of her problems, she just stayed with Mrs. MacDonald. Henry, her son, was delivered by Dr. Oven on September 2 in Mrs. MacDonald's home. By September 15, Ashley was feeling much better and started to visit Oven's office for an hour or two each day. During the third week in October, she returned to full time but came home three times a day to feed the young child.

In September, the M8 armored car was abandoned in a motor pool. It had hardly been used since early June. The attitude of the Allies and Germans changed and the recon group was assigned to help crack the black market operations. The 763 group started to find small black markets in almost every city and village that they cruised. They would arrest the marketers and turned them over to the provisional police, who generally fined the people and sent them to an old concentration camp for two weeks. By November, the small operations had disappeared. They were replaced by larger and more efficient ones. Since they had been trained for War and none of their training was of any use, the patrol normally reported the illegal incidents to the police and let them handle the criminals. The patrol was disbanded late in November and the men sent back to the USA. The Army preferred to use men who were better qualified to search for criminals than good recon patrols.

The patrol left their jeeps in a motor pool near Frankfurt and took the train to Antwerp where they were loaded unto an escort aircraft carrier. There were 6000 men on the ship, most of who were put up on the hanger deck where hundreds of bunks were stacked four or five high. The officer accommodations were a little better but not good. Four or five men occupied a cabin that was designed for two navy pilots. During the trip across the Atlantic, they ran into several storms and most of the men were sea sick. Fortunately, the trip only lasted seven days. The enlisted men stood in line for hours to be fed. The meals were never good and there were many complaints. The officers had little better food service. They usually got through the food line in less than an hour but it was not much better. There were twice as many men on the ship as it was designed but the commissary had the same number of sailors. Thus everyone was overworked and only wanted to get the voyage terminated.

Walt's group arrived in NYC on December 3 and was sent to Fort Bellaire, New Jersey, where he was discharged three days later. He called both Ashley and his parents. He told the latter that he was going to St. Louis to see Ashley and would try to visit Marietta before Christmas. He told Ashley that he would be in St. Louis in a few days depending upon when he could arrange the train connections. She offered to meet him at the St. Louis RR station but since the trains could be ten to twelve hours late, he insisted that she not waste the time trying to find him. He told her that he would travel to Winerfield as fast as possible.

He arrived in the village at 1 PM on December 10 and walked the two blocks to Dr. Oven's office. As he entered the waiting room, he saw Ashley taking data from a patient. She did not immediately see him. As she looked for new patients, she spotted him and virtually jumped into his arms screaming, "When did you arrive?"

"About ten minutes ago. My bag sits at the door." He pointed to his duffel bag. "When do you get off?"

"As soon as I check everything with Dr. Oven, I have been waiting for days for you and the doctor agreed to give me off the rest of the day when you arrived."

Ten minutes later, they reached Mrs. MacDonald's boarding house. She was babysitting with Henry while Ashley worked. She agreed to let Walt stay in the boarding hour until the newly assembled family could find an apartment. She was holding Henry when they entered the house. She tried to transfer the boy to Walt but he was awkward in taking the young man and the baby began to cry. Walt wasn't sure what to do. Ashley took the baby and cuddled him. He stopped crying as soon as his mother had him in her arms. Mrs. Mac-Donald offered Walt coffee and apple pie. Since he had not eaten since the previous day, he accepted. Ashley nursed Henry and told Walt about her work in Oven's office.

At 2:45, Mrs. MacDonald commented, "Why don't you two people take a walk about the town? I'll take care of Henry until you return. Will you be having dinner here?"

Walt asked, "Is there a place to eat in Winerfield?"

"Yes. I occasionally go to the *Hole in a Wall*. It is not much of a restaurant but it has good food."

"Why don't we have our first dinner together there? We can return by seven or seven thirty.

"I will not plan for either of you to be a dinner and will take care of Henry. You'll need to feed him when you get home. If he cries, I'll give him a bottle."

Walt and Ashley walked about the town and talked continuously. Ashley talked about their child, his delivery, and her caring for him during his first twelve weeks. He told her about his effort to use the 763 recon patrol to counter the black marketers and the many mistakes that they made. He explained that because of the goofs, the patrol was disbanded, and its members sent back to the USA.

At 5:15, they entered the *Hole in a Wall* and sat in the last booth at the rear of the café. Walt ordered a steak and commented, "This is only the second steak that I have eaten since I left the USA more than eighteen months ago. They served steak to the officers on the ship back to NYC, but it was not good."

Ashley laughed and ordered a BLT with the comment, "Mrs. MacDonald feeds us too well. I cannot eat everything that she sets upon the table."

Walt brought up the subject of his wound, "I have talked to several doctors. They tell me that I can take testosterone shots and have normal marital relationships."

"I wrote to Pastor Weidman and he told me the same thing. I asked Dr. Oven if he had any articles/books on sex. He loaned me a big book on male/female sex. There was not much on the loss of sexual function but apparently a number of soldiers' loss their sexual prowess during World War I. The doctors eventually learned how to help those who still had a penis."

"The doctors told me that we need to plan our love affairs. If I need testosterone shots, you can give them to me a few hours before we make love. Since the lost was due to the wound, the army will pay for all my medical needs for the rest of my life. I may need to go to military hospital if I need more than simple shots or pills."

"I'm glad that you understand the complications. I wondered what would happen but you never wrote enough to help understand me."

"Until four weeks ago I'm not sure that I knew. We need to talk about getting a legal marriage."

"I'd like Weidman to perform the ceremony. I expected him to return to Winerfield by this time. Have you heard anything?"

"No. After he visited me in April, I never heard from him. Maybe Pastor Schubert has some information."

After the Sunday morning service, Reverent Schubert told them. "Pastor Weidman will be discharge shortly. He wrote to me saying that his work was finished and only needed the approval of the chaplain colonel in Paris and to find transportation back to the USA. He hopes to celebrate Christmas here in Winerfield. If he makes it by Christmas, I will leave at the end of the month."

A few days later Walt asked Ashley, "Did you read anything about the three military personnel that were lost in New Guinea?"

"Yes, they were rescued at the end of June. There was a parade for Margaret Hastings, the WAC, in her home town. She was on a War Bond Drive before she disappeared from the news. Did you read James Hilton's book?"

"Yes. I read all three of his best books, *Lost Horizon*, *Good-bye Mr. Chips*, and *Random Harvest* while I was recovering in Germany. I guess I forgot to tell you."

"I have not read any of them. What are they like?"

"They are excellent stories and all have been made into movies. I saw Lost Horizons, which starred Ronald Coleman. It was one of the Signal Corps movies shown after the end of the War. Lost Horizon is the story of a plane that crashed in Tibet. The survivors were rescued by the people from a peaceful Tibetan village. No one dies in the village and some of the villagers are over 200 years of age. The hero falls in love with a pretty woman who was 200 years of age. He wanted to leave Shangri La and convinced her to go with him. She aged rapidly after they leave the valley and died of old age before they reach civilization.

"Good-bye Mr. Chips was the story about a school master who taught generations of students and finally retired. Everyone celebrated his leaving the school. He had many students who loved him. I never saw the movie.

"Random Harvest was the story about a British officer who suffered shell shock in World War I. He escaped from the asylum where he was being kept. He was rescued by an actress and joined the traveling stage group. He married the actress. He wrote a book and took it to the publisher in Liverpool. He was run down by a cab. When he awoke, he remembered who he was and returned to the home he occupied before the War and took up managing the family business. His wife lost their baby. When she found his name and picture in the newspaper, she traveled to where his business was located and became his secretary. He married her a second time. On a business trip he saw the play in which he and his wife starred while traveling years earlier. He retraced his steps and found his wife for a third time outside of the cottage where they lived when he disappeared in 1920. I saw the movie which ends at the beginning of World War II.. The book ends a little earlier.

"They are excellent stories and I recommend that you visit the library and check them out. I think Hilton received a Pulitzer Prize for his works."

"I will try. You always seem to read good literature."

"I make an attempt but some books that I consume have a lot to be desired. I just like to read and always carry a book with me. I had two or three in my jeep during the patrols. Unfortunately, I can't remember the titles of most of them."

The next week, Ashley came home carrying a book. She told Walt, "I found Random Harvest in the library. I asked the librarian about James Hilton. She told me that his three best books were published in the UK, thus they were ineligible for a Pulitzer Prize. He has recently received the award but not for the books you recommended. She thinks he now works in Hollywood writing scripts for movies."

A Dishonorable Discharge

During the first week in Winerfield, Walt tried to make love without a testosterone shot. He was unable to get a sufficient erection. It was his first attempt since he was released from the hospital in April. The doctors told him that he had to plan his love making and take the testosterone injection about two hours before going to bed. He was also told that some men produced sufficient testosterone in their adrenalin glands and did not need the injection. It was obvious that he needed the injections. They decided to try on a Sunday afternoons when nothing else was scheduled.

Walt visited the poultry plant at the end of his first week in Winerfield looking for a position as an engineer. They agreed to hire him as soon as he could obtain a copy of his degree. His job was checking production and looking for ways to increase the efficiency of the plant. The chicken bones were boiled for soup and then thrown in the trash. He remembered from his chemistry classes that they were high in phosphorus and suggested that they be send to a fertilizer plant. The fertilizer plant did not pay them much more than the cost of transportation but they saved the cost of dumping the bones in a land fill. He looked at the discarded legs, tails, and internal organs. He suggested that they be sent to a pet food manufacturer. Again they did not get much more than shipping but it decreased land fill costs. He could not understand why these simple recycling techniques had not been used. He was told, "The plant was built late in 1940. Our contracts were with the military. They wanted chickens to use in military meals. They did not want what we call waste. We just threw it away. Now we need to be more efficient to compete in the civilian world, "We like your ideas."

Weidman did not return for Christmas. Pastor Schubert officiated at the services. He held a candlelight service on Christmas Eve that was attended by Walt and Ashley. Mrs. MacDonald took care of Henry. It reminded Walt of the Methodist Service that he attended many years previous. There were a hundred candles set everywhere in the church. Schubert opened the service with the singing of "*Oh Come, Oh Come Emmanuel.*" He asked all parishioners to file past him and light their candle from his then go and light a candle or two in the church. As the congregation came forward the usher turned off all the electric lights except for those on the trees in the chancel. The choir sang "*Christ is the Light of the World*" until everyone returned to their seats. Schubert prayed a long prayer thanking God for the peace that had come to the world with the end of the War. The congregation sang *"Joy to the World"* during the offertory. Schubert preached a short sermon on the need to forgive one's enemies and to celebrate of the Coming of the Prince of Peace. The service closed with the hymn, *"This Child of God."* Both Walt and Ashley expressed their feeling of strong inspiration as they walked home.

On Christmas morning Walt and Mrs. MacDonald attended the Communion Service while Ashley cared for her son. The Service was out of the Lutheran Service book and was what Walt remembered from his childhood.

During the week after Christmas, the Steinbergs found an apartment and made arrangements to move in on New Year's Day.

Pastor Weidman finally returned to Winerfield during the middle of January and Reverent Schubert left the next week. Weidman explained that he was needed in a military hospital when he arrived back in the USA. His discharge was delayed a month while he assisted in the hospital.

The Sunday after his return, Walt and Ashley met his wife, Julie, for the first time. She was thirty years of age, had a rather pale complexion, wore glasses, and had platinum hair with a touch of yellow. She was slender but had no real figure. She had pigmented skin at the hair line on the left side of her face. She told the Steinbergs that she had it all her life. Henry Weidman explained that she was a majorette in high school and taught young girls how to twirl the baton at the YMCA. When asked why she left Winerfield, she stated, "When Henry entered the Army in 1942, I needed a job but could not find one in Winerfield. The YMCA St. Louis offered me one traveling through their branches, as so I stayed there until Henry came home."

They then asked about obtaining a legal marriage. Walt stated, "We have the certificate that you gave us."

Weidman acknowledged, "Almost any time that you desire, I can legally marry you. You'll need a county marriage license but you do not need a blood test. Just mark the application 'married in the Army' then add that you now want a church ceremony. No one will check anything."

"We'll write to our families and ask them when they wish to have the wedding."

"Good."

They held the wedding on Bright Saturday, the Saturday after Easter. Since Elaine Shook and Ed Smith were both back in the USA, they consented to repeat their previous eminence and be part of the wedding party. Mrs. MacDonald took care of Henry during the ceremony. The couple took two days to travel to the Ozarks for a second honeymoon. Even though it did not have the army or War restrictions, they felt that their short stay in Senlis was a much better entry into being a couple under the love of God.

At the wedding, Walt told his parents that he lost his sexual organs in a firefight near the end of the War. He also told them that he would receive an army disability pension of $8.25 a month for the rest of his life.

A DISHONORABLE DISCHARGE

Epilogue

Missouri

July 1953

AFTER settling in Winerfield, Walt stayed in the Army Re-
serves and became very active in the local American Legion
Post. He attend most of the local meeting, voted in every elec-
tion, stopped in the club three times a month for a beer, and led the
American Legion Post parades on National Holidays. He never gained
weight and could still wear his uniform twelve years after he was discharged. However, it started to develop holes and he finally discarded
it in 1960. At the time when he could no longer wear his army uniform, he bought an American legion uniform and wore it in all functions. Even though he could not play an instrument, he assisted the
Legion's youth band, especially with its marching and uniforms. He
also visited veterans and tried to get them to join the Legion.

He joined the Boy Scout troop committee at St. John's church.
Two years after he joined, he became an assistant scout master. He
served three years then became the scoutmaster. He served twenty five
years, had thirty two Eagle scouts, and was awarded a Silver Beaver
when he finally gave up being scoutmaster.

Walt and Ashley learned to schedule their love affairs. Ashley usually gave Walt his testosterone shot and they were able to show their
love even if they could never have another child. They worked with
the Lutheran adoption agencies and in 1950 adopted a girl whom they
called Elaine in honor of the army captain.

In the summer of 1953, Walt read an article in the Legion magazine
that anyone who had less than an honorable discharge from the military might apply for an honorable discharge. They needed to apply to
the Armed Service Record Department and attached all documents. He
showed the article to Ashley and suggested that she apply. Since they
were married before the discharge, he felt she had justification for an
upgrade in her discharge. The army would not recognize the marriage

because the ceremony was performed without proper approvals but it was irrelevant since the rules had changed since the end of the War. The church certificate was dated prior to the discharge. She made copies of all the records, sent them to the Records Department, and asked that they be reviewed.

Four months later, she received an honorable discharge in the mail with a note that she could apply for veteran's benefits and medals. She applied and six months later received three European theater medals. She became a member of Walt's Legion Post, became a very active member and was elected the post commander five years later.

HISTORY

Glenn Miller, b. March 1, 1904. He was declared missing on December 15, 1944. He was forty years of age. In 1988, a former B24 bombardier heard of Miller's disappearance. He remembered that on December 15, his squadron's raid into Germany was aborted because of bad weather. They dumped their bombs in a bomb dump off the SE coast of England. He remembered that one of the jettisoned bombs hit a plane and knocked off its wing. He assumed it had crashed.

In 2004, the Royal Navy explored the unexploded ordinance dump with a deep water midget submarine. They found Glenn Miller's plane and photographed the serial number. His disappearance was solved.

Ray McKinley, b. June 18, 1910: Ray McKinley and Jerry Gray took over the *Glenn Miller Army Air Force Band* after Miller's disappearance. Upon being discharged at the end of the following year, McKinley formed an excellent, modern big band that featured original material by legendary arranger, Eddie Sauter. But with the business decline in 1950, the band became history. McKinley evolved into a part time band leader, radio, and TV personality. In 1956, he capitalized on the popularity of *The Glenn Miller Story* movie starring James Steward and June Allison, and revived the Glenn Miller band. He led the band until 1966. He co-hosted (with band vocalist Johnny Desmond) a thirteen week CBS-TV summer series with the band in 1961. He died on May 7, 1995 at the age of 85.

Johnny Desmond, b. November 14, 1919. After the War, he took a job with *The Breakfast Club*, in Chicago. He made a number of hit recordings: *Don't You Remember Me?*, *Just Say I Love Her*, *The Picnic Song*, *Because of You*, *The High and the Mighty*, and many more. In 1957, Desmond joined Boris Karloff in a guest appearance on *The Giesele Mackenzie Show*. In 1958, he was casted as a regular in Joan Caulfield's

NBC sitcom, *Sally*. On Broadway, he appeared in *Say, Darling* and in *Funny Girl*. He died of cancer in Los Angeles on September 6, 1985, at age 65.

Marlene Dietrich, 27 December 1901-6 May 1992. Her performance as Lola-Lola in *The Blue Angel* (1930), directed by Josef von Sternberg, brought her international fame and garnered her a contract with Paramount Pictures in the U.S. Dietrich became a U.S. citizen in 1939, and throughout World War II she was a high-profile frontline entertainer. Although she still made occasional films in the post-war years, Dietrich spent most of the 1950s to the 1970s touring the world as a successful show performer.

Margaret Hastings (30). She was a corporal in the Army when the *Gremlin Special*, a C-47, crashed in the jungles 150 miles west of Hollandia, New Guinea on May 13, 1945; a valley called *Shangri La* after the James Hilton's village in *Lost Horizons*. The survivors were taken out in a glider on June 28, 1945. The other service men came out in gliders in the next three days. Hasting came back to the USA, a hero, and went on a *Victory Bond Drive*. She returned to Owego, NY, attended Syracuse University and married Robert Atkinson. She had two children but divorced her husband. She died in November, 1978 of uterine cancer at age 63.

Heloise d'Argenteuil, b. 1101, d. 1162. The story of Abélard and Héloïse premiered at the Shakespeare Globe Theater in 2006. Susie Salmon referred to the story of Abélard and Héloïse as the most tragic love story of all times. There are many legends about Abélard and Héloïse. A summary of the most authentic material is given in Chapter 6.

FICTION

At his twentieth high school class reunion, Walt asked one of his class officers, "What happened to Janet Moore?"

"I have not seen her for six or seven years. She married a Marietta man in the Lutheran Church. I think he was in college but I do not know where or what he studied. I think his last name was Chase. They moved away from Marietta. She was a very pretty girl and got prettier as she got older. A rumor said she was in a beauty contest but I don't know if she won a prize. She did not return her family profile for this reunion.

Elaine Shook returned to Fort Meade at the end of the War. She stayed in the Army for 25 years and retired as a Lieutenant Colonel.

She then took a position as the head of the Nursing Department in a large hospital in Cincinnati.

Ed Smith returned to Cleveland. He attended Fenn College and earned a degree in Chemical Engineering. He worked for Republic Steel until he died in an auto accident in 1961.

USAAF Douglas A-20 Havoc light bomber

USAAF Republic P-47 Thunderbolt fighter

RAF Supermarine Spitfire

US Army M7 "Priest" self-propelled howitzer
(Howitzer, Motor Carriage, 105mm)

A DISHONORABLE DISCHARGE

US Army M18 "Hellcat" tank destroyer
(Gun, Motor Carriage, 76mm)

British Army Humber Mk IV Armoured Car

www.ingramcontent.com/pod-product-compliance
Lightning Source LLC
Chambersburg PA
CBHW020325260626
47156CB00004B/1387